Gerald Locklin

Candy Bars: *Selected Stories*

Water Row Press
Sudbury
2003

Grateful acknowledgment is given to the editors and
publishers of all the periodicals and books in which some of
this material has previously been published.

Water Row Press
PO Box 438
Sudbury MA 01776
email waterrow@aol.com
www.waterrowbooks.com
write for free catalogue

ISBN 0-934953-69-4 paper

Printed in USA
Cover illustration by Bruce Hilvitz.
Book design and typesetting by Pride Printing, Nepean, Ont.

Library of Congress Cataloging-in-Publication Data

Locklin, Gerald.
    Candy bars: stories / by Gerald Locklin
        p. cm.
    ISBN 0-934953-69-4 (pbk.)
        1. United States--Social life and customs--20th century--Fiction. I. Title.

PS2562.O265 C27 2000
813'.54--dc21

00.020722

Acknowledgements

To *True-Gripp Press*, publishers of *Locked In With Gerald Locklin*, for "The Hippie Shirt," "The Monopoly Story," and "The Bummer."

To *Nausea Publications*, publishers of *The Four-Day Work Week*, for "Turkey Day," "The Story Story," and "The Four-Day Work Week."

To *Applezaba Press*, publishers of *The Gold Rush and Other Stories* for "The English Girl," "I Do Not Have Herpes," "A Sober Reading of Sigmund Freud," and "The Gold Rush."

To *Event Horizon Press* for "The Return of the Hippie Shirt."

To *Winners and Wind* for "To the Shores of San Clemente."

To *Tears in the Fence* for "Swing Shift," "Circuitry," and "Becalmed."

To *Chiron Review* for "Not to Worry" and Candy Bars."

To *Red Earth Press* for "The Gold Rush."

To *Minotaur* for "O Tannenbaum."

Dedication

For Bob Austin, Tom Gripp, Leo Mailman, Hubert Lloyd, Karl Kopp, Alex Scandalios, Jim Gove, David Caddy and Michael Hathaway, who first ushered so many of these stories into print, and to Jeffrey Weinberg, who is once again going to bat for me. And to Bill Fox, for the initial reading, selecting, and sequencing.

Contents

Jimmy Abbey Stories

Other Stories

THE STORY STORY

I go to visit my wife and kids. I take them out to lunch at a Mexican restaurant. The kids would prefer a drive-thru hamburg stand, one of those places famous for colorful balloons and soybean filler, but I am adamant about the Mexican restaurants mostly because I am feeling the need for a tall, chilled, delicately sweet bottle of Napa Valley white. The kids have long ago learned the futility of disputing their father when a bottle of wine is at stake. They resign themselves to the treat of being taken to a Mexican restaurant, where they order hamburgers anyway.

* * *

At home the children play at once inside and outside, alternating between their paints in the kitchen and their various vehicles on the walk. I sit in the front room with my wife, sharing another bottle of wine. Whenever I ask my wife to run to the store for me for a bottle of wine, she says, "Sure," and hops to her feet. Whenever I ask the girl I live with to run to the store for me for a bottle of wine, she says, "Fuck you; go get it yourself." Whenever I ask my wife to fix me a little salad or to throw on a steak, she says, "Sure," and hops up to do it. Whenever I ask the girl I live with to boil a hot dog for me, she says, "I'm tired; I don't feel good; I just don't feel like cooking: Let's go out to eat at the Jolly Roger." Furthermore, my wife never gave me much shit about getting a little on the side, whereas the girl that I am living with is insanely jealous and lies awake on Thursday nights timing my arrival home from the bar.

Sometimes I have difficulty remembering exactly why it was I left my wife for the girl I am now living with.

* * *

"I've got to get going soon," I say to my wife.
"How come?"
"I want to go home and try to do some writing."
"Have you been writing a lot lately?"
"I haven't written shit all summer."
"Well, you were gone for quite a while."
"Yes, I suppose so."
"What are you going to write?"
"I don't know. A story."
"Do you have an idea?"
"I don't know. No, I guess I don't."
"Then how are you going to write a story when you don't know what you want to write about."
"I guess I was hoping it would just come to me. I guess I was figuring that once I... I'll tell you what—you give me the ideas."
"Me?"
"Yes, you. Here, I will copy down with your ballpoint pen on the back of this envelope—which happens to be my pay envelope, so please have respect for its presence in the room— I will copy down the ideas you give me and then I will go home and write them up,"
"I don't know what sort of thing you're looking for."
"I'm not looking for anything. Just give me ideas. They don't have to be related."
"Okay... let's see... you could write about the rain."
"What rain?"
"The rain last week. The big rain. You could write about the twelve-foot waves and how they were breaking out beyond the end of the pier and..."
"I didn't go out in the rain. I didn't go to the beach. I stayed inside and watched the Olympics on t.v."
"Grant and I went to the beach. It was really something else."

"Okay, I can write about my wife and her boyfriend going to the beach during the big storm and about how romantic it was and…"

"Instead, why don't you write about the storm, about how the beach was covered with clamshells and all the little boys came and gorged themselves on the clams and their penises grew as long as Pinocchio's nose and they went running home to rape their mommies but their mommies just kissed their penises and made the hurt go away…"

* * *

I am thinking that what I should write about is how a man manages to leave his wife and yet hold on to her for a year or two. To have his cake and eat it too. It is a very unfair situation, of course, but he doesn't want to let go. For one thing he is never sure that he will not want to return home permanently any day now. For another, he finds that both his wife and mistress treat him better, knowing that they have a rival. Perhaps it is the very *unfairness* itself that lends a fascination to the arrangement — it makes him feel a little like a caveman.

But the people around them are disturbed by the unorthodox nature of the triangle. It is neither conventional nor conventionally unconventional. They are bent upon liberating the wife. They are forever introducing her to prospective lovers. At first he manages to intervene in time, showing up at unexpected hours and literally scaring some of them away, but finally she takes a liking to one preternaturally tenacious suitor, a kid still in his teens, a kid in some ways the polar opposite of her husband, while in others very similar to him. They get the affair under way while the husband is in Europe. He returns ill, discouraged, his confidence broken, and she breaks the news to him: she, Grant, and the kids are going to be living together north of San Francisco for a while. He nods; hands are shaken all around; he begins to admire his wife's young lover.

* * *

"Write a story about somebody who gets raped…"

"I'm always writing about rapes. People are going to start thinking I have a dirty mind or something."

"Write a story about a Lesbian mail-lady who rapes an old man sitting on his front porch."

"No, Monk, too many…"

"Write about King Kong."

"Everybody and his brother is writing about…"

"Write about a giant mandala that comes to life and rapes all the Buddhist monks and marries a giant panda…"

* * *

Their son went through the room carrying a handful of red straws.

"He's collecting straws. Isn't your son talented?"

"It's an inexpensive hobby at least. Encourage it."

"Write a story about a man who found God in a red straw."

* * *

I remember a story by Edith Wharton, a story entitled, "The Other Two." It is about a man who marries a woman who has been married twice before. It is about the impossibility of excluding the two former husbands from the new household. It is about a proud man's acceptance of compromise and it is about the ironically humanizing effects of compromise. The story ends in laughter.

I think my story about this later husband might bear structural resemblances to Edith Wharton's story.

* * *

"Write about a seamonster."

My little boy runs through the room chanting, "The monsters are coming; the monsters are coming.

"Kids aren't afraid of monsters," I say.

"Kids love monsters."

"Kids are always on Frankenstein's side. They cry at the end of the movie."

"They cry for King Kong too."

"Let's forget about fucking King Kong."

* * *

"Write about fish that are birds that fly both ways, into the night and into the day."

"That's good; that's very good; that's beautiful; it's... it's poetic... but it's somewhat limited in dramatic potential."

"Write about Cinderella as the original liberated woman... write about Rapunzel and how when her lover was halfway up to her window she cut her hair and he fell and broke his ass."

"Very clever... but self-contained."

"Write about a man who ate a watermelon and a woman who put her hand on another woman's shoulder."

* * *

It is earlier in the week and I am in the bar with a girl named Bonnie. She is only in California for the summer, to be near her boyfriend, and she is returning in two days for her last year at Duke. We like each other but nothing is going to come of it because of her boyfriend and because of the time-factor and maybe because she just doesn't like me well enough, although I prefer to think that she does.

Throughout the conversation, she is constantly touching me. I like it, and at first I attach great meaning to it, but then I begin to realize that she is just a touching sort of person. I kid her about it and she tells me how it came up in one of her psychology classes and a big discussion arose over whether it was queer or natural to be always touching people, especially when many of them are of your own sex.

I tell her that I love to be touched, although I am myself rather inhibited about touching other people.

As the afternoon wears on I get enough beer in me to tell her how much I like her, how much I think that she has going for her, how sorry I am that she is not going to be around in the fall, and how I would endeavor to give her boyfriend a little competition if she were to be around. She accepts the compliments gracefully.

When I am saying goodbye to her outside the bar, I find myself sufficiently drunk, sufficiently in love, to put forth a hand to touch her face.

She grabs my hand and shakes it heartily.

* * *

I go back inside the bar, order another beer, and settle down for a bit of romantic self-indulgence. Perhaps she will write me from Duke. Perhaps our love will survive the harsh winter, only to find itself strengthened for a rapturous future together. Since she is not really my type—that is, the type I have nearly always found myself with in the past—perhaps she will awaken whole undiscovered selves within me.

Or, better yet, perhaps she will free me at last from the prison of my self...

"Well, Jimmy," the bartender says, "you out for the evening?"

I remember that I am indeed out for the evening, that the girl with whom I live is having dinner with her parents. Hurriedly removing my address book from my pocket, I begin the search for a suitable date, as the young lass from Durham recedes into the shadows of time past.

* * *

"You could write," my wife is saying, "about our landlord, that fucker."

"Who's a fucker?" my young son asks.

"You are," his mother tells him.

"I am not a fucker," he replies. "I am a rattlesnake."

* * *

"Write about one of your girlfriends."

"I don't have any girlfriends."

"Bullshit. Throw in a scene about one of your girlfriends."

* * *

I go to pick Katie up at the hamburger stand where she works. She comes to the window smiling her perpetually mischievous smile.

"Hi, are you off in five minutes?"

"Unh-hunh."

"Your father isn't picking you up, is he?"

"Not tonight. My car is in back."

"I'll see you in five minutes then."

I return to my car where in five minutes she joins me. We drive a couple of blocks away and park.

"How long do you have?"

"I should be home in thirty minutes."

"But tomorrow night you can get away for sure?"

"I'm pretty sure."

"Try hard."

"I will."

"Okay. Well, what's new?"

"Oh, nothing's new. Gramma's going crazy again."

"What's she up to this time?"

"Oh, she's sleeping with her umbrella. She says the German family next door have been throwing water at her during the night. One night she slept under the piano. She goes outside and calls them Nazis and Krauts. You'd think she was a Jew instead of Irish but she doesn't like the Jews either. Thank God there aren't any Jews in her neighborhood or she'd be sleeping *inside* the piano. Also she's begun throwing her food against the wall. No matter what we fix her, she says, 'This isn't fit for human consumption,' and she hurls it against the wall. Mom and Dad are at the end of their wits and Dad says she hasn't been this bad since she shamed Grampa into going out to mow the lawn in spite of his bad heart and he had an attack and died and at the funeral she was furious and cursing him because she said that he had always planned to die first and stick her with the burial expense and..."

"Yeah, well, look, how was your weekend?"

"Oh, Friday night I went to a party with all my friends from high school and we went back to school and pelted the residence with eggs and all the brothers came running out and Brother Osmond recognized me and called my parents and I got in trouble for that but not too much trouble because my father hates the clergy anyway and I think he secretly wishes he could have been with us and hurled a few eggs himself and afterwards we went to the park and I was pushing Jack in his wheel chair and I hit a curb and dumped him out on his face but fortunately he wasn't hurt bad and later I fell asleep in George's van and the next thing I knew he was on top of me but I insisted he get off me and finally he did but not until I threatened to scream and he could tell that I was serious and..."

"Here," I say, reaching under the seat, "Let's have a couple cans of beer."

"...and Saturday night I went out with Bert and I hate him so, I just wish he would leave me alone and quit calling all the time wanting to come over and wanting me to go out with him but I feel sorry for him and he wants to marry me now and anyway it's a chance to see a few movies, I suppose, and we went to the drive-in and saw this new Woody Allen flick and it was really far-in but afterwards I had an awful time with

Bert because he wanted to smoke grass and..."

I take her in my arms and seal her mouth with kisses.

* * *

"No," I say. "No girlfriends. Please spare me that. Anyway, I think you've given me plenty of material for a starter. What we need now is a title."

"Call it," she says, "The King Kong Story."

"King Kong is not going to be in this story. King Kong is going to be thousands of miles from this story. King Kong may weasel his hairy cock into everyone else's story but he is going to have to stay the fuck out of mine."

"Call it," my little boy says, "The Hurricane."

"Call it," my wife says, "The Story about People who were Friends and then who were Not Friends and then who were Friends Again."

"Call it," my little boy says, "The Fuckerface Story."

And my little girl says, "Why don't you just call it The Story Story."

* * *

My wife is sitting across from me, slouched in a chair. She is wearing cut-off Levis with no panties underneath. Her ample pubic hair is amply visible. If we were still living together, I would not allow her to run around like that, not even at home. She senses this because whenever I take her out to lunch she changes into slacks.

I wonder why this immodesty does not bother Grant?

I add one item to the story list: Monk's pubic hair.

"What are you writing?" she says.

"Oh, I was just adding one last thing about you."

"What did you write about me?" she says.

"I wrote, *what a nice girl Monk is.*"

"Bullshit you did."

"I wrote, *Monk's pretty curly hair.*"

"Let me see what you wrote, you fucker."
I hastily begin to cross it out.
"Give me that goddamn list, bastard-penis!"
We struggle over the list. She bites my hand but I break away and run outside where I obliterate the final entry from the story list.
Monk is pretty pissed, but, true to her nature, she does not stay mad for long.

*   *   *

"I've got to go," I say. I pick the kids up, hug them tightly, kiss them. They run off to play in their fort in the alley.
I give Monk a momentary hug. "You solvent?"
"What's that mean?"
"Need any money?"
"No."
"I'll see you in a couple of days."
"In a couple of days. Write a good story."

*   *   *

I walk to my car thinking, You're the story, Monk, and someday, maybe someday, I will write it.

TURKEY DAY

Wednesday night goes badly. He puts Brenda on the plane to San Francisco, where her parents live. Hoping to avoid an evening of beer and pinball, he has scheduled dates with three girls simultaneously. He will have to weasel his way out of two of them, he realizes, but he has long ago concluded that the number of birds in the bush has a good deal to do with the chances of taking one of them in hand.

The first one calls him at the bar to beg off. She has decided that she can't go through with it. She is just too screwed up. She is behind on so many things, involved with so many people, burdened beneath so many present cares and ancient guilts...

He understands. Anyway it is one less apology that he himself will have to make.

The second girl brings her husband with her to the bar. He knows that she knows that this is not what he had meant at all. She raises her eyebrows as if to say, I just couldn't shake him, I didn't want to just leave you sitting here.

Okay, he understands. But he doesn't like it. He is cold towards both of them, and when he gets up to go to the telephone, the young marrieds prematurely rise and leave.

"Hello, Paula?... Jimmy... whatcha up to?... the turkey?... shall I ride on down and keep you company?... your brother?... your younger brother?... Paula, Jesus... yeah, okay, okay... but couldn't you have discouraged him?... okay, yeah, sure, I understand..."

*   *   *

At least he gets home early, logs a good night's sleep, awakens without a trace of hangover. He lies around in bed, spooning away at a leftover casserole and switching channels among three football games.

Miraculously, their half-times coincide and he is able to shower and dress.

After three quarters he calls his wife.

"Monk?... how you feeling?... good, the kids?... he isn't... is he all right to ride on up there?... just a cold, you're sure?... okay, okay, what time you want me over there?... okay, I'll be there... no, I'm just watching football... yeah, right, I'll see you in an hour..."

*   *   *

His daughter, Deena, is waiting by the curb when he pulls up in his weatherbeaten VW. She goes a little wild, and he waves to her, and making a U-turn he is almost demolished by a Lincoln Continental. By a hair the big car misses him, and he breathes a sigh, thinking, What an inauspicious start! Often it makes him nervous to be around his kids, because they mean so much to him, because he fears so for their safety. He knows he is a little crazy on this point, that it is all no doubt a mixture of guilt, paranoia, and genuine concerns, but life is too short for the sorting out of motives. Better just to smile and show there is a comfortable kind of scairdy-cat...

His daughter is wearing a Pilgrim's hat, made in first-grade, and the filmy maxi-dress he brought her back from London many months before. She takes his hand. It is arranged that she will ride up to Los Angeles with him; her brother, going on four, will ride with his mother...

*   *   *

"Okay," he says, "fasten your seat belt."
"Oh, Jimmy, I don't want to."
"I want you to."

"You never wear yours."

"I'm too fat for it."

"Then I'm too fat for mine."

"You're not fat, you're skinny. You're skinny, Deena, because you won't eat anything but hamburgers and ice cream."

"I don't like all that other icky stuff."

"Are you going to eat your turkey today?"

"If it isn't icky."

"Would your Nana fix an icky turkey?"

"She fixed an icky meat loaf once."

"Well, her turkey won't be icky, it will be delicious. It will be delicious because your daddy says it will be, and because your daddy is always right. Right?"

"Jimmy, you're wrong all the time. Remember when you took the wrong freeway on the way to…"

"Somebody must have given me the wrong directions."

"And remember last Christmas when you were drunk and you said you could fix the windshield wiper and you smashed the windshield with your fist and all that happened was that you cracked the windshield?"

Jimmy stares straight ahead through the still unrepaired pane of glass.

"And then you called the gas station man a donkey and tried to get him to fight but he wouldn't. Jimmy, why did you call that man a donkey?"

"Because it was Christmas and I thought his lube pit was the manger. Look, Deena, I'm really sorry that I was so drunk last Christmas."

"Oh, it didn't matter, you were funny."

"I promise this year I'll stay sober."

"No, don't. Get a little drunk. You're more fun when you're a little drunk."

"Is Poppop more fun when he's a little drunk?"

"Poppop is scary when he's drunk. Do you think he'll be drunk today?"

"I don't know. If he is, just stay out of his way. Now fasten your seat belt."

"Oh, okay..."

*   *   *

"Look, Deena, you can see snow on the mountains."

"I can't see anything."

"Why not?"

"Because I'm tied way down here on the seat by this icky belt."

Well, hell, he thinks, what good is a ride to L.A. on a clear afternoon if all you can see is the radio dial.

"All right," he says, "loosen your seat belt and look at the beautiful snow on the mountains." And immediately he thinks, are you crazy, letting a child talk you into something like this? How will you feel if you have an accident?

I'm not going to have an accident, he tells himself. I'm not going to have any goddamnned accident, but I sure wish I had a couple of beers before we got started...

*   *   *

"Jimmy, why isn't the snow white? It's icky yellow."

"We're looking at it through the smog."

"Pollution. Yuck!"

"Where'd you learn about pollution?"

"Monk told me."

"Monk is a good mommy. Are you always good to your mommy?"

"No."

"Well, don't sweat it, you're good to her enough."

"Does that factory over there cause pollution?'

"The steam plant? Yes, that causes some of it."

"I wish it wasn't there then."

"We need it."

"Monk says we don't. She says we could all go back to growing our own food... and growing herbs for medicines."

"Your mommy is always right, but your daddy is even more right. Daddy says we need the steam plant. Do you know which freeway we're on?"

"Yes, the Santa Ana."

"Very good. And which way is north?"

"Straight ahead."

"And what are those hills to the right?"

"The Rose Hills."

"And the ones up ahead."

"Hollywood."

"Very good, Deena, very, very good."

* * *

Where the Santa Monica and Harbor freeways meet, he gets trapped in the slow lane, is unable to make an adjustment in time, and ends up cruising down the off-ramp onto Pico Boulevard.

"Jimmy?"

"Yes?"

"You made a mistake, didn't you?"

"Wouldn't you rather take this nice route through the city?"

"Yes, but you made a mistake, didn't you?"

Jimmy sighs deeply: "Yes, lover, I made a mistake."

"It's all right, Jimmy," she says. "It's no big deal making mistakes."

* * *

"Jimmy?"

"Yes?"

"Is this a ghetto?"

"Kind of."

"Mexicans?"

"Mexican-Americans, Chicanos, Latins... people call them
different names... they call themselves different names..."

"Are you scared?"

"A little, I suppose. Are you?"

"They won't hurt us. They don't even want to hurt us.
When they're in a part of the city that is practically all whites,
they're probably a little scared themselves."

"Patricio is a Chicano."

"Yes."

"And Poppop is prejudiced."

"A little."

"Does Poppop hate Patricio?"

"Why should he?"

"For marrying Jenny."

"I don't think so."

"Does Poppop know he's prejudiced?"

"I don't think so."

"I like Patricio."

"Yes, Patricio is a good person."

"And I like Poppop too... when he isn't drunk."

"Poppop loves you, Deena."

*   *   *

"Jimmy?"

"Yes?"

"Where do you live?"

"I live in an apartment."

"I *know* that, I mean *where*?"

"I live in Seal Beach."

"*Where* in Seal Beach?"

"I live south of you. Do you know which way is south?"

"Yes."

"Okay, then you know where I live. Now no more
questions about it."

"Do you have a telephone number?"

"Mommy has a telephone number where she can reach me if she has to."

"Can I call you there?"

"No."

"Why not?"

"Because it's not really my number. It's somebody else's number, but I use it for emergencies."

"What's the somebody else's name?"

"That's enough, Deena. That's all the questions for now."

*   *   *

They arrive at the grandparents'. He doesn't see Monk's car and that worries him; given his own surface route through the city, she should have arrived here ahead of him. He begins to kick himself for not insisting that they all go in his car. But as they are standing on the porch waiting for Nana to come and let them in, Monk and Kubla arrive in their bulky old Chevy...

Nana seems happy to see them, but he can tell that something is wrong. The kids run off to their toy-closet, he puts a few packages away, and Monk follows her mother into the kitchen...

She returns to say, "Jenny and Patricio have left already."

"What happened?"

"My father insulted Patricio."

"What did he say?"

"Oh you know how he gets, calling everybody stupid and demanding all the attention and pretending he's going to beat everybody up, doing all the talking so loud and..."

"I thought that he was on the wagon."

"He had been."

"Do you want me to call Patricio and ask him to come back?"

"That won't do any good."

"Is there *anything* you'd like me to do?"

"Do whatever you want to do."

He looks at her tough little face. There are no tears in her eyes. He has only seen tears in her eyes on two occasions and both times she was able to rush to the bathroom and stop the crying in a matter of seconds. He has cried in front of her on many occasions—it is a thing he has never been able to stop once it gets a start on him. But she kept it all inside all her life... and he has seen it make her a little hard...

"What I want," he says, "is to go fix myself a drink."

* * *

He goes into the living room, where the portable bar is laid out. The old man is ensconced in his favorite armchair, not so old a man, sixty perhaps, and still quite handsome with his silver hair and baby-blue eyes and considerable expanse of chest and shoulders. He leans a bit off-keel, always in discomfort from the metal hip, vestige of a drunk-driving accident. Always a warm shaker of hands, he starts now to lift himself from the chair, and Jimmy hurries to spare him the effort. They shake and the father-in-law says, "Well, what are you waiting for? Time's a-wasting. Fix yourself one and fix me another."

"What are you drinking?"

"That bourbon will do."

"Water? Ice?"

"I said I wanted a drink, not a beauty treatment."

"Is this enough?"

"Come on, come on, I don't want to be begging for seconds every five minutes."

Jimmy hands him six or seven ounces of straight bourbon and fixes himself a gin-and tonic.

"Well, I suppose you heard all about my boo-boo."

"Give me the details."

"I don't remember them. I guess I said something that offended my second and most recent son-in-law."

"What did you say?"

"I don't remember. Honest. For God's sake though, he acts as if I'm some kind of bigot. He doesn't realize that in thirty-five years with Ma Bell, I've always treated our minority employees fairly. Like they said about Lombardi, I've treated everybody the same—like a dog. Why even back when I was playing ball for Loyola, we had a black kid on the squad and..."

"Well, it's over. No use crying over spilt..."

"Look Jimmy, do you think you can get him to come back?"

"You want me to call Patricio?"

"Your mother-in-law is fit to commit murder on me."

"Okay, I'll try."

"Good lad... tell him I'll apologize... even though he's the one that should be apologizing... for what he called me... do you know what he called me?"

"No, what?"

"He called me Archie Bunker."

* * *

He drains his drink, fixes another, and goes to the phone in the back corridor.

"Patricio?... Jimmy."

"Jimmy, good to hear from you... are you at the folks?"

"Yes."

"I couldn't take anymore of it."

"So I heard."

"I just don't find his racist humor funny."

"I understand."

"Sorry that you're stuck holding the fort by yourself. I'll make it up to you somehow."

"Look, the old man asked me to call you. He wants you to come back. He says he'll apologize."

"No way."

"It would make Nana feel better."

"I feel sorry for Nana... but what I really feel sorry about is that she's had to spend her life with that drunk."

"I can't persuade you then?"

"Is he still drinking?"

"Yes."

"Then he'll go from bad to worse. No, Jimmy, I've had it with him. I wish you luck."

"Okay. I don't blame you. I had to try."

"When are we going to get together for some boxing?"

"You'd kill me. How's school?"

"I take my comprehensives in the spring."

"Wonderful. How's my baby sister-in-law?"

"She's upset."

"It's a shame he couldn't have stayed on the wagon—not that I've ever been able to myself."

"You don't drink like he does."

"I will. When I start telling you about the nice Chicano kid that I played football with in high school..."

"Oh God..."

"Tell my baby sister-in-law that her dirty old brother-in-law still has the hots for her."

"I'm sure that will raise her spirits."

"Happy Thanksgiving, Patricio."

"Yeah, Jimmy."

* * *

In truth, Jenny *is* his sexual dream-girl. Even as she is now—married, twenty-five, beginning to put on a pound or two in the wrong places—she is as exciting to him as when she was seventeen, an ugly duckling just turning swan, lanky, awkward, small-breasted, embarrassed by her dark curly hair, terrified of men. He still finds himself from time to time in bed with another woman but making love in his mind to Jenny. On occasion he has had to stifle her name into a pillow...

* * *

He remembers now with shame the one time that he laid his feelings for her on the line. He had taken her to a jazz night-club to hear a new group she was interested in, Monk having had to go to a girlfriend's that night, and after a couple of drinks he tried to take her hand, and she yanked it away and turned upon him an expression of mingled horror and ire...

What a stupid thing to have tried, he reflects now, shaking his head in self-dismay, but if he hadn't tried it he would always have wondered.

* * *

His older sister-in-law, Marian, arrives, clad in mini-skirt, tights, and boots, a kind, warm rosy Irish girl, thirtyish and sensual, her face only beautiful after you have come to know her. He once made a pass at her also, back when his wife was in Europe. He had been visiting his kids, who were staying at Nana's, and Marian was there, and they went out for drinks at Barney's Beanery, and after five Irish coffees he tried to kiss her. She was neither horrified nor incensed; she simply wasn't having any. She told him that no matter what their feelings towards each other, there were some things that could never be. It was, in its own way, a very romantic evening. If it had been any woman but Marian, he would have doubted her perseverance in her resolve, but she was not an ordinary woman...

Now, in the kitchen, they embrace and he says, "How's your sex life, Marian?"

"Wonderful. The best in months."

"You seeing Jack again?"

"That creep? No, I have a brand new lover... but that's all you're going to find out about him."

"How am I ever going to make it as a writer without the vicarious experience you provide me, Marian?"

"How about your own sex-life, Jimmy?"

"I don't have one. I'm a married man."

"Unh-hunh."

"I sublimate."

"Into what?"

"Into fat. My whole sex life is preserved in this roll around my waist."

"Well, we'd better get off this particular subject before the old man wanders out here and brings down the wrath of the Puritan Irish on our brows... not that his Puritanism has ever extended to himself."

"He's feeling no pain."

"Monk told me."

"I guess we all just try to stay out of his way,"

"It's a shame that he doesn't pass out when he drinks."

"I know. He'll be flying for days."

"Well, let me fix us both a couple of drinks. What we drink, he can't."

"I've missed seeing you, Marian."

"I've missed you too, Jimmy."

* * *

Sometimes, when in bed with another woman, he will fantasize vignettes in which he rescues Marian and Jenny from Turkish rapists... and then screws them both himself.

The guests, the other relatives, begin to arrive

Kenny is Monk's brother, Jenny's twin. A strange kid, unattractive, doomed by bad eyesight to intellectualism or a reasonable facsimile thereof, he has never seemed particularly well-liked by the rest of the family, and even now Jimmy senses beneath Kenny's holiday well-wishing that he does not really wish anyone well at all...

He remembers back to the days when he had tried in some small ways to befriend the kid, to take an interest in him, play chess with him, listen to his classical records, endure his incessant praises of never-fully-read volumes by Kazantzakis and Dostoevsky. At first he had found Monk's brusqueness towards her brother curious, but Kenny began to drop in on them unexpectedly and with great frequency, interrupting their plans, making work impossible, boring them both up the walls... finally Jimmy came to avoid him as much as possible. Yes, he did prefer the women in the family... and Kenny seemed zealous to intrude himself whenever Jimmy had a few moments alone with one of the women. Doubtless, he had to admit, Kenny did have a right to be a bit nonplussed at this outsider who had taken one of his sisters from him, while so clearly coveting the other two, if not indeed the mother as well, that wrinkled but vibrant, stern but quick-witted, support-hosed but buxom old gal...

* * *

Robert arrives, Monk's older brother, with his lovely, tiny Lebanese wife and seven kids in tow. A beautiful family, a beautiful Catholic family, staunch supporters of Cardinal McIntyre. Serene as an onyx monolith, they stand against abortion, for Vietnam, against the Kennedys, for the Buckleys, against Welfare and for a greater availability of domestic help. They know the Hopes, the Crosbys, Mary Tyler Moore... Robert is a lector in the church on Sundays. A short, handsome firebrand of a man, he has risen at thirty-five to partnership in the most successful firms of corporation lawyers in Los Angeles. There is something indomitable about the man, a quality which has been known to crowd out sympathy for one's lessers.

For a time immediately after Monk's elopement with Jimmy, there had been a period of rapprochement with Robert and his family. They visited each other's place for drinks, the invitations were always open on holidays, Robert's children took turns staying with them at the beach, they all seemed able to discuss even the most controversial of topics...

Jimmy cannot remember at which point the change took place, or even began to take place... but now the children no longer come to visit, they greet him politely but look askance as if in the presence of the Abominable Freak... and they are not even at Nana's for the turkey dinner... they have stopped by to show off the kids' party clothes, to have a single drink, to rush off to the other grandparents' for dinner.

Jimmy is watching a ballgame in the den. Robert joins him with a drink:

"How's your college going to do against UCLA this year?"

"We'll give 'em a run for it."

"Well it's just a question of whether your niggers are better than their niggers."

Jimmy has heard it before, just as he has heard Robert's kids maligning Sister Corita and expressing their inherited joy at the assassinations of the Kennedys. It's all beyond the point of hope...

"Yeah," Jimmy says, "I suppose."

* * *

Robert and his family depart, Uncle Tim and his wife arrive, and dinner is served.

Tim is an art director in Hollywood, but in his forty years in the business he has somehow managed not to become a Hollywood type. Everybody loves Tim and everybody loves to talk with him, not only because of the people he has known, the places he has been, but because Tim wants to hear what you have to say yourself, he is genuinely interested in you. It seems, however, that no one is going to get to talk to Tim tonight, because the old man is already holding forth from the position of honor.

The table hears for the ten-thousandth time the saga of Poppop's non-military experience with Pacific Telephone in the Imperial Valley, 1940-45. There is absolutely nothing of interest to tell, but the words and pauses occupy the room like some colossal vacuum expanding at a rate superior to that of the universe itself. At the far end of the table Nana transmits glances sharpened with the chill of hell, but to no avail.

Finally Kenny brashly, cruelly interrupts his father, taking the conversation to himself. But the choice between Kenny's conversation and that of his father is the choice between cancer and a slow starvation: he tells Tim of his new job as a teacher's aide; he gives him his unsolicited opinion, as pejorative as it is uninformed, of some recent films with which Tim has been associated; he drops the names of a few atonal composers with whom no one at the table is familiar; he agonizes over his impending choice between the Peace Corps and an M.A. in computer programming...

None of them would have believed it possible, but they are all actually relieved when Poppop takes advantage of a prolonged swallow of potatoes on his son's part to continue the saga of the general who demanded an extension telephone within an arm's length of the toilet.

*   *   *

The dinner itself, however, is, as always, delicious. Turkey and dressing and gravy, mashed potatoes and peas and candied yams, rolls, real butter, salad, and cranberry sauce...

And he has his children, one on each side of him, and they are oblivious to Poppop's monologue. Deena eats so little— thank God she seems to remain healthy—while Kubla scarfs it all down, beautiful little Kubla with his incredibly long lashes, and his one slightly crossing, plaintive eye, and his golden hair the exact hue and only slightly shorter than his sister's... he appreciates them more, and is better with them, now that he no longer lives with them...

The most pleasant part of the day is after dinner. Poppop goes to the living room, and everyone else scatters to the other rooms of the house. Jimmy has a few minutes alone with Tim and Hattie, a chance for them to renew their mutual love of Paris, London, and the West of Ireland. Then he wanders into the kitchen where Marian is at work on the dishes and he surprises her with a big hug from behind, and they carry on their endless, teasing flirtation for a few minutes, and then they just talk of this and that for a while, and then he goes back into the den to watch the second half of the last ballgame of the day, and sip a drink, and let the enormous dinner digest...

* * *

He has good associations with the house, the innumerable fine dinners (especially back in the early days of the marriage when he and Monk were just about starving to death), the ambiance of loving, intelligent women, the drinks and laughter, the games of monopoly and euchre and hearts, the chance to watch a t.v. before they could afford one of their own (their first, in fact, a gift from Monk's parents), the fun that the kids have always had here, the sleeping late in the mornings and arising to pancakes or left-over turkey, the movies he would take his harem to...

He has always sensed a healing quality in the place; he used to insist that they drive up on those long-ago hungover Saturdays with the bad-ass black dog chewing on his liver...

And Poppop has had his sober, genial hours...

And for a while there he and Robert were hale fellows well met...

And even Kenny sometimes stayed in his room listening to Mahler...

* * *

Just as the Fourth quarter ends and he is rising from his seat to switch the channel, the old man looms up in the doorway, makes a funny face, limps heavily across the room, and lets himself down painfully into the chair.

"Well, whaddaya think of it all?"

"Of what?"

He swats the air vengefully with a liver-spotted paw.

"Awwww... the all of it."

From his long history of grinning and bearing it, always of course with the help of a drink, Jimmy has built a reputation for patience. Now, with Patricio a part of the family, Patricio who brooks no contumely, his role as quiet buffer has become accentuated, although it is regarded less as prudence, more as cowardice. But in his own mind he has always known that it is simply a matter of time .

"Ya know, I don't even know what's... anymore... your business, you... Monk... your mother-in-law won't... and your wife... even as a kid... oh hell who cares who cares... the Jebbies at least... you and I both... the Jebbies... those old boys... you got to agree... you got to admire 'em..."

"I don't admire them."

A stunned hiatus. Does the bear no longer shit in the woods?

"I think they're intellectually over-rated. They're living on past laurels. They can teach you your Latin or your English grammar, and they can make it stick—they're first-class drill instructors—but in anything that involves the free play of mind, history, literature, philosophy—they're straightjacketed."

"Now you listen to me! When I was at Loyola I learned the proof for the existence of God from those supposedly over-rated Jebbies, and I have yet to meet the self-styled intellectual who could refute it."

"You mean the one about the First Cause, the Uncaused Cause?"

"You're damn right that's the one I mean."

"I'll refute it for you in a sentence. It's no more difficult to conceive of matter and energy existing without a beginning than it is to conceive of a God who had no beginning."

An aching silence as the phantom of Aquinas haunts the room.

Then: "No... no... you don't understand... don't see my point... way back before... there wasn't anything, no matter, no whatever... but there had to be a..."

"Why?"

"Don't be a fool... never anything without a... any fool in third-year metaphysics... tried to argue it with Father Flaherty... thought I was a smart-ass whippersnapper just like... never had to work... not in the real world... they'd teach you in the company... spent your whole life in..."

"Jesus Christ."

"...and still you haven't learned to think... and I think it's time... I want to know... you tell me just what's going on around..."

"MICHAEL!"

Nana's small frame dominates the doorway. She waves a finger fraught with exasperation towards her husband as she says, "Are you determined to bore us all into submission? Can't you be satisfied you drove Patricio away, you spoiled dinner, you've spoiled everything as far back as I can remember... you just sit here by yourself now and you hold your drunken tongue the rest of the evening. I don't want to hear so much as another belch out of you, do you understand?"

Jimmy remembers once before when she stood up to the old man in his drunkenness. It was in the kitchen and he shoved her across the room and Jenny leaped between them and, her eyes aflame, drove him to his room with the pure fury of her filial indignation. Perhaps age is taking its toll, because this time he does not rise to strike her; instead, childishly, he brushes his glass to the floor where it fails to break.

"Come on, Jimmy," Nana says, and he follows her quickly out of the den.

* * *

In the other room he says, "It was partly my fault, Nana. I'd better be running along now before he gets started a—"

"Monk wants to see you in the front bedroom first."

"What's the problem?"

"It's Kubla. He has a bad cough."

                          *   *   *

Monk says, "He can't stop coughing."

"Did you give him any cough syrup?"

"What I could find. It wasn't very good. He threw it up."

He props himself up on the bed next to his son, holds him tightly: "You're gonna be okay, old guy. My big old guy is gonna be all right."

To his wife, he says, "Go call the clinic. See if there's a pediatrician on duty. Have him call in a prescription to the all-night pharmacy."

While she is gone, he continues to hold the boy, who feels warm to him. The child coughs violently, spits up on his father's shirt. When the spasms subside, he says, "I'm sorry, Jimmy."

"It's okay, old guy. It doesn't matter."

"I'm tired, Jimmy."

"I know you are."

"Are we going to the hospital?"

"Oh, I don't think that will be necessary."

"You won't leave me at the hospital, right? You'll take me home to your house, right?"

"You're gonna be better real soon, old Kubla."

"Monk and her mother return from the other room:

"The doctor said to give him candy."

"What?"

"He said to sit him up and give him candy."

"No cough medicine?"

"He said that candy would relieve the coughing."

"Did you tell him how bad the coughing was?"

"I tried to."

"Did you say he has a temperature?"

"Yes. He asked me if we had a thermometer and when I said we couldn't find it he just kind of snorted."

"He snorted huh?"

"Yes. He acted superior the whole time, the way they always do."

"Well give old Kubla some candy and let's keep our fingers crossed that it works."

After fifteen minutes it is apparent that the candy is doing no good. Kubla coughs it up, he spits it up, he throws it up on Jimmy's lap. In between spasms, he twists and writhes miserably. But he does not cry. He says, "I'm sorry, Mommy; I'm sorry, Nana. I'm sorry, Jimmy." It is Jimmy who has tears in his eyes.

"Hold him a minute, Monk," Jimmy says.

"Where are you going?"

"I'm going to call the clinic."

* * *

"My name is Abbey, James Abbey."

"Yes, Mr. Abbey."

"A little while ago my wife talked to one of your doctors concerning our child who is sick with a very bad..."

"Yes, Mr Abbey, I am the doctor who talked to your wife."

"Yes, well, my wife tells me that you prescribed some sort of 'candy cure'?"

"I suggested to your wife that she sit the child up and..."

"Now listen to me, Doctor, I have had it with the Kerner Clinic. You people act as if you are running sore sort of charity ward. Let me remind you that there is nothing charitable about your operation whatsoever; you are a profit-making pre-paid health insurance plan and tonight is just one more in an extended series of examples of your failure to provide the services which you have contracted to provide. Now I have a kid in the other room coughing and puking and running a fever and I want you to do something for him."

A protracted silence. "Bring the child in, Mr. Abbey."

"You want me to bring the child to the hospital, coughing and exhausted, in the middle of the night?"

"It's the only way I can give your child the proper care, Mr.

Abbey. As you were so kind to remind me, he is certainly *not* a charity case."

"You couldn't simply prescribe a cough syrup and give that a chance to work?"

"I wouldn't take the chance. You see a cough syrup may suppress a cough but it may also suppress the child as well."

"I suppose it's completely out of the question to suggest a house call."

"We have no doctors free to make house calls."

"I'll be seeing you shortly, Doctor... Doctor..."

Jimmy sighs, bites his lip...

"Doctor Price."

* * *

While Monk and Marian are bundling Kubla warmly, Nana says, "You better use a mouthwash. They're going to know that you've been drinking."

He returns from the bathroom, asks, "Is that any better?"

Marian says, "Here, take this," and she shoves a cartridge of Binaca in his pocket. Then she hikes Kubla up in his daddy's arms and they are off. It is a twenty minute ride up to La Brea, across Hollywood Boulevard, then farther up the slope of the Hollywood Hills. They have trouble finding the Emergency entrance, end up parking about a hundred yards away. The wind out of the canyons is as a thousand scimitars. They hurry past the entrance, back-track, finally bluster their way into the crowded waiting room.

They check in, take their seats on a day-glo plastic bench, begin the inevitable siege. Kubla hacks, clutches Jimmy's collar, blinks in the fluorescent lighting...

"I don't want to stay here, Jimmy."

"I doubt that you'll have to, big guy."

"I want you to take me home with you."

"You and Mommy and Deena will be staying at Nana's tonight. That way you can have fun tomorrow at the park or the..."

"Will you take me home with you someday?"

"Yes, someday."

"And Mommy too?"

"You'd better rest now, Kubla."

* * *

A man in a wheelchair and his wife are arguing with the receptionists:

"I must have your Kerner card,"

"We can't find it. He had it in his hand when he went in, but now we can't find it."

"I'm sorry but it's impossible for me to check you out without your card."

"It must be in one of your examining rooms, I'm sure it will..."

"You'll just have to sit down until we have a chance to..."

"We have been here since eight o'clock, I've got to get my husband home to..."

"I'm sorry but I can't allow you to leave until..."

"Stop us!'

The woman rolls her husband towards the door. The receptionist heads out from her glassed-in office. Jimmy hands his son to Monk, rises quickly and opens the door for the woman, who is therefore enabled to escape the premises before the receptionist can prevent her. The frustrated bureaucrat turns beet-red, the sinews of her turkey-neck all a-strain, and she stammers, "But... but... but... but... but..."

Jimmy sits down, presses Kubla to him.

* * *

A superannuated virago leads them to the examining room: "Remove his clothes and place him face-down on the table."

Jimmy lays his son down, touches his head: "He's burning up."

"You probably brought his temperature up two degrees the way you've got him bundled."

Jimmy wheels on her in amazement.

"Oh yes, we've had actual examples of that happening."

"Take the kid's temperature."

"I am about to do just that, sir."

Three minutes later she removes the thermometer, reads it, shakes it, scribbles on a chart.

"What was his temperature?"

"The doctor will…"

"WHAT WAS HIS TEMPERATURE?"

"One-hundred-three-point-two."

*   *   *

When she leaves, Jimmy sprays about ten shots of Binaca in his mouth and goes about the room spraying every nook and cranny. "Jimmy," Monk says, "this is serious," but a smile plays at the corners of her mouth.

The nurse returns with a handful of baby aspirin. She sniffs the air, wrinkles her brow, hurries through her task, withdraws. She is followed shortly by a youngish man, short, handsome, probably just in his residency.

"I'm Doctor Price."

"My name is Abbey. I believe we just talked on the…"

"Yes, Mr. Abbey, you talk too goddamn much."

Like a rocket from Cape Canaveral, Jimmy rises straight into the air. "No." Monk cries, grabbing his arm. "This child is sick!" she hisses at the both of them.

"All right," Jimmy says, "she's right. A truce while… while…" and, restraining himself from continuing, *while you do what you're paid to do*, he settles for, "…while you do your work."

*   *   *

The Doctor examines Kubla thoroughly, saying nothing. He sends him for a chest x-ray. When they are all together again in the examining room, he sits at a small desk and says, "He doesn't have pneumonia."

"Thank God."

"He has a lot of congestion. I'm going to prescribe some Phenergan and..."

"Phenergan? I could have prescribed Phenergan three hours ago."

"You couldn't have prescribed anything, Mr. Abbey, because you are not..."

"But you are. *You* could have."

"Mr. Abbey, as I explained to you over the phone, a cough medicine will often suppress the cough but it will sometimes also..."

"And so you never prescribe a cough medicine over the phone?"

"I use my professional discretion and in this case..."

"In this case you preferred your famous candy cure."

"As I explained to your wife, Mr. Abbey, sugar is an excellent demulcent. It also has properties which..."

"...which make the child throw up."

"What sort of candy did you give the child?"

"It was peppermint candy."

"You see: that was probably the problem. What I specified to your wife was candy suckers! Here, take a couple of these little fellows with you." He reaches into his shirt pocket and produces a handful of varicolored suckers. Jimmy stares at them.

"Dr. Price, I see you but I don't believe my eyes."

"I've treated forty children for coughs tonight, Mr. Abbey."

"Doctor, I have no doubt you are overworked but..."

"I am *not* overworked. The major difficulty I face in my practice is in fact, uh, the dissemination of, uh, information to, uh, the layman."

"Doctor, I am not a physician . ."

"I'm surprised to hear you admit it."

"I do, however, have a doctorate in English and I have been teaching English for eleven years and I am perfectly capable of understanding the English language, even as stultifying a corruption of it as you seem to pride yourself in having mastered. Furthermore I intend to enter a formal complaint against you on Monday with the state personnel board through whom I unfortunately have been enrolled in the Kerner Health Plan."

"Feel free."

"Let's go, Monk."

"Don't forget your prescription. And, listen, Mr. Abbey: I think you will find, if you shop around, that you can do a lot worse than our health care here."

"I doubt it, Doctor. In fact, every independent doctor I have ever spoken with in Southern California has assured me that Kerner scrapes the bottom of the barrel for its doctors. I think they're right."

Dr. Price sighs and turns away.

"I don't know, Mr. Abbey. All I know is that it's nearly four a.m. Let's all go home."

*　　*　　*

Bringing the car around to the emergency exit to pick up Monk and Kub, Jimmy passes the doctor, now all bundled up himself and trudging to his car. Their eyes meet momentarily and it occurs to Jimmy at first to open the window and say, "You fucking turkey." Then relenting, he almost says, "Hey, buddy, let's bury the hatchet and have a drink sometime." Instead he just drives on.

In the car he asks Kubla, "How'd you like the hospital?"

The little boy, groggy, supple, says, "I liked it."

"How'd you like the doctor?"

"I loved him."

"And the nurse?"

"I loved the nurse."

"He loves everybody," Monk says. "He's a nice boy."

"He's in for a hell of a life." Jimmy says."

* * *

They pick up the medicine at the pharmacy and, at home, fifteen minutes after taking it, Kub is comfortably asleep. Then Monk and Jimmy and Nana and Marion have one last drink in the living room.

"Will you really file a complaint against that doctor?"

"Nah, I'll never get around to it."

"You really ought to."

"I guess I'm either too chickenshit or schizoid or maybe just plain lazy, but I never follow through on threats like that."

"He'll have the last laugh then."

"Yeah. I hope I at least spoiled his weekend."

* * *

When Jimmy rises to leave, Nana says, "Why don't you stay over?"

"Oh, I better be getting down to Long Beach,"

"It's nearly dawn. Stay and get a fresh start tomorrow."

"Do you have room for me?"

"The studio couch is yours."

"Okay. Thanks. It's been a long day,"

* * *

He lies alone on the studio couch, his wife two rooms away. He supposes they could have slept together but his pride would not allow him to suggest it. It doesn't matter; he feels no sexual need for her.

He did at one time. She was beautiful and young and different from any other girl that he had known, and he loved her madly and reduced himself to poverty for her. He still loves her, and the male in him vows to protect her always, and the male in him is wounded by her sleeping in the other room, but he no longer feels that stinging need for her. He slips easily into sleep.

* * *

In the morning he awakes to find Deena in her nightie by the side of the couch.

"Hi, Jimmy, You were uncovered. I covered you up."

"You're a good girl, Deena."

"You looked funny lying there without any clothes on, Jimmy."

"Yes, I bet I did "

"You looked like a fat turkey."

"A fat turkey? Well, maybe I am a fat turkey. How's your brother?"

"He's fine. Mommy says you had to take him to the hospital,"

"You slept through it all."

"I was as tired as a turkey."

"And Kubla was as sick as a turkey."

"And Poppop was as drunk as a turkey."

"Shhhhh... and Nana was as pissed as a turkey."

"...and Kenny talks like a turkey..."

"...and Uncle Robert wears turkey shoes..."

"...and I love you, Jimmy. I love you and I like you."

"I love you and I like you too, my little lover."

"Are we the turkey family?"

"All families are the turkey family, Deena. But the great question that philosophers have never been able to resolve is whether we are all equally turkeys or whether some of us are even bigger turkeys than others. I lean to the latter opinion when drinking, and to the former when hung over."

"Happy Day-after-Turkey-Day, Daddy."

"Thank you, Deena. Let's go see if Nana can manage a stack of pancakes for her grand-daughter and a can of beer for her son-in-law..."

THE FOUR-DAY WORKWEEK

The sequence opens Tuesday evening when they get home from the banquet at the Chinese restaurant. Jimmy sits down, has a drink, gets up, turns on the t.v., watches it for five minutes, goes back in the other room, has two more drinks, goes to the bathroom and discovers that he doesn't need to, has another drink, goes back to the bedroom where the Cavett show is on, sits on the bed and sips a drink...

Brenda is already in bed, trying to watch the television, but her eyes are beginning to close.

She touches his arm, and he tries to smile and be nice, but his heart isn't in it.

"What's wrong?" she asks.

"Ahhh... nothing important."

"It's Hank that's bothering you, isn't it?"

"Yes."

"I could tell. I tried to discourage him without actually hurting his feelings."

"I know."

"I'm sorry."

"I know. It's not your fault. I don't know where ol' Hank's head gets to sometimes."

"He was drunk."

"I know."

"And stoned."

"I know."

"You don't consider that an excuse, do you?"

"No."

"And if the roles were reversed?"

"No."

"He didn't actually try anything."

"I was sitting there all the time."

"He may have just been trying to be nice to me."

"Does he know me well enough to know I don't appreciate that sort of favor?"

"Yes."

"Is he among my very closest friends, my three or four close friends?"

"Yes."

"Do I treat my friends that way?"

"No."

"Okay. You go to sleep, love. I want to drink a little more before I come to bed."

"Don't let it make you sick, Jimmy."

"It's made me sick already."

*   *   *

He turns the light off and she falls asleep almost immediately. He fills his glass and watches Gore Vidal come on the Cavett show.

Vidal is making hay at the expense of Norman Mailer who is not in attendance. Jimmy hopes that watching Gore Vidal will dull his mind to slumber, and it helps a little, but finally it doesn't do the job. The show ends and he watches the late, late news.

At half-past one he goes back to the other room and sits there drinking, trying to, as they say in these days, get his head straight. Something will have to be done. He can request a change of office from the one he is sharing with Hank. He can give Hank a chance to explain himself, but that seems supererogatory, his behavior having been so forthrightly offensive. He can simply tell him not to consider him a friend from here on in. He can leave him a note to that effect. If he answers with impertinence he knows he won't be able to refrain from hitting him. He can just shine it on, but at the moment that seems inconceivable.

Jimmy, he tries to tell himself, you're sure to feel a little different in the morning. Go to bed now or you won't be able to function at all.

This is how it always starts, the killing of the nerves—it starts with the drinking of himself to sleep in the middle of the night. If he goes to sleep now, then it's sure to be better in the morning regardless of what course of action he eventually decides upon. If he doesn't get to sleep now, he may simply not be able to cope.

He finishes his drink, turns off the kitchen lights, and goes to lie down on the bed. He lies there stiffly on his back and then he turns upon his side and throws an arm around Brenda. He turns upon his other side. He rolls back on his back. He holds his testicles first in one hand, then in the other.

His mind is racing, a kaleidoscope of Polaroid stills from the evening: what they have in common is the insolence, insouciance, the utter disregard Hank wears upon his face.

Be sensible, he tells himself, you have a poetry reading to give at noon tomorrow. That girl's supposed to meet you after class tomorrow night. If you don't get to sleep you're going to be sick. Bad sick.

He gets back up. It's two a.m. I'll drink till three, he says. I'll drink every goddamn drop of alcohol that I can find around this place, and that's a lot. I'll read the newspaper and I will drink myself into oblivion. By God, by three o'clock there won't be enough adrenalin in the whole human race to keep me from falling asleep.

He commences to put his plan into operation. At three he staggers to the bed. He falls one hundred stories into sleep.

* * *

When he awakes, Brenda is long gone to work. He stumbles to the kitchen, takes a couple of gulps from an open bottle of coke, tries to focus his eyes on the clock. Ten o'clock. Thank God for that at least—he'd been afraid it was much earlier.

* * *

His alarm is still set for eleven. He lays himself back down upon the bed and kind of dozes for an hour. He doesn't really go to sleep; he isn't feeling very well at all.

The alarm goes off, scaring the cat, who, if she were human, would be an inmate of a mental institution. He rises, silences the ringing, turns some music on. He opens the refrigerator, removes a beer. He drinks half of it, gags, spits in the sink. He finishes the beer, opens another.

In between swallows of the beer, he dresses, washes his face, runs a toothbrush three times through his mouth. It's time to leave for school.

It takes ten minutes driving to the campus, twenty looking for a parking spot. The day is hot and windy. It's a hot and windy walk to where the reading's being held.

There are a handful of students milling around the lecture hall. "The reading's been postponed," they tell him.

"Oh," he says.

"Gwendolyn Brooks is reading at the Speaker's Platform."

"Oh.

"Your reading's been postponed till next week."

"Oh fine."

Well, he's here now, so he goes up to the office. Maybe Hank will be there—he would like to get it over with. He is surprised to find his anger has subsided little with the passing of the hours. Maybe he is still a little drunk.

Hank isn't there, so he goes down two floors to check his mail. He finds two manilla envelopes there waiting for him. One is from Marvin Malone at *Wormwood Review*, who has taken three of his poems and scrawled him a customarily gracious acceptance note. The other is from an unknown magazine in Baltimore, whose address he had gotten from the *Directory of Little Magazines*. The editor has rejected all the poems submitted and has penned a note on the back of a Campbell soup can label. It reads: "Thank you for submitting more of your work, and a large batch at that. Unfortunately I did not like any of your poems. In fact I found them totally lacking in even that minimal promise which I had seemed to perceive in your earlier submissions. So..."

He gets back on the elevator and descends to terra firma.

At the Speaker's Platform Gwendolyn Brooks is reading from her early works. There are a number of black students and the English professors are occupying the spaces on the grass nearest to the Speaker's Platform. Farther away, groups of white students are coming and going. It is not very good poetry, although no one seems ready to acknowledge that. Everyone seems to be rooting for it to be good, but it is nonetheless bad poetry. He stays for as much as he can stand of it, and quietly leaves in the direction of the coke machine.

He sips a coke and thinks, "It had all been going so well." He had been keeping the booze within reason, sleeping well, getting exercise, teaching responsibly, working on old manuscripts, turning out an occasional new poem. Ah well, he tells himself, today the piper must be paid, but I'll be back in stride tomorrow. Then he remembers the business with Hank and his gut goes sick again.

A couple of his students come by, both girls, one a tiny, highly cultivated and intelligent Eurasian girl, Dutch-Indonesian, and the other an immense and cheerful drama student from the back row, a regular Mama Cass.

"Coming from the reading?"

"Yes."

"Is it over then?"

"No."

"What'd you think of it?"

"Well..."

"Well..."

"Yeah, that's what I thought too. C'mon and have a beer with me."

"Sounds great. Okay with you, Pam?"

"Wonderful."

"Let's go. I'm parked behind the library."

*　*　*

They take a table in the sparsely populated beer-bar and he buys a pitcher. He lifts his glass, clicks it against theirs, and mutters "Kill or cure."

"Aren't you feeling well?"

"I am not feeling well at all."

"Should you be drinking then?"

"Oh yes, I should be drinking."

"Oh dear," says Pam, the dark one, "are you hungover again?"

"I am suffering, my dear," he sagely nods, "from a light touch of the existential flu."

The beer stays down, the next one does, the pitchers start to flow as on an invisible conveyor belt. "Ah brave new world," he suddenly announces, realizing he has warded off catastrophe for one more day. The problem now is just to last the day out slowly, get to bed a good deal earlier, sleep long and well, and start on life anew.

He feels so good now and the big fat girl especially is fun. They talk about her tastes in music and her taste in movies. It turns out that she likes just about everything. She goes to movies every Friday, Saturday and Sunday, and the only one she hasn't liked in two years was, for some inscrutable reason, *Women in Love*. She owns practically every album of every rock group of even the dimmest of reputations and the only one she hasn't liked is, inscrutably, *Sergeant Pepper*. She is a very inscrutable girl for a Westerner.

Pam has gone inside herself. She doesn't drink very often and it seems to affect her like pot does others. But he talks to her about Wordsworth and Coleridge, her beloved romantics, and she comes out of herself a while and converses brilliantly, her agile mind darting from Frye to Lovejoy, Abrams to Livingston Lowes. He hears her speaking names and notions that he hasn't heard since graduate school. He hears it all with a certain nostalgia.

He has taken her out before, at which time she was very frightened. She is a virgin in her early twenties. She has told him that she is in love with a friend of his, a student in a couple of his classes, a bright and worthy lad, but one who unfortunately is shacking up with someone else, someone upon whom the boy is very dependent, he not being among the most emotionally stable of young men. Of course she has never spoken to the boy of her love. In fact she has never spoken to him at all. It is all so literary that he can't believe it, but it has a certain adolescent charm. A pity that de Maupassant is not alive to write of it.

The afternoon wanes quickly. Pam has gone inside herself, a wanderer in her private Xanadu, while Sue is wafting herself heavenward upon a monumental cumulo-nimbus of her words and memories.

"I've got to stop by class," he says, "but why don't you just stay here and I'll be right back."

"Oh no," Sue sadly intones, "we've got to get home soon to start the supper."

"Yes," says Pam, "we have a permanent dinner guest, a starving artist."

"Why don't you come by for dinner too?"

"I can't tonight, but let me have your address and I will sometime."

"Good. Wonderful. And thanks for the beer. It was a lovely, lovely afternoon."

"You raised me from the dead."

"You're feeling better now?"

"Yes, yes, I've quite recovered."

* * *

His freshman class is doing term papers. It is simply a matter of showing up. There are four students there. He has corrected papers for three of them. The fourth is there to hand his in.

"Where are the rest of the class?"

"I saw a couple of them in the library still working on their papers.

"Oh. Good. Good place for them. Any questions?"

A silence prevails.

"Read the rest of the poetry in the anthology. Class dismissed."

* * *

He returns to the bar and is about to order a pitcher when the bar-maid says, "Your wife called. She wants to see you."

"Oh. Thanks. I'll take a six-pack to go, please."

He goes out to the car, opens a bottle of beer, wedges it into his crotch, and starts down the highway to his wife's place, which is only a few blocks from his and Brenda's. He turns on the staticky radio and says to himself, "What are you doing drinking in the car? Don't you know what they'd do if they caught you?" He takes a long swallow of beer which helps him to forget what they will do to him if they catch him.

Monk answers the door in an old robe and sweater. She is as cute as ever, a twenty-eight-year-old who looks about sixteen, but she is obviously well under the weather.

"You still sick?"

"I'm worse."

"The penicillin didn't help?"

"Not yet."

"Did you go back to see the doctor?"

"Yes, I went back to see the doctor and I went to see a different one as well, a friend of Grant's."

"What did this other fellow say?"

"He said I had an abscess and I should be in the hospital."

"So did you tell the doctor out at Kerner that?"

"He said I didn't have an abscess and I didn't need to be in the hospital."

"What do you want to do?"

"I want to die."

"We all want that. What do you want to do about the doctors?"

"I'm going to call tomorrow and see if I can get a different doctor."

"Good idea."

"I want you to sign a note admitting me to the hospital in case they want to and they can't get ahold of you."

"Okay."

"You want a drink?"

"Yes, please."

"Have you been drinking all day long?"

"Show a little respect for your old man. Here's the note."

"Thanks. Are you hungry?"

"No, but I'd better eat."

"There's cheese and cottage cheese and stuff in the refrigerator. Can you fix it?"

"Yes. Look Monk, I'm really sorry that this had to happen. I hate to see you sick."

"Those bastards—you know what one of them said when I went into the emergency—he said, 'The way you young girls run around these days there's no telling what you might have picked up.' And another one said, 'Yeah, yeah, I know, you're afraid you have gonorrhea, aren't you?'"

"Do you want me to call them?"

"What could you do?"

"I don't know what I could do, but I might be able to put the fear of God into them."

"Oh it would only make things worse."

"You've got to lean on them a little, Monk."

"What do you mean?"

"I mean keep emphasizing that you have a different opinion from a private physician. Let drop a few hints of malpractice suits. Be firm with them."

"You're thinking firm because you're drunk."

"Thanks."
"Well you've never been a Ralph Nader exactly."
"I know."
"I'm sorry, Jimmy. Here's your drink."

* * *

Surprisingly, or maybe not surprisingly, his seminar goes excellently. For one thing, they are discussing Susan Sontag's *Death-Kit*. For another, these are really a bright young bunch of people, much closer readers than himself, much closer to the discipline of literary study. The class runs almost to the time that it says in the catalog it is supposed to run to.

Afterwards they all go to the beer-bar.

This has become something of a tradition, the Wednesday night post-seminar. It has little to do with literature. It is devoted to beerdrinking, preferably of a hard-core nature.

He is waiting for Chris to show up. He had called her for the first time in nearly a year last Sunday. She had said that she was busy then but that she would show up for sure tonight.

They have been drifting together for a long time, ever since he met her through a girlfriend of hers that he was dating. She was dating someone else then, a guy who turned up later as a student in his classes, a guy he liked but who he knew was dating someone else now. She was attractive, very much so, and a funny, obscene, and outspoken conversationalist. That had always been a part of the problem, her total lack of discretion. His better judgement said no; a different part said yes.

He chats with the others at the table. Over at the bar, a bunch of guys are listening to the Lakers' playoff game on the radio. He doesn't want to hear it. They have been beaten badly by Milwaukee in the opener, and he wants so badly for them to win this one that he is afraid he will jinx them. He won't listen to it, but, win or lose, he promises himself that he will watch the t.v. replay on at midnight.

Chris comes in, then, but of all the impossible bad luck, she is with Bill, the guy that she used to date.

"Dear Jim," she says, "it's been an impossibly long time. And look who I found on my doorstep just as I was leaving."

Well it doesn't matter, nothing matters now that he is mellow. It is nice to have her sitting next to him, holding his arm from time to time, rubbing affectionately against him, even with Bill across the table. She is as funny as usual, funny at his expense, at Bill's expense, at her own—she is a born catalyst, and everyone is happy around her. It is a warm, good-natured Wednesday evening.

Then ol' Hank comes in.

Hank buys a beer and wanders over to the table: "The Lakers are ahead," he says.

"Listen, Hank," Jim says, as softly as possible, "what got into you last night?"

"What do you mean?"

"I mean you were a real pain in the ass to me."

"You're kidding."

"I'm serious."

"Come on, you *are* kidding me, aren't you?"

"No, I'm not."

"What did I do?"

"You were just making an utter Hank out of yourself."

"My God, I know I was drunk but . . , Jesus Christ..."

He turns and goes back to the bar, apparently stunned, apparently sincerely... while Jimmy asks himself, Why couldn't I have sloughed it off? Why do I have to make an issue out of things?...

He drinks a lot of beer down quickly and it numbs him. Once again it doesn't seem to matter.

Hank is back beside him though: "Jimmy, have you got a minute?"

"Of course."

He follows Hank out of the door:

"Did it have anything to do with Brenda?"

"Yes."

"Do you seriously believe I would do anything to jeopardize the friendship?"

"It looked as if you would..."

"For God's sake, man..."

"You didn't seem to give a shit..."

"I'd cut my balls off first..."

"It just seemed like you didn't give a shit."

The tears have come into his eyes now, which is something that he does not want. One thing to cry at home, that's bad enough, but how intolerable to bring childish sorrow with him to the bar...

"All I can say, old buddy, is, Forgive me."

He puts a hand on Hank's old bony shoulder, turns away, once more the ostrich. "Let's forget it; I've forgotten it."

"I've never felt so awful in my life."

"Forget it, please. I'm just a little crazy. Write it off to temporary madness on my part."

"I've got to go on home now—please, let's not let anything be spoiled."

"It won't be. I'm sorry I said anything. I just couldn't seem to shake it any other way.

"I'll see you Friday if not before."

"For sure."

*   *   *

He goes straight to the men's room, rinses off his face, adjusts it to conceal his softness. He is glad it's over, glad that nothing's really changed. No reason for him not to enjoy a good night's rest.

Except that he's already kind of drunk again. The Lakers win and he orders up a celebration round of pitchers. Chris is telling him she hopes he'll call more often. And now he notices that Jane is at the bar, the one who waited for him last week when he was with someone else.

The clock begins to melt now, as it passes through his mind that this is maybe what was meant by Dali's watches. Chris gets up to leave with Bill—they share a long kiss and agree to get together soon. Another good friend, Wee Geordie, and his girl arrive. There's talk of a basketball game on the outdoor courts and who was supposed to show up when and why they didn't and when they will...

Now Jane is sitting next to him. Now they are kissing amidst sympathetic laughter from the others at the table. Now they are going to her car. Now Jane is saying, "Let's go to a motel," and he is saying, "No, I have to see the Lakers' game at twelve," and she is saying, "We can watch it there," but he's insisting, "No, you say that now but I can't trust you not to distract me when the chips are down." So she goes down on him, and he says, "Yes, that's good, yes, that's very, very nice," and when it's over he rests ten minutes in her arms, then says, "I better be getting back inside." "You bastard." "Yes, I know, but..." "Do you think you'll ever take me for a fool again?" "I don't know, Jane, I'm really much too drunk to think." "Get out of here!" "Yes, certainly and thank you very much..."

*   *   *

He goes back in the bar where Geordie and his girl are nearly all that still remain. The Lakers replay has just begun.

At the first commercial break, Wee Geordie says to him, "You know where Linda works?"

"Unh-unh."

"You better ask her."

"Linda, where do you work?"

"I work at a massage parlor in Huntington Beach."

"You're shitting me."

"I'm not."

"She has a girlfriend works there also."

"Linda?"

"Yes?"

"*Where* do you work?"

"I work at a massage parlor in Huntington Beach."

"That's what I thought you said. Now let me ask you one more thing."

"Yes?"

"*Where do you work?*"

"She isn't kidding. She and her girlfriend have invited us for freebees Thursday night."

"Tomorrow night? I'll never get away."

"You've got to."

"Any other night."

"I had it all set up."

"Go back to work on the negotiations. Any other night I'd love to, but on Thursday nights I'm always faithful to my mistress."

* * *

Now the customers are drifting homewards. He is left with the bartender and one of the owners to finish off a pitcher or two for the road and savor the final moments of the Lakers' victory.

He leaves a little after two a.m.

He drives carefully, slowly, down the highway, no weave to the best of his knowledge.

He drifts into a parking space.

The door is locked. He reaches one arm through the window to unlatch it.

Brenda is asleep, a test pattern on the t.v.

He turns off the lights, leaves his clothes in a heap on the floor and is literally asleep before he hits the pillow.

* * *

He slides from sleep. He knows already what is happening, but gets up anyway and checks the clock. Six-thirty. Yeah.

He goes back to bed, hoping, but it is no good. He's wired. He might as well have dropped a handful of amphetamines.

He gets back up, takes a couple of Excedrin P.M.'s. After that, he relaxes slightly; his mind wanders; a couple of times he almost dozes off.

He gets up, takes a couple more pills. These don't seem to work at all.

He'd take a sleeping pill, a strong prescription pill, but he's supposed to box and lift weights with his buddy, Rog, at noon. If you take a sleeping pill, you've got to have plenty of time to sleep.

Soon it is time for Brenda to get up. He lies there while she puts herself together for her job as a third-grade teacher. Every so often she comes in to see if he has gotten back to sleep. He hasn't. "I'm sorry," she says. "Me too," he says.

She leaves, and he gets up, turns down the heat, drinks some coke, and tries to read. He can't concentrate. He feels like gagging. He can't relax lying down and he can't relax standing up. A beer might help, but you've got to break the cycle sooner or later and, since he hasn't any classes on Thursday, he'd better make this day the bad one.

He lies back down and then it hits him bad, the fear, the fear that he is losing his mind. He berates himself for not having laid in some tranquilizers from the doctor. Any reason would probably suffice. He remembers the girl he visited so often at Norwalk Metropolitan Hospital a year ago, that dread asylum. A voice insinuates, Turn yourself in. He has to warn himself that that is neither necessary nor would it most likely offer any comfort. He remembers the ex-alcoholic in the bar who told him about the d.t.'s and being in a straight-jacket and about waking in the night and having a few drinks to put him back to sleep.

He sweats; his feet are cold.

He gets up and dry heaves. It makes the stomach hurt. There's nothing down there.

Then he relaxes slightly, not enough to fall asleep, but

enough to pass the morning hours. He entertains erotic
fantasies, almost enjoys himself...

* * *

At eleven his alarm goes off. He gets up, pulls his clothes
on off the floor, splashes water on his face.
He calls his wife:
"You feeling any better?"
"Not really."
"Did you get an appointment with a different doctor?"
"No. I called her but she said that I should just go to my
appointment in the morning."
"Can I do anything?"
"No."
"Are you depressed?"
"Yes, I'm depressed."
"I'm sorry. Really."
"How are you?"
"Not good."
"Hungover?"
"A little more than that. Look, I'll get in touch again a little
later."
"All right."
"Can Nana keep the kids a little longer?"
"Sure. Unless you want them."
"Monk..."
"I wasn't serious."
"Oh... get some rest."
"Sure. Thanks for calling."

* * *

Rog is working on his patio, but he is in his sweat clothes,
ready to get started.
"How you feeling?"

"Not good,"

"Want to call it off?"

"Not this time. It should do me good."

"Let's go then."

They take their warm-up jog around the neighborhood. On the return stretch, Jimmy tells him what's been going on with Monk. Back at the garage-gym, Rog says, "Go on home; you don't want to work out today."

"No, I would like to."

"Go over to your wife's. Get on those bastards' asses."

"It's hard to even find a starting point."

"Get on the phone and tell them that you want to talk to the guy in charge and don't take no for an answer."

"Okay."

"Tell them you've already talked to your lawyers."

"You're right."

"It's too important a thing to go easy on, Jimmy. If anything happens and you didn't do everything possible for her, you'll never forgive yourself."

"I know."

"Then get out of here right now."

*　*　*

"I didn't expect you so soon."

"Neither did I. Look, where is Grant?"

"He's over working at his mother's."

"See if you can get him over here."

"All right."

So they all get together—he and his wife and the twenty-year-old kid who's living with her—in the front room of their hippie pad. "Okay, Grant," he says, "what do you think we ought to do?"

"I think we've got to get the two doctors to consult."

"Monk, what do you think?"

"I don't think there's anything we can do."

"Okay, I think I should try to light a fire under them at the clinic."

"I think you're right," Grant says.

"They'll be on their lunch hour."

"How soon should I call?"

"An hour maybe."

"All right."

"Do you want a drink?"

"No, thanks."

"I'd better go back to bed and get up again. I could have sworn I heard you say you didn't want a drink."

"A little respect, please."

"Something to eat?"

"Cottage cheese."

"You hate cottage cheese."

"I would please like a small goddamn dish of cottage cheese."

"I think I'll try to call Doctor O'Neill," Grant says.

"Who's he?"

"He's the other doctor that she went to. He's my mother's doctor."

"Good idea."

So he nibbles on his cottage cheese, and slumps back in the nearly bottomless wicker chair, and tries to hold his nerves together. He tries to plan what he will say to them at the clinic. He listens to Grant on the phone...

"Yes... hello... Dr. O'Neill's office... his secretary?... yes, well, this is Grant Travis... Travis... Yes, Grant Travis... v-i-s... no, no, I'm calling on behalf of Mrs.... yes, that's right, two days ago, yes, well, you see, she is also a patient at the Kerner clinic and, that's right, her doctor there insists there isn't any abscess, yes, that's right, no abscess, and he won't hospitalize her and, anyway, I wonder if I could talk to Dr. O'Neill... He's not in?... Well, could you have him call me?... An hour and a half?... All right... yes, I'll be here, the number is..."

Jimmy gets up, takes his dish out to the kitchen, takes a swig out of a bottle of organic apple juice, considers the cupboard full of vitamin pills... reconsiders... goes out on the steps... observes the miniature banana tree, and all the time there is a pit of cowardice within his gut, he has to tell himself repeatedly, "Hang on, hang on, tonight a sleeping pill, a good night's rest, and you will be all right..."

* * *

"The gynecology department, please... Hello?... My name is Abbey and I would like to speak to the doctor in charge of your department... Yes, my wife has been a patient with you and I am very severely concerned over what I consider to be the inadequate treatment she has been receiving... Dr. Stargell isn't in today?... Then I would like to speak to whoever is in charge *today*... Dr. Mimes... What time do you expect him back... okay then let me talk to his nurse..."

"Hello?... Yes, uh, my name is Abbey, James Abbey, and I am extremely concerned over the treatment, or the lack of it, that my wife is receiving in your clinic for what we have been assured by a private physician is a very serious... yes, Abbey, A-B-B-E-Y... and I would like to talk to Dr. Mimes at the earliest possible... An hour?... From lunch?... All right, all right, I'll give you my number and... yes, I will be here most of the afternoon, but please have him call me just as soon as..."

"He's calling in an hour."

"Look, man, I've got to run back over to my mother's. I'll be back to talk to Dr. O'Neill."

"Okay."

"You don't look good, man."

"I'm okay."

"Your stomach?"

"Kind of."

"Honest, man, you ought to try a little garlic."

"No thanks, Grant, but maybe later..."

* * *

Monk goes to her bedroom where she falls into half-sleep on the mattress on the floor. She is feeling pretty good on codeine pain-pills. Maybe he should take a hit himself. No, not today... today has got to be cold turkey.

He sits with her a while, then goes into the front room, plunges in the wicker chair, and listens to the f.m. jazz...

Eventually the hour passes, but there is no call.

Thirty minutes later, the phone rings. It is Monk's sister. He has to ask her to hang up.

Grant returns. They sit there in the living room abusing the medical profession. Eventually they run out of things to talk about, having little in common except his wife...

...who finally wakes up to join them in the silent afternoon...

The phone rings.

"Hello?"

"Mr. Abbey?"

"Yes."

"This is Dr. Gauthier."

"I was expecting..."

"Dr. Mimes? Dr. Mimes is very busy, we are all very busy, he has asked that I return your call, I am the doctor Mrs. Abbey has been seeing."

"Yes, all right, well, Dr. Gauthier, you understand that we have had a separate diagnosis from a private physician and it does not jibe with yours, in fact it is considerably more serious. He feels that my wife should be in the hospital..."

"Mr. Abbey, there is no need for your wife to go into the hospital."

"And you are sure there is no abscess?"

"Mr. Abbey, I have been a gynecologist for twenty years and..."

"Doctor, I'm not questioning your credentials. But no matter how long you have been a doctor you may still have made a..."

"If you have no confidence in me..."

"I do not even know you but..."

"What we are following is the established practice of the American Gynecological Community..."

"Apparently this other doctor is a member of some other Gynecological Community because he says that he would drain the abscess..."

"We no longer drain the abscesses, we do the major surgery."

"You do the what?"

"We do the hysterectomy. We take it all out—the ovaries, the tubes, the..."

"Listen, Doctor, couldn't you call Dr. O'Neill and consult with..."

"Dr. O'Neill can consult with *me* if he would like to. Dr. O'Neill can take over the care of the patient if he likes to. Dr. O'Neill..."

"Dr. Gauthier, we're paying Kerner lots of money so that *you* will take care of the patient and I am asking you..."

"I am a busy man. You want to bring your wife in here this afternoon, I will examine her. Otherwise..."

"Thank you for calling, Dr. Gauthier."

* * *

Grant puts him on the phone to Dr. O'Neill. Except that it is really Dr. O'Neill's receptionist. She has him hold the line. He holds for almost ten minutes. Finally Dr. O'Neill is on the line: "...He wouldn't call me?... No, I'm not surprised, that tribe out there are a world unto themselves... I've handled their mistakes before... No, you will have to stick with them, I'd put her in the hospital but it would run into the tens of thousands... Yes, she's a very sick girl... Yes, keep after them... You see that's what you get when you get mixed up with that sort of medical protection, they're supposed to give you proper care but they won't put you in the hospital till you're half dead... No, I won't call him... but if the roles were

reversed I certainly would call... Yes, just keep after them...
I'm sorry that it has to be this way... That's all right, Mr.
Abbey; yes it's quite all right..."

*　*　*

They stand around another hour trying silently to
formulate another plan. His nerves are jangling. Monk asks,
"What are you doing?"
"Just thinking."
"You've done more of that today than in the last five
years."
"Yes, I suppose so."
Finally they call their pediatrician at the clinic. They have
always trusted him, and his wife once took a class from Jimmy.
The pediatrician says that Dr. Gauthier is highly
competent. He says that Dr. Gauthier delivered two of his own
children. He says Monk should just continue seeing Dr.
Gauthier.
Jimmy thanks him.
Thanks for nothing.

*　*　*

It's five o'clock and all the offices are closing.
Time to go on home.
"A wasted afternoon," Monk says.
"I don't know," Jimmy replies, "maybe we shook them up
a little."
"We didn't shake them up," she says. "We didn't light any
fire under them. We didn't do anything."
"Thanks for trying anyway, man," Grant says.
As he leaves, Grant and Monk are on the phone to her
sister. Her sister wants Monk to drive up to Hollywood to be
examined by a different gynecologist.

* * *

Brenda is already home from school.

He tells her the story of the afternoon.

She isn't pleased. She doesn't like to hear of anything connected with his wife.

She feels he should have gotten legally divorced two years ago. She feels he should have married her two years ago.

She sits on the couch and grades arithmetic tests.

Later he takes her out to dinner but he is too sick to eat anything. He is so shaky, panicky, that he at one point tells her they are going to have to leave. But it passes and he sticks it out.

At home he watches t.v., trying to concentrate on the programs, trying not to think about the necessity of his sleeping well tonight, trying not to think of his manhood-failure with the doctors in their telephone encounters, trying not to think about the failures of his inner life back down the previous decade, back, perhaps, down through his lifetime...

Trying to get interested in Marcus Welby and to tell himself that everything is going to be all right.

At eleven he takes a sleeping pill and turns the t.v. off.

He lies there for two hours.

He is almost on the point of getting up and taking a second one when, belatedly, it hits him and he goes to sleep.

* * *

He doesn't dream of renaissance utopias or hippie communes.

* * *

He awakens feeling great, has a good lunch, teaches well.

Does an hour's work in the office, goes to the gym for a couple hours of basketball.

Goes to the bar, plays pool, but sticks to Coke. "Don't make a habit of that stuff," the bartender says. "I'm sure I won't," he says.

He gets in touch with Monk. She has been back to the gynecological clinic, which she has found in an uproar. She has been examined by the head of the department and other doctors. Dr Gauthier is outraged. But, ironically, it now appears that Dr. O'Neill was the one who was mistaken. She's already feeling better.

He goes to Hank's to watch the Lakers' game. They pull it out of the fire in the last ten seconds.

When he leaves, Hank hands him an envelope. He opens it in the car. It contains a brief note: "I think what I was doing was trying to be as 'charming' and 'witty' as I could to my friend's girl to make her feel good in a situation where she may not have felt comfortable. You are the boundary to my existentialism. Why am I such an asshole? I've never felt so shitty in my entire life. For Christ's sake, let's bury our hatchet in the Milwaukee Bucks."

At home he finds Brenda affectionate, needing his affection, ready for a nap.

Afterwards she falls asleep. He watches *The Cabinet of Dr. Caligari*, which, amazingly, he has never seen before.

He falls into an easy sleep, one eager for the morning.

THE ENGLISH GIRL

She doesn't appear in class until the third week of the semester. Southern California is in the midst of its annual Indian Summer heat wave, and she is wearing running trunks and a t-shirt and sitting in the first row. She is a big girl, a bit chunky about the middle, but with shapely legs and bosom and an intriguing face. From the way she glances at him it's impossible to tell if she is coy or shy.

At this point he doesn't know who she is, where she's from, or what she's doing here, so he launches into a discussion of Simon Ward's play, *Otherwise Engaged.* She seems surprised that this is the work assigned, but she takes notes assiduously.

The class is sluggish from the heat and time of day—this is the third Tuesday of a Tuesday-Thursday 5:30 to 7:00 schedule on the third floor of a poorly ventilated building. He is forced to do more of the talking than he'd hoped, especially since he has a limited number of points to make about this obvious play.

At the end of the period she approaches the podium: "I'm here as a part of a foreign exchange program from England. I hope my attending will be all right with you. I'm sorry to have missed the first couple of weeks, but we're on a different academic calendar back home, and I only arrived in California this weekend."

In truth, Jimmy doesn't mind anything that doesn't complicate his life, and so he says, "No, I don't mind, but you'd better pay a visit to the Records Office first thing in the morning and make sure you're properly enrolled in the course."

"That's all been taken care of between my school and yours. My name won't appear on the printouts you receive, but at the end of the semester you'll be given a separate form on which to report my grade. I realize the procedures are somewhat unorthodox, but I can promise you I won't be any great problem."

"Do you have the book list and the work you've missed?"

"Yes. The lady sitting next to me in the front row was exceptionally helpful. I've read most of the works already, but I don't mind in the least rereading them."

"I should think you would have read them. What in the world possessed you to come six thousand miles to study the literature of your own country?"

"I didn't choose the course. My department back home selected it for me. My program—my major I suppose you'd call it here—is teacher training. I'll be practice-teaching in one of the local schools. They wanted me to take one classroom course as well. So here I am."

"Okay, fine, I'm glad you're in the class. Just as long as you take care of all the technicalities and formalities yourself. I hate technicalities and formalities. I'm just no good at them."

"Everything will be seen to without any bother to you."

"Great. I'll see you on Thursday then."

Afterwards, over a pitcher of beer across the road, he regrets he hadn't had the presence of mind to have asked her along. The heat must be getting to his brain. Well, time enough for that. Might have frightened her off.

No doubt the English university system has come a ways since John Henry Newman's time, but Jimmy supposes faculty-student relations there may still involve a bit more distancing than in California.

* * *

Catching her at the bottom of the stairs after Thursday's class, he asks, "Where are you from in England anyway?"

"Are you familiar with Winchester?"

"Oh, sure, I could sing a few bars of Winchester Cathedral if you'd like, but since you probably wouldn't like, I won't.

Truth is I've never been to Winchester, but I've been to Salisbury. Not far apart are they?"

"Less than fifty miles. Salisbury is more what you'd think of as Hardy country. Winchester's not far out from London."

"You can give me some advice. I'm on sabbatical in the spring, and I don't have any plans yet, except I'd like to spend as much time as possible in Europe, but all I hear are horror stories of the prices. Where would be my best bet? You know, someplace that would be less expensive than London and yet not totally without interest. Maybe not too far by rail from London."

"I have just the place for you—Bristol. There's a university and the sea and it's on a direct line to London."

"I'm glad to hear you suggest Bristol because it had occurred to me on my own. I passed over Bristol and Bath on my way to Wales once and I've never forgiven myself for not spending some time in each."

"Or to go to an extreme, there's Newcastle-on-Tyne."

"You're not putting me on?"

"No, Newcastle's a lovely place. You must at least spend a few days there."

"Well, that's a new one for my consideration. Look, I'm going to wander down to the Nugget. Will you join me?"

"What's the Nugget?"

"It's the campus beer bar."

"Oh, well, I'd better not. I have my first lesson plan to do for tomorrow morning."

"Some other time then."

"Some other time."

She seems to be looking at him as if she would like to read his mind.

* * *

It's only a few days later that he ends up drinking with the English girl's "mates" in the Gold Rush Tavern. It seems there are only five of them at State on the exchange program, of whom four are young men specializing in Physical Education. There was supposed to be one other girl, but she flew back homesick three days after arriving. The English chaps are good lads: fun-loving, but well behaved, interested in beer and conversation, and what little there is to be had in the way of female companionship. Of the three Jimmy talks to, one is Welsh, and one is Irish, and one is from the North counties. They are full of advice for Jimmy on his sabbatical, and of promises to provide him with helpful addresses. The evening wears long, however, and it is only a few days since the launching of Lord Mountbatten into orbit and Jimmy's tongue is loosed to discourse upon his standard proposal for the reunification of Ireland. His newfound comrades have, however, learned at home the advisability of being circumspect in their comments on that particularly volatile subject, so Jimmy gets off it. He then spends forty-five minutes trying to understand cricket, a few of which he may even remember in the morning.

When his tutor, the Welsh lad, initiates an attack upon American football, Jimmy responds with a blanket condemnation of British athletics, recreations, cuisine, weather, politics, religion, family life, and sexuality. The diatribe is accepted in surprisingly good temper.

During the course of the increasingly drunken evening, the subject of the English girl is raised. The Irishman says, "We hear you have Ainsley Richardson in your class." Once they ascertain they are discussing the same person, the Irishman says, "She's a very intelligent girl."

"She seems so," Jimmy says, "but she also seems a little shy."

"Shy?" the Welsh lad interjects, "so shy that she nearly took me by force at the dorm party last Friday night."

The Irishman, who seems the unofficial leader and moderator of the group, mentions softly that Ainsley can be "rather physical" at times.

So the next morning, as he is downing Excedrin with ginger ale, Jimmy sorts out the implications of that disclosure.

The English girl is heterosexual.

She is not shy, not always at least.

She goes to parties; is most likely not a teetotaler.

She is apparently unattached.

She is a good student, would perhaps find a semester's liaison with her American instructor not totally without interest.

Her name is Ainsley Richardson.

So far, so good. It does not exhilarate him that she finds pretty, skinny Welsh lads with unpronounceable names attractive, nor that she is sexually forward, perhaps promiscuous.

Still, he shrugs, as the third of the Excedrin successfully evades his gag reflex, at least she fucks.

*   *   *

There is, however, one massive obstacle to be removed.

Elizabeth.

Elizabeth weighs at least three hundred pounds. Elizabeth is in the same class as the English girls. Elizabeth was in a class of his in the spring. Elizabeth is an excellent student, but Elizabeth wants him, and if Elizabeth cannot have him, Elizabeth does not want him to have anyone else. Elizabeth has a sixth sense for developing developments. Elizabeth is loud, pushy, unscrupulous, and devious.

He senses what's happening when, in the next class, the English girl is no longer sitting in the front row, but has moved back to the middle of the classroom next to Elizabeth.

As usual Elizabeth has been drinking in the Nugget before class. As usual Elizabeth draws attention to herself with loud and not-very-funny remarks. As usual Elizabeth interrupts his train of thought with cavils over some peripheral point of data in his lecture.

After class, Elizabeth comes up to him, with the English girls at her side: "Are you going to stop by the Nugget?"

"For a little while, I guess."

"Good. I've talked Ainsley into joining us."

* * *

Jimmy drops his books off in his office and drives from the upper faculty lot to the one adjoining the bar.

It's only four years since the legislature passed a measure allowing beer and wine on state campuses, but the food service people have done a creditable job of endowing what used to be a brightly lit section of the cafeteria with a modicum of atmosphere. He purchases a pitcher of light beer with three glasses, only to find, when he joins the women, that they are already drinking wine. Elizabeth is asking Ainsley, "Well, how do you find America?"

"You know the Beatles' famous reply to that question?"

"Yes, but I was interested in yours."

"Do you know how many people have asked me the same question?"

"I can guess but I haven't heard your answer."

The English girl sighs, and resignedly scowls: "First, I'm not quite sure why Americans are so concerned with how the rest of the world perceives them. You're doing quite well for yourselves, so what do you care?

"Of course everyone has been wonderful to me. Americans have a passion for hospitality to foreigners. It's more than a passion; it's an obsession, a national trait. It's so predictable I'm not even sure that it's necessarily praiseworthy. I'm already committed, for instance, to go home with my roommate to San Francisco over Thanksgiving, even though that's weeks away. I absolutely must be shown off to her parents."

"What do you think of the school you're working at?"

"I think the children are incredibly beautiful little spoiled brats who need to be told once in a while that they're wrong. Everyone tiptoes around the place in fear that they might irrevocably damage an incubating psyche. Most of the kids would benefit from at least one solid paddling or knuckle-rapping or a vigorous twist of an earlobe.

"On the other hand, I'm amazed at how old-fashioned the curriculum is. So little attention to art or music or plays or..."

"That's a very recent reaction," Jimmy interjects, "to what was seen, accurately or not, by the public as a swinging too far in the direction of 'permissive' or 'progressive' or 'smorgasbord' education. The battle cry the last couple of years has been 'back to basics.' The three R's. Little red schoolhouse. Which incidentally is thought of by the taxpayers as cheaper. No frills. More specifically, a voter's initiative known as Proposition Thirteen limited property taxes, and resulted in budget cuts in the schools. These shifts back are so new that it's still something of a shock to hear a product of the English system criticizing our schools for their rigidity."

"What do you think," Elizabeth asks, with a delicious malice of intent, "of Doctor Abbey's class?"

"I think that most students are lazy, inarticulate, unmotivated, and unfit for college. Mind you, I'm not speaking of you, Elizabeth. You're terrifyingly bright, and I doubt there are ten books you haven't read, but I'm surrounded by more sloths in that class than on my visit to the San Diego Zoo."

"Here, let me pour you another glass of wine. If the wine is having the same effect on you as on me you should be sufficiently emboldened to tell us what you think of the professor himself."

"It's too soon to tell about our illustrious instructor, but I would take exception to his choice of *Otherwise Engaged* and *Lucky Jim* to be included in the reading. In my country Ward and Amis are considered lightweights."

Jimmy feels his face heating up: *Otherwise Engaged* was a

last-minute substitution for Osborne's *Look Back in Anger*, which is out of print in paperback.

"I hadn't seen it or read it in advance, but I'd seen *Butley* both here and in London and had been impressed by it. I wanted one play to lead into a quick survey of the flourishing of British theater in the last few years. Ward, Nichols, Stoppard, Orton, Griffiths, Shaefer, Mortimer, and the rest. For that matter, I think *Otherwise Engaged* is well done. I've used *Lucky Jim* for years as an introduction to the whole social revolution which carried from the Angry Young Men and Beats up through Civil Rights, drugs, rock, Vietnam, students and feminism, the gays, and all the accelerated social change of which Jim's popgun of a protest is the first shot fired. It's at that point, you see, that someone finally caught on that his failure to adjust to the system might not be his fault but that the system might need overhauling. I went over all that before you'd landed at LAX. I'd also explained that I adamantly refuse to defend or even to discuss my reading list."

"It wasn't my fault I missed the first two weeks of class."

"My, my, you two are off to a great start," Elizabeth intercedes. "We're off and running on another semester of fireworks." She rearranges the conversation with herself at the center.

* * *

Elizabeth loves to talk about herself. Jimmy has heard it all many times now. How she nearly flunked out of UCLA because she couldn't spell. Her studies in Arabic. Her involvement with Arabic and Persian students. Her alienation from her Glendale family. Her travels in Europe. Her illness. Her brilliant uncle, only a couple of years older than herself. Her bachelor's in anthropology. Her dilemma of choosing between literature and linguistics. Ah well, Jimmy tells himself, we all repeat ourselves when we're drunk.

The boredom of it frees his mind for other calculations. This campus bar closes early. He'll invite the English girl to continue drinking with him at the Gold Rush, but Elizabeth will want to tag along. As he knows from past performances, she will try to make it appear that she is with him, maneuvering herself to his elbow whether he is playing foosball or pool or just drinking beer. Then, around midnight, she'll remember she has to get up early for work and she'll ask him for a ride home. At her apartment, she won't get out of the car unless he does. Then she won't go through her door unless he precedes her. Then... he doesn't even want to think about what will happen then. By the time he gets back to the bar, the English girl will have left with someone else. Most of his life, he has found himself caught off guard, but this one triumphant time, after Ainsley says that yes, she wouldn't mind getting a look at the Gold Rush, and Elizabeth adds that she guesses she could stand a glass of wine there also, Jimmy says, "I won't be able to give you a ride home later, but Ainsley and I can drop you off now, if you'd like." Elizabeth, too startled to be angry, stammers, "Oh... Oh... Okay."

In the car he does his best to pretend he needs directions to Elizabeth's apartment.

*   *   *

A tableful of his friends is already at the tavern when he arrives with the English girl. He hasn't seen any of these guys in a week and, in some cases, it's been a lot longer than that. As a result they have quite a bit to talk about, everything from literary schemes to the Rams' declining fortunes. He realizes that he isn't paying the girl as much attention as he should be, but he rationalizes that she's getting plenty of attention from other quarters. There will be time enough for the two of them later in the evening.

He's getting higher now, high enough to rise at one point and lead the traditional sing-along with Sinatra's "My Way."

He knows he may be making a fool out of himself in her eyes, but if so, fuck her. There's more fish than her in the sea. Or so it seems at least at this level of blood alcohol, although there are damn few fish to be spied in the bar.

They do begin to draw closer near the end of the evening. His arm is resting comfortably and apparently unresented around her waist when a fight breaks out. Some guy nobody knows has slapped the owner of the bar in the face. The owner, an old friend of Jimmy's, has dragged his assailant by means of headlock along the length of the bar floor and out into the parking lot. He's pinned to the asphalt there, but Jimmy has leapt to his feet, and rushed out with the bartender and a couple of other guys in case some allies of the stranger should suddenly materialize. They don't, and after reasoning with him for a while, the owner releases his attacker. The man winds to his feet, scowls at the assembly, and takes a measured but undelayed leave.

It wouldn't surprise Jimmy if the guy returned with a gun. Nothing would surprise him anymore. It's just as well the bar is about to close. Jimmy returns to the bar to find the English girl talking with Ted Rowe, a young guy Jimmy has known over a long period of time although not very well. They once played a drunken one-on-one basketball game on an unlighted court—well, Jimmy was drunk at least—which Jimmy managed to win, two games out of three, only by committing every foul in the book plus inventing a few that had never been written down. Other times Ted had been thoughtful enough to drive up to L.A. for poetry readings Jimmy had given. They'd had many sports conversations, and a couple of monumental bets. As the baseball season draws to a close, Jimmy is about to foreclose on the forty dollars owed him for their most recent wager, a highly imaginative and involuted affair involving the unsuccessful comeback bid of Andy Messersmith. Jimmy's always thought of Ted as a buddy, and it should have been obvious that the English girl was with Jimmy, and he can't remember ever having seen Ted with a girl before, let alone having perceived any sexual aggressiveness, but it looks as if this buddy is in the process of moving in on the girl, and that she reciprocates his interest. So, as the opportunity presents itself along about last call, Jimmy says to her under his breath, "If you want to leave with someone else, feel free."

To which she defiantly responds, "That's big of you."

"I'm just trying not to stand in your way."

"That's all right. I can arrange a ride back for myself."

Jimmy throws up his hands. Whether she believes it or not, it looks as if her version is that Jimmy's dumped her. She gets up, and seats herself next to Ted. A few minutes later, they all stream out the door, she goes with Ted to his car, and they drive off. Jimmy tries not even to look their way. As is their custom, Jimmy and his friends have purchased a couple of six-packs to go which they now consume leaning against their cars parked on the side street. About half-way through the second six-pack, Ted pulls up, alone. Jimmy hands him a beer and says, "Thanks for relieving me of my burden."

"What do you mean?"

"You know goddamnn well she was with me."

"I didn't know that."

"Horseshit you didn't. You're a trusty friend to have around. Remind me to introduce you to my wife sometime. In fact, I'll give her your number in case she ever needs a ride anyplace when I'm not around."

"Sure, I'll give your wife a ride anytime."

"You shut your fucking mouth or you'll give my fist a landing pad smack in the middle of your fucking face."

Ted shrugs. He still seems half-abashed, half proud of himself: "If it comes to that, I'll do what I have to do."

When Ted first arrived back, the other guys there had done their best to take the whole scene as amusing, but now they're setting their empty bottles on the curb, and getting in their cars. They wave, and Jimmy waves back. As the others drive away, Jimmy and Ted stand there finishing their beers, not saying anything, not looking each other in the eye. There isn't much to say or do. Jimmy is bigger and Ted is younger. If they fight, Jimmy will probably win the same way he won the basketball match—by fouling. But what's there to fight about? Ted was back so quickly he couldn't have done anything except drop the girl off. Jimmy's no longer interested in her anyway.

From a sense that Ted shouldn't get off scot-free, Jimmy says, "I owe you one, and you owe me forty bucks," and he walks to his car.

In the morning, he's sorry he even bothered to say that.

* * *

The next Tuesday he makes a point of arriving at class early, so he can greet the English girl with a smile as she takes her seat, letting her know, as he has always scrupulously maintained it, that their social relationship, for better or worse or even in its now non-existent state, in no way alters, affects, modifies, or impinges upon their academic relationship. From the propriety—not to mention sobriety—of the smile she returns him, he takes it she understands this.

* * *

He avoids the campus beer bar after this class and after Thursday's. When he sees the English girl is in class the next Tuesday, however, something moves just a bit inside him. It's not any cover-girl pulchritude. If anything, she's looking dumpier than usual, but there is still the variety and ambiguity of her expressions. Beyond that, they could be, for a time at least, so goddamnn perfect together.

Maybe just for the fall... maybe to carry over into the spring in England... if they went about it with the right attitude... taking it for what it could be for the time being... he could bring California alive for her. She could do the same for him in England. Whether it were to turn into something longer lasting than that, they would just have to see.

The farce of the Thursday night in the Gold Rush has already faded into the recesses of his past.

He decides to stop by the Nugget after class.

* * *

She's there with Elizabeth. Along with his own pitcher of beer, he purchases a small carafe of rosé which he brings to their table.

"Mind if I join you?"

"No, please do."

He notices a bandage on the inside of her elbow. "Ah, shooting heroin! That's going American with a vengeance. Or were you giving blood? In return for that our dear boys shed at Omaha Beach."

"You're close," Elizabeth says. "But she wasn't *giving* blood; she was *selling* it."

"Are you serious?"

"Just plasma," Ainsley says. "Twice a week. My grant has been held up and it provides me with pocket money."

"Isn't it bad for your health?"

"Do I look like I'm withering away?"

"No, I won't try to tell you you're sylph-like, gossamer, and evanescent. If I were to fall on hard times in the spring, though, do you think I could pick up a few shillings the same way in England?"

"I'm afraid not. Different system, you know. The National Health, and all that."

"Well, it would make one appreciate one's wine, knowing it was paid for with one's own blood."

"Unfortunately it doesn't seem to have slowed my pace a bit."

"Well, I'm buying tonight. Can't promise I'll always be able to, but I can't allow you to shell out your cash with a bandaged arm."

*   *   *

The conversation is going fine, and he and Ainsley have exchanged a couple of deep looks that seem to say all is forgiven on both sides, when two young drunks insist on joining them. Jimmy has managed to avoid these guys for six months. He's polite now, but not encouraging. One of them, a light Chicano named Jaco, immediately launches into a flirtation with Ainsley.

Another girl, a student of Jimmy's from the previous semester, comes to the table to say a few words to him. Jaco, whose advances have apparently been repulsed in the past, turns his malicious tongue on her. He's not witty, just crude. Jimmy has a hunch the performance is for his benefit. If the girl was with him, if anyone at the table was his responsibility, he would have to say something. Which might be playing into Jaco's hands.

Jimmy gets up and goes to the bar. He buys another pitcher, and spotting at a different table a couple from the same class, he joins them. The guy says, "You're leaving your friends?"

Jimmy replies, "The two who just sat down aren't friends of mine. Some people I'd rather not drink with."

He chats with these two about their jobs and backgrounds. When he glances over his shoulder, Ainsley is standing at the bar, flanked by the two assholes, while Elizabeth and the other girl have left.

A little later, as the bar is closing, he notices that Ainsley and the assholes have left also.

Outside the bar he finds Ainsley still flanked by Jaco and Maury and looking as if she could use a friend. Jimmy bids the couple he's been drinking with good night and swings towards the trio. Jaco says, "We've been trying to talk this lovely British thing into smoking a little dope with us."

"Yeah? Ainsley, I'm changing venue to the Gold Rush. You want to come along?"

"I don't want to stay out late."

"You don't have to. I can give you a ride back."

"You said that once before."

"You found a different chauffeur."

"Out of necessity."

"That's not my recollection... but come on, I'll drive you home when you want to go. Promise."

"Hey," Maury says, "We're going, too. We can ride along, can't we?"

"Okay," Jimmy says, "I'm parked in this lot."

*   *   *

It's only a couple of minutes to the Rush. Jimmy positions himself next to Ainsley at the table, letting Maury buy the first pitcher. Jaco runs across the street to a fast food place for a hamburger. While they're alone at the table, Jimmy says, "I thought you could use an alternative."

"I wasn't sure. Are they basically all right?"

"They're basically awful. We're not going to be here long. In a few minutes I'm going to get up from the table to buy the second pitcher. When I return, I'm going to say, 'Here, you guys finish this, we've got to get going,' at which point you get up quickly, and we're out of here before they know what's happened." And that is exactly how they bring it off.

*   *   *

In the car, Jimmy says, "There's a place we can have a drink just down the road."

"Tell me about those guys."

"Maury is intelligent but a bore. Jaco has big problems. I don't know the causes. Maybe being Chicano. Maybe being short. Maybe something to do with being in the service. Maybe he always wanted to play pro basketball. I don't know. He has a fair intelligence and he wants to be a writer, but he ain't no genius and I haven't seen any sign of literary talent either. He's very resentful of authority, so I made a point of trying to be complimentary to him at first. As soon as he'd get drunk, he'd become so insulting to me I finally got sick of it one night, and warned him to cut that shit out. So the next week he's in the Gold Rush again, and he's trying to get me into a pissing contest but I'm in a terrible mood, and not even listening to him. Finally he pisses off a friend of mine who tells him, 'Look, you think everybody hates you because you're a Chicano, but I'm a Chicano myself, and I can't stand you either.' Later, when the bar closes, the bartender lets the rest of us stay in for another round, but he tells Maury and Jaco they have to leave.

"When we come out of the bar we find the windshield and hood of my buddy's old Mercedes all smashed and dented. Some people come out of a house, and say they saw this little guy do it with a big hunk of concrete, and then run away.

"Well, to shorten the narrative, my buddy put the word out he was going to cut off Jaco's nuts and stuff them down his throat. He filed a report with the police, but two days later Jaco called him up, and said he'd been in jail, he must have gotten busted wandering drunk down the highway that night, and that he'd pay for all the damages.

"He did pay for everything, five or six hundred dollars, although it would have been more if Rafe hadn't gone to a lot of trouble to get the repairs done as cheaply as possible.

"Now, you'd think that would make a happy ending to the story, but instead of figuring he really stepped on his dick, and maybe he just can't drink, Jaco decides it's all my fault, and I turned two Chicanos against each other. Since I never enjoyed his company anyway, I let word filter back to him through some mutual acquaintances that I think it would be a good idea if we just go our own ways socially.

"And we have, until tonight."

Ainsley nods and says, "Mmmm," but Jimmy can tell she's decided to keep an open mind. Jimmy may be a liar. Jaco may be a great guy.

* * *

Over vodka tonics at the bar of the cocktail lounge, they get a lot closer quickly. Jimmy kisses her for the first time and for the second and the third. They are practically the only customers except for a pair of German businessmen staying at the adjoining motel. Unfortunately, the Teutons are very drunk and the younger one decides he must engage Ainsley in conversation, even though he does not know more than ten words of English.

She is very polite to the guy. Her German is good. Jimmy's is spotty, and learning she is a fellow European, the German insists he and she exchange addresses, which she does, on the proverbial match covers. Jimmy is beginning to wonder if he has allowed himself to become somewhat attached to the legendary girl who can't say no.

Throughout this, the German is maintaining a constant aren't-we-all-citizens-of-the-human-race smile whenever he glances in Jimmy's direction. While Jimmy is abandoning any pretense of amiability. When Ainsley leaves for the lady's room, the German points to where she has been sitting and more through gestures than words communicates the question, "She is yours?"

"Yeah," Jimmy replies. "So fuckenzee off."

That has only temporary effect.

The bartender doesn't like the Germans either, but he has his own way of handling them. He asks them whether they want to order a round, and when they make an affirmative wave of their hands, he pours drinks for Jimmy and Ainsley as well. "These are on the krauts," he tells Jimmy. "And so are any more you want."

"Are you sure?"

"Sure I'm sure."

When Ainsley suggests she shouldn't stay much longer, the bartender says, "Stick around. You'll be doing me a favor."

They stick around until closing. The younger German

fawns over Ainsley, while the bartender and Jimmy talk the older German out of his plans to visit San Francisco and Hawaii. They assure him neither place holds a candle to Long Beach in beauty, cuisine, sophistication, or night life.

When Jimmy and Ainsley finally leave, the Germans are in a state of shock over the tab that has just been presented them, while the bartender is offering the information that twenty percent of it will be an adequate gratuity.

* * *

In the car, Jimmy says, "Did you give him your real address?"

"Why not? He'll never get to England."

"He got to America."

"Do you really mind?"

"To tell you the truth, we have a custom here in the West, dating back to the discovery of gold at Sutter's Mill, that you don't give out your address or phone number to one guy when you're out with another. Or if you do, you do it on the sly."

"You'd rather I act like a sneak?"

"I'd rather you didn't encourage every man who puts the make on you."

"I think your ideas are old-fashioned and ridiculous."

"They may be but they're mine."

"You want me to behave as though you're my Lord and Master?"

"No, I just want you to behave as if you're with me when you are with me. Otherwise I don't find the experience a pleasant one."

"You didn't enjoy this evening?"

"I enjoyed it very much up to a point. Then I didn't care much for it."

"Well, it seems obvious to me that you shouldn't repeat unpleasant experiences."

"You're goddamnn right, I shouldn't."

"It's this driveway."

"And it doesn't usually take me two doses of the same bad-tasting stuff to cure me of it."

"You can let me off right at that walkway."

"And I can assure you that I won't make the same goddamnn mistake again."

"Come here," she says, and as they kiss, it's the first time she shows anything approaching passion.

"Are you still angry with me?"

"Yes."

"Oh fiddle!" she shoots back, as she removes herself from the car and slams the door behind her.

Jimmy thinks, I'd better sit here and watch her get safely inside. Otherwise, with my luck she'll get murdered and the bitch will be responsible for my going to the gas chamber.

* * *

The next morning Jimmy swears off her again.

That Thursday night she is not in class for the midterm.

The following Tuesday she is in class and she waits outside for him afterwards: "I didn't take the test because I haven't been here long enough to catch up on the work I missed."

"I don't give makeups."

"It would have been an insult to your intelligence and to my own."

"It doesn't count either for you or against you."

"I didn't think you'd want me to fake it."

"Just do well on the next test."

"I have a very high average at the college I came from."

"Look, it's no big deal. It wouldn't be whether I knew you or not. It's only one test. Now are you or are you not going to the Nugget?"

"All right, but just for a little while."

* * *

Jaco is in the bar again. They're not at their table for long before he wanders up with a literal drunken Indian. This guy is an unfortunate stereotype who is stumbling drunk whenever Jimmy sees him in a bar, and who is even more unfortunately very big and rumored to have pulled a knife on occasion. Once, a year ago, Jimmy had a brief oblique exchange with him in the Gold Rush. Now the Indian stands above where Jimmy is sitting, and Jimmy suddenly realizes the Indian would like to say something provocative, but he is too drunk to speak.

"Go ahead," Jaco whispers, "follow your inclination. Do what you think you ought to."

Jimmy breaks whatever truce may have existed with, "You got someone doing your dirty work for you these days, Jaco?"

"No. I always do my own. Unlike some people."

"Some people don't do dirty work."

The Indian wanders off to the bar then and Jaco follows him, only to return a few minutes later to Jimmy's table. He plops himself down across from Ainsley and leers at her.

"I really wish," she says, "you wouldn't look at me like that."

"Oh," he says, momentarily abashed, "excuse me." After a couple of swallows of beer, he recovers himself and says, "I'll look at you any way I damn well please, and you know you love it."

"I find it repulsive."

"You love it because you can tell I have balls. You can tell I have big balls, that I'm a..."

"Listen," Jimmy fires at him, and he leaps to his feet, and punctuates his sentences by banging his chair on the floor. "This is two weeks in a row you've sat down without being invited and caused trouble. I've warned you before about taking advantage of the fact I'm limited in what I can do on campus, but I'm leaving campus now, and you know where you can find me." With a final bang of the chair, he storms out of the room.

* * *

He has to remind himself to drive cautiously in spite of the adrenalin. Jaco will have the last laugh if he gets into an accident or gets a ticket. He's never been able to stay pissed off for long, though, and by the time he gets to the Gold Rush he's calmed down a lot. It's only over his first beer that he realizes he should probably have taken the time to invite Ainsley along.

He's on his third beer and talking to one of the bar guys about the Rams when Jaco comes through the door, goes to the far end of the bar, and orders a schooner. Jimmy ignores him.

A couple of minutes later, Ainsley arrives. "I wanted to be with you," she says.

"I'm glad you came. I should have waited for you."

"It's not a long walk."

He gets them a pitcher, and they go to a table. Ainsley sees Jaco: "What do you think he'll do?"

"We'll have to see."

"I hate violence. It makes me sick to be around it. That was one of the problems the first night when you went outside."

"I'll try to avoid it."

They try to talk of other things: her teaching, a movie they've both seen, but he's distracted, of course, by Jaco's presence. He's just as glad it isn't too long before Jaco approaches their table.

Jimmy says, "I really wish you wouldn't sit down."

Jaco says, "You can't tell me what to do."

"Look, Jaco," Jimmy sighs, "everything was fine for six months because we stayed out of each other's way. Why don't we just keep it like that?"

"You can't talk to me the way you did in the Nugget."

"I can talk to you any way I like, but let me say this: I don't dislike you. I respect the things about you that deserve respect. But you get all fired up when you're drunk, and you end up doing things that you regret the next day, and that cost you a lot of trouble and money, and since you have this great hostility towards me, I think it would be to both our advantages to keep away from each other."

"I'll leave. But only because I want to, and I want you to know that in my eyes you're a nothing, a zero, a cipher."

"What you don't seem to realize is that's exactly what I want to be in your eyes. I don't care what you think of me. I don't want to be a part of your life nor of you to be any part of mine."

Jaco returns to the bar with his schooner and throws over his shoulder, "Where are your friends tonight?"

Of course there are several of Jimmy's friends in the bar, but he doesn't bother to point that out. In order not to let the remark hang unanswered, he says, "Go beat up someone's car."

Jaco lets that pass, but Jimmy is sure there will be more to the evening. He keeps one eye on the guy as Ainsley says, "You were right about him. He is awful."

"Thank you for allowing me that much at least."

"Proves that nobody's wrong all the time. I'm glad there wasn't a fight."

"There may still be. And that may be for the best. I think I made a mistake in trying to be diplomatic. Like dealing with the Russians—it's only taken for weakness."

Jimmy takes a swallow of beer and stares deliberately in Jaco's direction. Just then a very dear old friend of his shows up, a fellow he hasn't seen in months who has come by especially looking for him. Jimmy explains why he's on edge, but it's unnecessary: his friend remembers Jaco from playing pool against him the year before and what he remembers most is that he couldn't stand him. Jimmy goes to buy another pitcher, making sure he does it close enough to give Jaco a chance to start something if he wants. Jaco looks the other way.

Ainsley, of course, is already getting along famously with Jimmy's friend, and for once he's glad to have the chance to partake only minimally of the conversation as he collects himself.

He goes to the men's room which involves cruising past Jaco. There is still no response. Finally, just after he has returned to the table, Jaco pushes his schooner away from him, turns to them for a quick attempt at a swaggering wave, and leaves the bar.

* * *

Jimmy's friend is such an intelligent and entertaining guy that it turns into a good evening for the three of them. Roy has gone to the trouble of memorizing every stanza of "What shall we do with a drunken sailor?" that he has been able to research. Jimmy expends the poisoning adrenalin on his part in their rendition of the chanty. Recently back from France and England, Roy has also mastered the representative British dialects. He gives them an amazingly professional performance. Then, they all have Paris anecdotes to trade. The empty pitchers multiply as the hands of the clock race to closing.

* * *

They park in the lot outside the dormitory. Ainsley says she won't go to a motel with him, not tonight at least, and she says he can't come to her room because of the roommate. His car is not designed for intercourse, especially not for people their size, and especially not with the campus police periodically circling them, but they become very close in the car. They are close till nearly dawn.

* * *

The next morning he again swears off of her. Everything is progressing too slowly. Who needs her brand of grief?

California is overrun with better-looking girls than she is. Plenty of them would treat him better than the English girl does.

But the next week he is with her again, leaving campus in the car.

"Where do you want to go?"

"Anyplace but the Gold Rush."

"How about to a motel?"

"No."

"Why?"

"Well, for one thing because I spent the weekend catching up on the collected works of Jimmy Abbey."

"Oh."

"And I don't want to be your seasonal lay."

"I don't think in those terms."

"You don't? Elizabeth says she was your spring lay."

Jimmy nearly drives into a telephone pole: "THAT CUNT SAID WHAT?????"

"She said you were lovers last spring, and last fall you were sleeping with Margaret."

"She introduced you to Margaret?"

"The three of us had lunch on Saturday. Well, did you?"

"Did I what?"

"Did you go to bed with Elizabeth?"

"Look, there's a big difference between going to bed with someone and being lovers."

"Then you did."

"God... how shall I put it... okay, let's paraphrase your countryman Sir Edmund Hillary: She was there. I was drunk. I wondered what it would be like to wallow in that much flesh. I found out. My regrets were immediate and profound. I wish I could obliterate the experience from memory, but she won't let me. Don't you see? She told you because she knew it would keep you from going to bed with me."

"Actually, she told me she thought I should. She even said to put in a good word for her."

"Oh, my God... I can't stand it... it makes me sick... I'll murder her... I'd run her over in my car, but it wouldn't make a dent... I'll have to rent a Sherman tank... order a B-52 strike... call for the multi-warhead ballistic missiles..."

"She really cares for you."

"But I don't care for her, and she's purposefully sabotaging things between us. She's set it up in hopes that, if she fails to keep you out of bed with me, she'll at least be present right there between the covers with us. God, I loathe her."

"She's got it figured out that you seduce us fat, intelligent girls by flattering us that we're attractive..."

"Ainsley, you're a big girl, but you're not fat in the sense in which Elizabeth is fat. Nobody is fat in that sense. If Elizabeth were a lady wrestler she'd be in a weight class by herself. Elizabeth *is* a lady wrestler."

"Well, her friendship is very important to me. At this point in my life, true friendships with women are more important than trivial relationships with men."

"So, she's done it then. She's succeeded. Thou hast conquered, Pale Elephantine."

"If you're going to talk that way you can just take me back to the dorm."

"No, I'm not taking you back to the dorm until I have a drink in that bar right over there."

"I can walk back, you know. I can hitchhike."

"You can fly back, for all I care, but you'd better have a drink with me first. Those air corridors can chill the bones."

It's a whiskey bar, and the English girl, who's given blood again that afternoon, gets drunk fast on the hard stuff. She grows abusive, but has trouble pronouncing her polysyllabic attempts at invective. The person she is attacking, he realizes, is the person she thinks he is from his poems and stories, and from the amateur analyses of the women she's discussed him with. None of it matters. He's enjoying his drink, and her diatribe frees him from the task of conversation. After a while, though, he does interrupt her to inquire, "Where'd you get my books anyway? I hope you didn't pay good money for them."

"What? Spill my life's blood for your solipsistic indulgences? I borrowed them."

"From Elizabeth? I think she only has a book or two."

"I borrowed them from someone who has a more complete set of your *oeuvres* than Elizabeth. Someone who, inexplicably enough, admires you tremendously."

"Obviously I don't have a clue."

"I refer to Ted."

"You're still seeing him!"

"Of course I'm still seeing him. I've been seeing him regularly ever since that first night. He took me to see *Yanks* Saturday night."

"*Yanks*? I'd hoped to take you to that one myself. I figured it could be 'our movie'.."

"Well, you needn't get all jealous over it. It did have significance for me, but my nostalgia was for neither you nor Ted. It was for a Yank I knew back home."

"Only one?"

"We're no longer an occupied land, you know."

"No, you're a preoccupied one. Anyway, that sure relieves my mind—knowing your tears of sentiment were shed for someone other than Ted. Let's get the fuck out of here."

"Oh, dear, you're actually angry, aren't you? Could this be a genuine emotion from the regressive rake?"

"I'm leaving."

"I'm not finished with my drink."

"You're finding your own way home anyway."

"Wait a minute. I'm having trouble walking. Let me lean on you."

Wonderful, wonderful. He's got a big sick broad on his hands, about to sit down on the sidewalk just a few blocks from the apartment to which his wife may even now be returning from visiting her parents.

Or is she less drunk than she seems? Just faking?

He gets her into his car, and drives as quickly as he can, without risking a ticket, to the dormitory parking lot. Since all the legal places are taken, he pulls into a red zone.

"So you've had it with me."

"Let's go," he says, and he exits the car to open her door for her.

Standing on the asphalt, she leans heavily against him. They're in each other's arms when a campus police car enters the lot and comes to a halt with its lights on them.

"Shit," he says, "let's get out of here." They get back into the car, and he drives to another lot, a nearly empty one. She lies back across the seat with her head resting on his lap and he reaches into her blouse.

"Small ones, aren't they?"

"Actually they're rather good-sized. Comparatively speaking."

"Tell me more. It's an area in which I must concede you a certain amount of expertise. I've been self-conscious about my small breasts ever since puberty. My mother always told me I was flat. Flat and fat."

"You're neither, but, believe me, Elizabeth is entirely wrong—I do not conceive of myself as God's gift to the fat girl. In fact, it's surprising I'm as attracted to you as I am, because my taste has generally run to the petite. My wife has trouble keeping her weight up to a hundred pounds."

"Why do you portray her as such a bitch in the things you write?"

"Because she can be a real pain in the ass."

"The people I know who've seen her say she's beautiful."

"I suppose that's why I've stayed with her so long. That and because we're so used to each other by now."

"How long have you been with her?"

"Over eleven years."

"Of unstinting infidelity."

"I've stinted as little as humanly possible."

"And she?"

"Who knows? I think she's more interested in the baby than in fooling around, but it wouldn't be hard for her to get away with something if she wanted to. Tonight, for instance."

"And you'd mind?"

"I'm sure I would."

"And you don't think that's wrong?"

"Whether or not it's wrong is less significant than that's the way it simply *is*."

"And she doesn't mind you going off to Europe on sabbatical by yourself."

"I don't know whether she minds or not. I think we got involved in a certain amount of game-playing over the sabbatical—my version is that the games were hers—and now we don't seem to be able to extricate ourselves from the moves we've already made. It wouldn't surprise me if she's expecting us never to get back together once I leave. We haven't been communicating much for quite a while now."

"Well, your divorces must get easier for you each time."

"No, they get harder. I'm older and less sure of myself. And, as my lack of success with you partially demonstrates, I don't have the luck with women that I did for a while."

"If you'd stop wasting your time on me I'm sure you'd get a leg over someone much more desirable than myself."

"Is that the English term for it—getting a leg over?"

"Yes, to get a leg over is the national striving of our lads."

"Do you think that's all I'm interested in? You don't believe me that I've all along been thinking of the places I'd love to show you and..."

"You don't have any time to show me any places. Besides, you won't like me at all once you get me naked. I have a spare tire. And I may not like your varicose veins."

"Who said I had varicose veins?"

"You said so in one of your stories. No, don't bother telling me how everything you write is made up."

"Goddamnn it, I would have rendered my protagonist more physically attractive if I knew his flaws were going to cost me a... a leg over."

She laughs. Then, knowing he shouldn't ask it, nonetheless, in a voice that's dropped back somewhere behind his Adam's apple he says, "Didn't Ted want to get a leg over?"

"Oh yes."

"Did he succeed?"

Without hesitation, she replies, "Of course he did."

Well, there it is.

"Okay," Jimmy says, "get up now so I can drive you back."

"You mean you're no longer interested in me?"

"You have cured me of my obsession."

"Just like that? All of a sudden you can go from being all turned on to being totally turned off."

"I'm afraid so. Let me start the car."

"Wait, we've got to go to bed at least once."

"No we don't."

"But you always knew we'd end up in bed eventually."

"No, I didn't. And, as I tried in vain to tell you, I was never interested in a one-night stand."

"What about in England? You will come to visit me in England, won't you?"

"And go through this all over again?"

"It won't have to be this way."

"Are you sure you want me to look you up there? I won't be interfering with whatever you have going?"

"I can handle any of that. Promise me you'll come to see me."

"Okay. I promise I'll visit you in England."

"Do you still want my body at least a little bit?"

"Jesus Christ, Ainsley." His lips move to her nipple as he pushes his hand down into her panties.

Later, he asks again, "You're *sure* we can't go to your room."

"No. My roommate."

"Where... where did you go with..."

"My roommate was gone for the weekend."

"Is this whole fucking city conspiring against me?"

"You're never free on weekends."

"You've never given me a chance to be. You're correct that

I do spend about half my weekends with two of my children, but that leaves a lot of weekends."

"What about this Saturday?"

"You're forgetting something: We're kaput until England."

"You're still serious about that!"

"You have your lad."

"We wouldn't invite him along with us, now would we?"

"He'd be just one of the many spirits that seem to haunt our quasi-but-never-quite assignations. He'd be just one too many, I'm afraid."

"I don't believe you."

"I'd like to say I don't believe you either, but you have only reinforced my longstanding faith in the law of reverse psychology."

"What do you mean?"

"Never mind."

"God, I want to be with you. I really do. Come here..."

They are at it again until she finally says, "I really *have* to go inside."

"Fine." He drives her to the other parking lot. This time, however, he accompanies her to the door, keeping her aroused until the second she manages at last to tear herself away, and shut the dormitory door behind her.

"You'll reconsider?"

"I can't think any more tonight," he says. "I'll talk to you in a couple of days."

"After class in the Nugget?"

"All right," he says.

So it looks like he has finally brought her around. He's only disappointed in himself that it took him so long to hit upon the most obvious of strategies. And it doesn't seem to matter that much anymore that he'll be, in a sense, sharing her with Ted. After all, when he first became interested in her, he had taken it for granted she was seeing other men. He just hadn't planned on one of them being a friend of his, but he's no good at holding grudges. He feels no strong animosity to

Ted. Besides, one of his friends has told him that this may not only be Ted's first woman in a long time—it may be his first woman ever. If so, Jimmy can hardly begrudge him Ainsley. He must be getting one hell of a crash course.

*   *   *

Unfortunately, the English girl is not in class that Thursday. She sends word by Elizabeth that she's been sick two days with the stomach flu.

The next time he sees her she is largely recovered, but must go straight to her room to catch up on her work.

When they finally do get together in the Nugget it is at a table with a large number of other people. Elizabeth, Ainsley, and another girl from the class are getting very drunk very quickly on bad wine. Before long, Jimmy cannot believe his eyes at the four empty carafes lined up in front of him. That's not wasting any time even by his own standards.

The three girls have been singing the most banal of camp songs. Although Jimmy is seated next to Ainsley, he's been talking mostly to other people at the table. Finally she turns to him: "I've got to have a few words with you. Can we go outside?"

"No."

"You have your eye on that young one with the red hair, don't you?"

"Is that what you wanted to say?"

"No, what I wanted to say is that I've decided that the only relationship I'll have for the rest of the time that I'm in California will be with Ted. But I like you very much, and so does Ted. I enjoy your company very much, and so does Ted, so I don't see why we all can't get together tonight at the Gold Rush, have a good time, and behave ourselves like civilized people for the rest of the fall."

"Fuck no."

"You won't grow up and begin to act your age?"

"Fuck no."

"In other words, if I walk into the Gold Rush tonight with Ted, you'll punch him in the nose?"

"I have no intention of punching anyone in the nose."

"And if we join you at the table?"

"I'll move to another table."

"Can't you be nice to him as a favor to me?"

"FUCK NO!"

"I don't mean that much to you?"

"You can't have it both ways."

"What does it matter to you?"

"It matters."

"Can't you be a little gracious... or generous... or self-sacrificing... just this once?"

"FUCK NO!"

"Well, Ted and I can go anyplace we want together, and we are going to the Gold Rush at ten o'clock tonight."

"Suit yourself."

"And I have a feeling that your nobler instincts will prevail and that you will behave like a gentleman."

"Don't count on it."

She turns back to the other women and refills her wine glass. It's obvious now to Jimmy that everyone at the table has overheard the greater part of their exchange. Minutes later, jaws fall again. A young guy in the class is kidding Ainsley about her English accent. She says, "Frankly I've about had it with people mocking the way I speak," and Jimmy says to the guy, "Go ahead. Make fun of it some more."

The angrier she gets, the more she sounds like Jude the Obscure's shrew wife, and she says, "If you are going to make fun of the way I talk, I will call attention to your droopy drawers." Of course—big-bellied, narrow-hipped, and thick-thighed as he is—his pants do have a tendency to slide down his buttocks, but it is a subject to which no one has previously had the nerve to allude.

He thinks it is a very funny remark, though, and Ainsley follows it with a comic monologue about the crack of his ass being a tourist attraction second only to the Queen Mary among Southern California's splendors, and, while the others are still a bit reluctant to laugh out loud, he is laughing so hard that she probably thinks she has won him over to her way of seeing things.

But when, a little after ten, she and Ted do arrive at the bar, he moves to a table at the far end and totally ignores them. They get very drunk and make a scene of themselves, necking passionately, while Jimmy goes about his conversations and his games of pool. Then, just about the time Ainsley has decided to sit on Ted's lap, when, given their comparative sizes, the positions should be reversed, Jimmy has one of those rare strokes of perfectly timed luck. The young girl with red hair, to whom Ainsley referred in the Nugget, has also made the transition to the Gold Rush. It is becoming increasingly obvious that she is not with the guy who's been accompanying her all evening. When her escort announces that he has to get going, Jimmy senses that the red-haired girl, whose name is Janet, doesn't want to leave. "I can give you a ride to your car when you're ready to go," he tells her, and she decides that will be just fine with her. The guy she came with, who obviously is not her boyfriend, leaves, and she is now with Jimmy. The next time Jimmy goes to the men's room, he notices Ted and Ainsley have left the bar.

* * *

At the next class she looks a little embarrassed, but he acts as if nothing at all has happened. He joins her and Elizabeth in the Nugget after class, and the three of them have a chat and some more laughs at the expense of his posterior cleavage. Everything is detached and in good humor, and he leaves early.

You'd think that would be the end of the affair that never quite occurred, but it isn't over yet.

* * *

About a week later she manages to get his goat by making vague plans in front of him at the usual table in the Nugget for still another young acquaintance of his to pay her a visit in England. When Jimmy leaves early this time, he does it less good-naturedly.

* * *

Consequently, a week later, she suddenly makes a sharp comment about his having deserted her when she had something she needed to discuss with him, and she storms out of the bar herself.

When Elizabeth says to him, "What was that all about?" he laughs and replies, "That's called 'giving me a taste of my own medicine.'"

He's dating the red-haired girl now. A couple of times he misses the usual postmortems in the Nugget because he's with her. When Ainsley asks him, with a sly grin, where he was, he says, "I had to be somewhere else." One time he brings Janet to the Nugget with him, and they leave early. He isn't using Janet to make Ainsley jealous—he's interested in her for herself—but he doesn't mind it having that effect. Eventually Ainsley asks him outright whether he is seeing Janet, and he tells her that he doesn't kiss and tell.

Let her blow the thing out of all proportion in her fertile imagination.

The truth is, he and Janet are not that comfortable together. Sober they are ill at ease, and have almost nothing to say to each other. Usually it takes them so many drinks to loosen up that they pretty much repeat conversations one or the other has forgotten they've already had. Jimmy can't remember having had such conversational difficulties since high school. Which is really the problem—she's only a couple of years out of high school, whereas it's just beginning to sink in for him how very far from his high school years he is. He can tell Janet isn't sure she likes being seen with him, because he's so much older than she is. He realizes he does look closer to fifty or fifty-five than to forty. This semester isn't making him look or feel any younger.

He's not familiar with any of the new wave bands Janet goes to see.

She thinks Shakespeare is a bore.

Conversation was the only problem he never had with Ainsley.

He bets they would have had even better conversations in bed.

Probably have laughed themselves half to death.

*   *   *

So, the last couple of weeks of the semester, he drifts back to the table in the Nugget with Elizabeth and the English girl. They are already waxing sentimental over her impending departure for home. He knows Elizabeth is not kidding when she says how lonely she will be without either of them to drink with all spring, that she might as well go on the wagon and drop a hundred pounds.

One night, he and Ainsley do go off alone to a bar for a couple of hours. They get very drunk on Scotches, and laugh and hug conspiratorially. Ainsley tells him how Elizabeth interrogated her about "Why Abbey kept shouting FUCK NO!" They laugh over the looks on the faces of the other people at the table when she berated him for his droopy drawers.

She confides in him that what she really wants is to have babies.

She says she's insanely possessive with men, and that Jimmy wouldn't have been able to stand her.

She says she couldn't have taken it if he had her and then dumped her. Ted she could manage.

Neither of them can believe how time has flown when the bartender calls last call.

Outside her dorm they exchange uninflammatory kisses.

* * *

After the final class, she presents him with a present: a pair of orange suspenders... or braces, as they're called in England.

Then he takes her and Elizabeth out to dinner at the most expensive place he can afford. It may be the first time, outside of the classroom, that he has managed to impress or move her. From the restaurant they drive to the Gold Rush where, not to Jimmy's surprise, Ted is waiting for him with the forty dollars from what Ainsley calls "the wager on the one-armed pitcher." They all play pool.

The one concession he will not make is to give Elizabeth a ride home. Ted has to go out of his way to drop her off.

Early next week he receives two envelopes. One contains the take-home final. Jotted on the top is "I hope I have avoided the dreaded a-and-b construction."

The second note contains Ainsley's address at her college in Winchester. She thanks Jimmy for "the best meal, perhaps the only decent meal, I had while in the States," and she invites him to get in touch with her, should he care to when he gets to England. She promises to buy him a pint of English beer, if his buds have not already been dulled to the point of insensitivity by years or oceans of "that tasteless Budweiser, and that other stuff from Pisswater, Washington."

He smiles, but there is something half-hearted about the invitation.

He's not at all sure he will ever try to see her again.

* * *

And that, once more, is where the story should end, conveniently inconclusive in the contemporary mode, but it goes on a bit because he does look her up in England.

Not right away. After the fall semester, he remains in California for a couple of months logging what are for him long hours at the typewriter to insure he has fulfilled at least the minimum requirements of his sabbatical project. Then, in February, he flies to London with two of his children, the ones aged fourteen and eleven. It's a trip he's always wanted to make, one he's saved for, their introduction to, their initiation into, London and Paris. The three-and-a-half weeks of this father and his two kids abroad is another story entirely, a long one that will most likely only be told in bits and pieces. It's a trip he will be glad to have made, one that for some reason he was convinced he had to make. When the time comes for them to leave, he knows he doesn't want to be away from home any longer. He misses his year-and-a-half-old daughter, with whom he has had a chance to become close during the weeks he has not been teaching, and, as much as he reminds himself how terrible life with Brenda can be, he can't help missing her also. He doesn't need the experience of being alone in London, of being down and nearly out in London— it's an experience he's had years before, has written about at great length, and has no desire to repeat. For two reasons he does not fly home. First, that would be admitting defeat. It would prove to Brenda that he can't get along without her, and would give her an edge that would make her power over him intolerable. Second, another of his children is scheduled to visit him in a month for the two-week spring vacation. This is his oldest child, his first son, now nearly eighteen, a boy with whom he fought tooth and nail when he was much too young to be a father, a kid from whom he was separated for thirteen years, but with whom he has hit it off famously on the couple of occasions since then that they have been together.

So he is committed to sticking it out another month by himself.

The day after he puts his kids on the flight back to L.A., he drops a card to the college address Ainsley his left him. He explains that he has yet successfully to negotiate a phone call in England, gives her his address and number, and says he'd love to get together with her in London or Winchester, as she chooses, if she likes, at her convenience, et cetera...

Since it is taking eleven days for air mail to reach California, twenty-four hour first class delivery within England catches him off guard. He returns from a play the next night to find a message waiting for him. Yes, Ainsley would love to see him, and she is sure he can master the Saxon pay phones, and here is her number. He spends the next days losing a fortune in the phone booths at the Exhibition Center end of the Earl's Court tube station, as the lorries thunder westward down the Warwick Road until, with an operator's assistance, and at an increased tariff, he at last connects with her. "Do you suppose," he asks her, "Forster had the English telephone system in mind when he came up with 'Only connect'?"

"Where are you? What's all that noise in the background?"

"I'm in hell, sometimes known as Earl's Armpit, nor am I often enough out of it. The noise is the fabled Indies tea trade. I have to speak quickly because I'm almost out of coins. When can I see you?"

"Well, not during the week because I have classes."

"Saturday?"

"All right."

"There or here?"

"Here, I suppose."

There is something so tentative about her responses that he says, "Look, Ainsley, you don't have to see me if you don't want to."

"No, I want to see you. I'm looking forward to it."

"Okay, I'll take a train out on Saturday. Probably arrive about noon. How do I find you?"

"Call me from the station, and I'll come get you. I'm only a couple of blocks away."

"Oh, God, another encounter with the less than rapid pips."

"You'll manage. Don't be too late or the pubs will be closing."

"I'll invest in an alarm clock. Saturday then."

"Yes, Saturday."

*   *   *

He puts the strangeness in her voice out of his mind, and goes about ordering his life in such a way as to keep his spirits a degree or two above despair while mixing high and low culture, which amounts largely to equal hours of playgoing and pubcrawling. Unfortunately, the Friday evening before the trip to Winchester he devotes to the latter, including an introduction to the glories of Barley Wine, and he awakens so shaky on Saturday morning that he can barely shut off the cheapest and loudest alarm in Albion. He washes down three Excedrin with ginger beer, showers hastily, and sets forth by tube for Waterloo Station.

*   *   *

The hour's ride to Winchester is similar in scenery or the lack of it to the one he's recently taken with his kids to Salisbury, so he allows himself to doze over a newspaper. That helps his nerves enough that he is able to postpone the Librium he's tucked in his shirt pocket.

On about his fifth attempt he connects with Ainsley from the booth outside the rail station. There's still something wrong with her tone of voice, something almost businesslike, courteous, but detached, and one thing their relationship has never been is diplomatic.

She joins him within ten minutes. She's changed her hair to short and frizzy. It's made her look younger and more slender, although she insists she's added a couple of pounds on the starchy English diet. She asks him about the weeks with his kids, and how he's been doing since then, and he answers briefly. They set out on a tour of the city.

The Cathedral has the longest nave in England, or is it the world? He can tell at once he prefers Salisbury Cathedral, but he doesn't tell her that. He does make a couple of anti-ecclesiastical remarks, especially regarding the admission fee and the worldly and political flavor of the Church of England in general, but she chides him. Apparently she has found consolation during bad times in the English churches. He assures her he has nothing against the buildings themselves, especially the oldest ones.

Tess of the D'Urbervilles was captured on St. Catherine's Hill (or was she put to death there?), and the Hampshire meadows inspired Keats' "Ode to Autumn." Jimmy tells her that he's oft expressed to colleagues in the Nineteenth Century his theory that Keats would not have died quite so young if he had only started drinking earlier in the day. He would have died of alcoholism in his late thirties or forties, like Dylan Thomas or Brendan Behan, but he would not have died in his twenties of psychosomatic consumption. She laughs for perhaps the first time that day, although it is nothing like the raucous, boisterous, coarse, and insulting laughter they used to share. She says there's a young man in her Romantic seminar who shares Jimmy's view. She's showed him one of Jimmy's books of poems, and he said he preferred it to the Oxford Keats. Now there is a true minority of one.

St. Catherine's Hill (or is it St. Giles') was a point of reference for medieval pilgrims. It is too wet to climb the farther of the hills, so she leads him, puffing, up the nearer. The brisk walk is clearing away the cobwebs. They lean upon a stone fence, and enjoy a view of Winchester and environs that would have given Rupert Brooke a fortnight's hard-on.

He wonders if he's supposed to make a pass at her now. He's never made a pass at her this early in the day. It's been years since he's made a pass at anyone this early in the day. He starts to put his arm around her—why else has she brought him to such a romantic place?—then something makes him think better of it. He gives her a feeble hug around the shoulders and goes back to leaning on both elbows.

"Your wife isn't joining you then?"

"No, she decided not to... her job... the baby..."

"How are you getting along?"

"We were still talking to each other when I left. In fact, we were behaving in a rather civilized manner towards each other the last couple of weeks, but I fully expect to find my possessions in a small heap on the doorstep when I get back."

"That won't happen. She's invested too many years in you."

"I seriously think it may. I'm not just saying it for your benefit. My being away will give her a chance to see what life is like without me. I think she'll find that life goes on quite well without me, that life without me may be a good deal preferable to life with me."

"If that does turn out to be the case how do you think you'll handle it?"

"I don't think I'll be happy about it, but I'm trying to prepare myself."

"Well, you deserve anything you get. You've been a bastard. You are a bastard. You must have hurt her terribly over the years."

"Sometimes in self-defense. Please go on. It's the first time you've sounded like the Ainsley I know and love. Why don't we have a good row?"

"Not on an empty stomach."

"Do you know a place with good pub fare? I've yet to find a place in London that serves anything but cheese-and-tomato sandwiches."

"I have the perfect place for you. It's called the Wykeham Arms. I help out there on Sundays. Wykeham was the founder of Winchester College, which is third only to Eton and Harrow in prestige among English public schools. Anyone connected with the college is known as a Wykehamite. End of lecture. I hope I haven't bored you too awfully."

"I loved it," he says without irony. "It was great not having to wander around trying to read a guide book while bumping into things."

He's been putting off his drinking till the sun goes down, but when Ainsley orders a local bitter, he's glad for the excuse to indulge himself. He's drinking pints to her halves, and a bit ill at ease in the crowded pub, he's drinking them fast. She's right about the food. There's a good Shepherd's Pie with vegetables, reasonably priced. The bitter is mellow. Soon he's mellow enough to ask her, "When are you coming up to spend a day with me in London? Or a weekend?"

She sighs, her shoulders collapsing into a shrug of resignation. She looks him in the eye and says, "There's something I've got to tell you, and I hope you won't get angry. Ted is here with me."

For a second he can't even remember who Ted is. When he does, he says, "He flew over to visit, too?"

"He came back with me. We decided at the end of the semester, and everything was so hectic I couldn't bring myself to tell you. I'm sorry."

"Ah, fuck it. No sweat."

"You're not mad?"

"No. Shit, if I'd known you two cared that much about each other, I would have bowed out months ago. Not gracefully, perhaps. I don't do much of anything gracefully, but I would have left you alone. Where is he?"

"He's right here. In the kitchen, that is. Working. He doesn't have a work permit, so he has to take whatever jobs he can get for whatever they're willing to pay him. He works terribly hard."

"Jesus, he's a better man than I am."

"I know he misses California. He was so excited when I got your card. He'd been asking whether I thought you'd really get in touch while you were over here."

"When does he get off work?"

"About three. I thought I'd go to the store and cook dinner for us, and you two could talk. Then we could all come back here for a few beers tonight before you have to catch your train."

"Sounds great."

"I'm so glad you aren't angry. You used to get so violently angry."

"I'd go to bed that way, but it was always gone by morning."

"I know. *That* used to make *me* mad, because I'd stay upset with you for days, and it seemed to be water off your back."

"It has its drawbacks. It makes it hard, for instance, to deal with someone like Brenda who can nurture a grievance, real or imagined, for years, plotting her revenge. By the time I get my just deserts I've forgotten what I did to deserve them."

"Come over here with me now. I see a couple of my friends I want you to meet."

* * *

He meets her friends, two in particular. One is a don at Winchester College and the other a big, tough, gentle ex-shipbuilder. It's typical of the institution of the English pub at its best that the two bachelors, so different in nearly every conceivable way, mix easily over their lunchtime bitters in this place that may be the nearest either comes to a social life. They try to teach him the intricacies of the "fruit machine," the English equivalent of the one-armed bandit, but the permutations and combinations are too much for him, at least on this particular afternoon.

After drinking-up time, Ainsley prevails upon the don to forego his afternoon nap in favor of giving them what turns out to be a very learned tour of the drenched-in-history college grounds. Then Jimmy and Ainsley return to the house she and Ted share with another couple with whom they don't get along. On the way, they stop at a not-so-supermarket. Jimmy knows the meal in his honor is going to be an expense for them they can ill afford. Ainsley won't allow him to chip in on the food, so he tries to stock up on more beer, wine, and cider than he figures they can possibly consume in an afternoon.

At home, Ted is waiting for them.

*   *   *

While Ainsley fusses in and out of the kitchen, the two men, once teacher and student and at least ten years apart in age, sit on the edge of a bed knocking back the alcohol, and talk mostly sports. Jimmy says he has traveled to England specifically to renew the notorious Andy Messersmith bet, and this time not in dollars, but in pounds. Ted asks if Andy is even still on the active roster, and Jimmy replies that is beside the point—the bet was, of course, of a perpetual nature, and who's to say that Andy, like Jim Bouton, is not apt to embark on another comeback in any given month of any given year. Jimmy does his best to pass on the news of the Lakers that he has been able to garner from the single sports page of the Herald-Tribune.

Ted says that he was coaching the basketball team at Ainsley's college for awhile, but finally gave it up out of frustration. No one would pass the ball. The second a player got his hands on the ball, he either put it up in the general direction of the hoop from whatever posture he might find himself in, or else he went in a mad dribble, often with both hands at once, towards the end of the line and usually into the stands.

Time passes with a deliquescence reminiscent of the best of Virginia Woolf and the worst of Thomas Wolfe.

*   *   *

By the time dinner is served, both men are starved. They don't actually lick their plates, but they do sop up every drop of the beef carbonade with the last crusts of bread.

*   *   *

In the meantime, Ainsley has had a call from the Wykeham asking her to tend that evening. She is in a nervous hurry, and barely able to partake of her own cooking. When she leaves for work, more made-up than Jimmy has ever seen her, and looking exactly as an English barmaid should, Ted and Jimmy remain behind until they have consumed every drop of every bottle in the house.

*   *   *

It seems to take hours for Ted to find his way across town to the Wykeham. There they buy rounds with the scholarly, but good-natured don and the jolly land-locked shipbuilder, while Ted loudly declaims his Bristolian imitation— "Up chew, nit?" Jimmy observes to himself that he is among people who could have stepped right out of Chaucer.

It's hard to break away in time to catch the train because the rounds keep coming. When he finally manages to detach himself from the bar, Jimmy goes a few feet away to have private words with Ainsley. He leaves her a couple of pounds to buy a round after he's gone, and says, "I feel as if all the battles have been fought. It's a nice feeling."

She gives him a squeeze and a quick kiss, and Ted leads him back, by some incredibly serpentine route, to the station. Jimmy cannot find his return ticket, and the ticket-taker is reluctant to let him board without one, but as the train is about to pull out, the old functionary relents. Once on the train, the ticket emerges from a cranny of his wallet. It has already been decided they will all get back together in a couple of weeks, when Ainsley will be finished with her quarterly exams and on her spring vacation.

The weeks before they do get together are again a story, perhaps a novel, in themselves, just as are the two weeks with his son. They do not get together as soon as Ainsley is out of classes. One weekend it is out of the question for Jimmy, the next weekend Ainsley and Ted both have to work, and the weekend after that will be the day after Jimmy's son flies in, and they agree he may need the rest. As it turns out, though, it is not a very restful Saturday. The underground workers are on strike, and Jimmy starts the two of them out on what he intends to be a brief sightseeing walk, but which turns into a trek from Earl's Court to and through the Victoria and Albert, across Hyde Park to the Speaker's Corner, down Park Lane and back up to Carnaby Street, through Soho and Covent Garden to the Old Curiosity Shop, and down the Aldwych to the river.

Crossing Waterloo Bridge, in the midst of one of the most populous cities in the world, they run into Ainsley and Ted. Jimmy has tickets for a Keith Jarrett concert at the Royal Festival Hall, and the other couple, coming to London on the spur of the moment and unable to reach Jimmy at his hotel, have lucked into tickets for *Death of a Salesman* at the National Theatre. They just have time, the four of them, to seek out a pub on the Strand for an hour's drinking.

Ainsley takes well to Jimmy's son, as he knew she would. She'd probably like to take him to bed, Jimmy figures, which would be fine with Jimmy. He wishes he could arrange it. He wonders if Ted would mind. He wonders whether Ted has ever been jealous of the time Ainsley has spent with him, or how many of the times he even knows about. He always assumes other men's minds work roughly the same as his, even if they usually manage to put forth a calmer front, but maybe he's wrong. Maybe it is possible for a guy to care enough for a girl to follow her to England and work his tail off for wetback's wages and still not be jealous of her being with others. How about the three of them in bed with Ainsley, or maybe her taking them on in succession. No, not bloody likely.

They also meet for fifteen minutes of drinking after the shows. They arrange to share the expenses of renting a car for a four-day, Easter weekend tour of the West country. Jimmy's not sure his son is all that crazy about the idea, but Jimmy wants him to see more of England than just London, and it seems that neither of them is apt ever again to have the chance to tour that part of the country under such favorable conditions. Ainsley is entrusted with making the arrangements.

* * *

He and Ainsley are alone for a few seconds at the bar.
"What do you hear from home?" she asks.
"Nothing. I haven't had a letter in a month."
"I'm sorry."
"I'm living with it. How are things with you and Ted?"
"His visa will be up this summer. We'll go to the States for awhile, but I doubt he'll be able to come back. Or that he'd want to."
"Transfer to State."
"There's no telling how many credits I'd lose. I should finish my degree first. Maybe my teaching certification also. That could be two or three years."
"I'll see what I can find out for you about transferred credit, residency, scholarships..."
"I'd appreciate that, but I'm not sanguine."
"Something will work out for you."
"I hope so, but right now I can't see how."

* * *

The first day of their motoring jaunt, they spend the afternoon in Bath, with its river and Georgian crescents and Roman ruins and Pump Room. They even follow Ainsley through the wardrobe museum housed in the Assembly Rooms, the three men trying not to hurry her while secretly stifling their yawns. That evening they stay over at Ainsley's mother's house on a hill overlooking Bristol.

Saturday they spend some time in Wells and Glastonbury, briefly touring cathedrals and ruins and the alleged burial spot of King Arthur. They kill a bit more time over lunch than they should, all but Ainsley, their driver, consuming pints of Bass Special in a back street working-men's pub. Jimmy gets them out of there when he senses the thickest of the men evincing a dangerously intense interest in Ainsley. They cross the Dartmoor. At a farmhouse near its highest point, they all but overdose on a Devon tea of scones, clotted cream, and jams. They arrive before sunset in Plymouth, where Ainsley worked, and was in love a couple of years ago.

They find lavishly appointed bed-and-breakfast accommodations in the house of an old lady who insists she only lets rooms to the "best" people, by which they later ascertain she means she won't let Pakis, "with their greasy hair," past her threshold. They have time to promenade along the waterfront with its plaques and monuments to Drake and the pilgrims. Ainsley and Ted seem to want some time to be romantic, so Jimmy and his son stay well ahead of them. It's nearly nine o'clock by the time they hit the pubs for their evening's drinking, and they never do find a place they can afford to eat in until after hours when they settle for donner kebabs in the red-light district.

Easter Sunday, after one of the last truly enormous English breakfasts, they make their way slowly along the hedge-lined back roads of Cornwall to the little fishing harbors of Looe, Polperro, and Fowey, then by the quicker route through Truro to The Lizard, where they walk along the cliffs. The coastline reminds Jimmy a good deal of the Sonoma and Mendocino coasts in Northern California. Then it's on through pirateless Penzance and past St. Michael's Mount to Land's End in time for Jimmy and his son to have their picture taken together in front of a sign adjusted to point the direction and mileage to Rochester, New York. The road now twists through the moors of Poldark country to St. Ives, so much like the beautiful-people, former artists' colonies of the California coast, the Carmels and La Jollas and Sausalitos. Ironically, in spite of the perfect weather they've had all weekend, it is still early enough in the tourist season that they get the best of room bargains of Jimmy's time in England at a hotel overlooking the ocean atop a ridge named, of all things, Fern Hill.

The place even has its own small bar for residents. It's been so long since any of them has been able to afford a hotel with a bar they return there early from the pubs, and drink till midnight. Jimmy's son is already making wishful reservations with the owner-bartender to return for a longer stay in a year. Ted retires to his room with the whirlies. Jimmy and Ainsley have another few moments in which to talk freely:

"I finally had a letter from my wife. Apparently she'd been mailing earlier letters to the hotel I moved out of. This letter wasn't dripping with sentiment, but it was sufficiently encouraging that I've made reservations to fly back two days after Jimmy leaves."

"I wish Ted and I were leaving with you. "

"You'll find a way soon."

"Anyway I'm glad for you that things are going to be okay with your wife."

"I'm not at all sure they will be," he says, and he silently doubts Ainsley is all that glad. She's probably been as glad to have him off on the periphery as a distant prospect, as he formerly was to harbor the possibility of a European romance with her. She's behaved so perfectly to him and his son that he says, "Look, if you do get back to California, with Ted or on your own, you have a friend there."

"Thank you. It helps to know that."

"You'd better go look after your lover now, and I'll see to my son."

"He's a lovely boy."

"Thank you. I think so, too, and he hasn't had an easy life."

"I hope we old folks haven't bored him with our plaques and ruins this weekend."

"We all have to eat our peck of culture. He's not bored now."

"No, he's flying. We all are except you. "

"I've been less the eagle of late than the penguin. Or the grounded albatross or whatever the fuck that bird of Baudelaire's was. Fish out of water sort of thing."

"We've all mellowed considerably in a short time, haven't we?"

"Yes, haven't we though."

At two a.m. Jimmy's son locks himself out of his room, and has to spend the rest of the night curled up in his jockey shorts on a sofa in the poorly heated t.v. lounge. He takes it in the right spirit, as a tale to tell, and what would our memories be like without them.

*   *   *

Monday they drive back through the Devon of Fowles and the Dorset of Hardy. Jimmy has tickets for the evening performance of *Evita*, and they will have to find a room before then. His son sleeps it off in the back seat, and they arrive in Winchester in time to catch the five o'clock train.

They make it to *Evita*, which turns out to be a disappointment.

At the Winchester station, though, he has given Ainsley and Ted his California address and phone number, and Ainsley has given him a hug and kiss a few degrees beyond that appropriate for comrades.

*   *   *

A week later he returns to his wife and child, and to the lowest-spirited month of his life. It is a month during which he cannot summon the time, strength, or sobriety to write, as he has promised, to Ainsley and Ted.

He wonders if the story's finally finished.

I DO NOT HAVE HERPES

He is awakened by his five-year old daughter bouncing on his ribs: "Get up... get up... get up... get up..."

"Sweetheart, please, take it easy."

"You sleep too much... you eat too much... you drink too much... you get too fat."

"It's not time for me to get up." He glances at the alarm clock. "It's time for you to go to your swimming lessons."

"Yes," her mother calls from the other room, "come here, and let me fix your hair."

His daughter reluctantly gives up using him for a trampoline, and goes to join her mother. He gets up anyway, headachy, and makes his way stiffly to the bathroom. He emerges in a few minutes to say crossly to his wife, "The toilet isn't flushing. Or just barely."

"Oh, that's because I had to turn it down because the water was rising too high in the tank."

"What good is a toilet that doesn't flush?"

"All right," she snaps. "All right." She flies from her daughter's hair to the back of the toilet where she makes a quick adjustment. Jimmy watches the water rising towards the top of the tank. "That's great," he says to her. "Now it's about to flood."

She flushes it, and makes another radical adjustment: "Why don't you fix it yourself?"

"I'm not a plumber," he says. "I've never pretended to be. You should have called the manager in the first place."

He ends up doing it himself. He's watched her closely enough to tell what valve it is she's been fiddling with. While she rushes the kids out the front door to the public pool, he adjusts and readjusts until the water level is even with the old water mark.

He starts back to bed until he feels the itching, touches his neck near his right ear, and remembers he has to call the dermatologist. First though, he has to swallow two Excedrin with a Seven-Up. He would much rather take the Excedrin with a Coke. The citric acid in the Seven-Up sometimes upsets his stomach, but there is no Coke in the refrigerator. He will have to hope the Seven-Up stays down.

He gets their personal telephone directory, and finds the number of *Dr. Parker: Dermatologist: For Messages*. He dials.

"Yes, I wonder if it would be possible for me to talk to Dr. Parker sometime this morning."

"What is the problem?"

"A skin infection of some sort. On my neck. It itches and it's sore, and it's been getting a lot worse every day."

"When did you first notice this?"

"I noticed it when it was just a couple of pimples about a week ago. A couple of days ago, it started getting much worse."

"Have you seen Dr. Parker before?"

"Many times."

"All right. Let me have your name and Medical Record Number, and Dr. Parker will call you back in about half an hour."

* * *

He has to sit by the phone. He can't even take a shower. He can't take a nap. He can't go to the corner grocery for a newspaper or some Cokes. He can't take a chance on missing the doctor's call.

It is mercifully and surprisingly prompt though, just about the promised half hour.

"Mr. Abby?"

"Yes..." Jimmy repeats his description of the ailment.

"Okay. How soon can you be out here?"

"I haven't had a chance to shower. Should I bother?"

"No."

"Forty-five minutes."

"Come right out then. If you can be here within an hour, I can see you before lunch. If you're late, I'm gone."

"I'll be there."

He finishes dressing, throws some water on his face, sticks some chewing gum in his shirt pocket, and makes sure everything is turned off in the apartment before vacating it. He remembers his car has been barely starting. He gets behind the wheel, and delicately inserts the key in the ignition. He takes a deep breath, pumps the accelerator twice, and turns the key. The engine turns over haltingly, but catches. Jimmy guns it in neutral, a ten second warmup, and backs out into the alley.

He has gone only a mile up the highway when he simultaneously hears and feels the bumping. He has not had a flat tire in the three years he has owned the car, but there's no kidding himself that he is not about to have his first. He manages to cross the highway and coast into an Arco station, coming to a stop right behind an empty service bay. He gets painfully out of the car, and limps to the station office. The man behind the counter is of Middle Eastern ethnicity. Jimmy tells him, "I'm rushing to an important doctor's appointment, and I need a flat tire changed. I have a bad back. I'll pay, of course."

The swarthy man in charge says, "We don't change tires anymore. We don't do repairs. We only do tune-ups."

"You don't have anyone free for five minutes to change a tire?"

"There's no one here but me right now."

Jimmy returns to the car and fumbles with the manual from the glove compartment. He has to look up where the jack is kept. It turns out that it's under the panel in the rear of the station wagon. He will have to unload all the boxes of books he's been hauling around. The spare tire is attached to the bottom of the car. He has to read in the manual how to get it down, and where to jack. When he tries to recall the mnemonic device for which way to turn the lugs, he blocks it out with "Spring forward; fall back."

He has managed to remove the flat, getting filthy, but without crippling himself, when a younger Middle Eastern gentleman in coveralls parks a sports car nearby and approaches: "You can't work on your car here. Our insurance doesn't allow it."

"Why don't *you* do it then, and I'll pay you."

"Our insurance doesn't allow that either. And you're blocking our service bay."

"There's no car to service in the service bay with the notable exception of mine."

"Move your car."

"I can't move my car. I just took the flat tire off. There's no point in putting the flat back on. As soon as I get the spare on, I'll be only too happy to leave."

* * *

Miraculously enough, with the help of the manual, Jimmy somehow manages to do the job without any hitches, let alone catastrophes. His head is throbbing. Since no one is watching, he goes to the men's room to get as much of the grease off his hands and arms as he can in sixty seconds. The place is in a condition in which it is hard for him to keep from vomiting. He just can't afford the time to puke.

A careless driver as a kid, Jimmy, at forty, has done an about face: he does not believe in driving recklessly in vain attempts to save a minute or two. However, this morning he must run at least a few yellow lights if he's to have any chance of salvaging the appointment. As always the Wilmington air stinks of sulfur from the oil refineries. Probably because of the working class clientele it serves, this prepaid medical chain seems to have its clinics in the most insalubrious locations of the metropolitan area.

He does an imitation of a man running from the parking lot to the registration desk. He is ten minutes late, but Dr. Parker is just finishing with his last scheduled patient.

* * *

Jimmy has more confidence by far in Dr. Parker than in any other doctor he has ever been to. Time and again the other doctors have diagnosed as psoriasis or eczema or even syphilis what Parker has been able in seconds to spot as poison oak or acne or a penicillin allergy. Now the middle-aged, but spruce doctor folds his hands behind his back and examines Jimmy's neck: "There's a secondary infection. I can't get a good enough look at it to tell what the original problem was. Did you put anything on it?"

"Everything. I tried everything in the medicine cabinet."

"You made it worse. Don't use anything else, except what I prescribe, which will be Erythromycin and a poultice."

"A poultice?"

"It's a dressing to dry it out, and help the itching. Just follow the directions. Have you been fooling around again?"

"Why?"

"Have you?"

"Yes. Two weeks ago. I went to bed with this girl, and she started biting my neck, and then she seemed to get carried away, and she bit the shit out of it. She thought the noises I was making were sounds of pleasure. I couldn't tear her off without ripping my own throat open. Honest to god, she swore in advance she didn't have anything. She made me swear *I* didn't. She's an intelligent girl, a..."

"That doesn't matter. She could be a carrier, and not even know it. She wasn't a virgin, was she?"

"Hardly."

"She didn't sound like one."

"Shit, then you think it may be..."

"Herpes? No. I think it's a bacterial infection, probably from her biting you."

"A Venereal Disease?"

"Venereal diseases are diseases of the sexual organs. Can't you tell your penis from your neck?"

"Then I don't have to worry about..."

"This will have no affect on your sexual activity. It's like a cut on the finger getting infected. You should notice improvement in seventy-two hours. If it gets worse instead of better, call me back. Otherwise there's no need to check back."

"Look, I appreciate your fitting me into your schedule like this."

"That's perfectly all right. Make sure you read the directions on the poultice."

* * *

It's a long wait for the prescriptions in the pharmacy. The waiting patients comprise what is euphemistically referred to in London as "a cosmopolitan gathering." The Working Class, except when unemployed. There is not a wealthy person in the place. Teachers are at the top of this social ladder.

* * *

He rewards himself with a weisswurst and sauerkraut, over the sports section, at Alpine Village. The sausages could not have been any better in Munich or Zurich. Or could they? It's been ten years.

Getting up from the table he feels the pinch of his back going out. So little pain, and yet he knows what that pin-prick augurs: several days of getting out of bed on his hands and knees and, shuffling around bent and twisted at the groin. He had better get to the back pills in his office drawer as quickly as possible.

* * *

He is no sooner at his desk than the phone rings. It's his girlfriend, just off work. He tells her the events of his day, leaving out his now-assuaged fears. Just a bacterial infection. She does not know, of course, about his dalliance with the girl who bit him. He knows it has never occurred to her that the skin problem could have been something communicable, in spite of all the current fuss in the papers and on TV. She showed absolutely no hesitation to make love with him two nights before, when the infection was already getting noticeable. He hadn't dared hesitate for fear of giving her ideas.

* * *

And her day? She has given two weeks' notice to her landlord and boss. She will be going a thousand miles away for graduate school. Neither of them ever thought it would end up this way. Her applications at two local schools went awry. He will not tell her not to go. He does not think she should sit out a year before continuing her education. He will not take any responsibility for her decisions. He still hopes it will be possible for him not to have to leave his family. Yet, for the year before they started going out two years ago, his life was awful. It had not been very happy for a couple of years before that.

Will he be able to come over this evening?

Yes, he has some things to get done at his desk, and then he will be over.

* * *

A woman calls to set up a publicity photo session. She says she wants an erotic theme to it. Can he bring something erotic?

"I only have my dick," he says, "and plenty of women have managed to find that not especially erotic."

Then, relenting, he asks, "How about if I come as Quasimodo?"

* * *

He picks up a borrowed copy of "Vanity Fair," and begins to read a story by Thomas McGuane about a man who is not being allowed to see his son, and who is doing all the wrong things in trying to get to see him. Like all McGuane's work, it is about a world in which being a man no longer makes sense. Finishing the story, he is overcome by a rush of a nameless emotion that leaves his hair follicles tingling. It is not self pity. He knows he is responsible for most of the things that have occurred in his adult life. He feels no desire to live his life over differently. Yet, for just a second, he almost covers his eyes to sob.

Which would be a stupid, silly, and self-conscious thing to do. Instead, he uses his arms to raise himself from his chair, noticing the pain in his shoulder is starting again. Ah well, the back pills will help the shoulder, too, but he can't take another for a few more hours. It's nearly time to take the second Erythromycin though, which reminds him he does not have herpes. He's tempted to shout it through the corridors of the empty building: "I'm okay. Everything is going to be all right. I've been given a reprieve. I DO NOT HAVE HERPES!"

He decides to pick up a bottle of champagne on the way to his girlfriend's. He wishes he could tell her what they are celebrating.

A SOBER READING OF DR. SIGMUND FREUD

"Go ahead," he says, "relax."

"It was a big meal," I say. "Lately, I seem to have to take a nap after any big meal."

"Where were we?" he says.

"Oh," I say, "I was telling you about the time that..."

I can't remember what I was telling him. I think I was narrating the bizarre sequence of combinations that accompanies one's falling off to sleep. Maybe something about my mother got mixed in, but I may just be adding that now. I haven't seen my mother since 1964. She would like me to fly home across the country to see her this summer, but I doubt now that I will. A couple of months ago I thought such a trip a probability, and I made the mistake of telling her so.

It was very difficult for me to make the break from my mother's influence. When she all but disowned me after my first divorce, I felt no longer required to worry much about her. I talked to her on the phone the other day. It was a cordial enough conversation. I don't let her bother me any more, at least not as much as before. At least not on the surface. I put my one-year-old son and my three-and-a-half-year-old-daughter on the line. She'd talked to them before. Then I put her thirteen-year-old grandson on the line. They'd never spoken. I doubt he remembered at first he even had a living grandmother. Afterward she said how sorry she was that she didn't know him or his older sister, the children of my second marriage, at all.

I guess she's managed to forget that she would not even hear of them for years, and that one time on receiving pictures of them, she said, "I think I'm able to deal with them now." So I never sent her pictures of them again.

While I was in Washington, D.C. this summer, my present (third) wife sent my mother pictures of our two young children. She probably thought it could mean an inheritance for them some day. Maybe I'm being unfair; maybe she had a genuine impulse to do something nice. What do you think, Dr. Freud? Do I underestimate the innocence, spontaneity, and altruism of our race? What do you think, Mr. Mencken?

My mother has no money anyway.

*   *   *

No, I don't remember what I was telling my ex-brother-in-law, who is a psychohistorian at a famous university, and a trained analyst, but suddenly he is holding my balls in his hand, as if using them for a lie detector, sensing contractions or changes in temperature, or maybe just testing my reaction. When I react with concern, he says, "Okay, let's try it this way then." Now he presses his forearm in such a way that there is pressure on my balls and on the crack of my ass.

"Unh-unh," I say, but it is no longer a question of any sexual encounter. I am apart from the analyst on my couch. It is the analysis itself I'm embarrassed by. I stop in the middle of whatever I'm telling him, which I can no longer remember, and say, "I'll only feel bad about it later if I say anymore. If I keep talking, it will only force us not to be friends anymore."

Maybe I am thinking of it as a sort of rape, but it seems more that it is not my nature to be psychoanalyzed, anymore than it would be my nature to, let's say, go skiing.

*   *   *

I have a mistress, Tina, who inserts her finger in my anus. In other words, she sticks her finger up my ass. I like it very much.

I put my finger up her ass. She seems to like it, too.

I have not been with Tina in about ten days because my son has been staying with me. I have not had sex with my wife during this period either.

I have on this evening delivered my son to his aunt and uncle for a week's stay. My son's mother and her lover are in Hawaii.

My son's aunt, the younger sister of my second wife, has invited me and all my third family to join them for a barbecue on the evening I drop my son off there. My ex-brother-in-law-the-psychohistorian-and-analyst and I have always enjoyed each other's company. We always have a lot to talk about, all the more so now that we see each other only about once a year.

Many years ago, for instance, in response to an innocent question about what was going on in his field, he got me started studying structuralism. I'm only now beginning to have some idea what the structuralists are, or were, talking about.

This Saturday evening I am not feeling well because my wife twisted my arm to go with her and the kids to the Seal Beach Lions Club Annual Fish Fry for lunch. I don't like fried fish much, and I especially dislike eating it in the sun near the beach in July. I went because my wife said our daughter had been asking to go, and then I spent the rest of the afternoon consuming antacids and trying to burp. When Dave asks me if I'll have a gin-and-tonic, I say, "If you're having one, but not as strong as usual."

We end up having four. I stuff myself on hamburgers and salad. I have a beer and a large glass of white wine.

Back when Dave first married into the family, I would not even have felt this amount of alcohol, but tonight I am conscious of having a buzz on, and a not altogether pleasant one, from the first sip. I am not as articulate as I would like to be or as I should be. I notice Dave has no difficulty in staying with me drink for drink now. He alludes to some of my legendary drinking feats. I say, "I don't drink like that anymore," and I don't, although I still drink plenty.

I tell him I have recently read *The White Hotel*. When he asks me what I thought of it, I say, "I liked the dirty parts," and he laughs.

I tell him I am teaching a course in Contemporary Literary Theory in the fall. I tell him about a couple of reviews I've recently had published in surprisingly (for me) prestigious places. I realize I'm trying to impress him. The opposite used to be the case. A shift in transference valence has taken place.

He asks if I would speak at his university in the fall, for an honorarium, on "The Artist and Self-Destruction." I say I would, and begin to tell him what I probably would say. I realize what I have to say is not at all what he has in mind. He has in mind the psychological roots of self-destructiveness, and a sort of Wound and Bow theory of the inseparability of neurosis and talent. I'm saying that the audience, who allows no middle ground between the mad genius and the bourgeois, destroys the artist. The conversation drifts off in two different directions.

I express concern about the recent infiltration of controversial university classes by fundamentalist religious fanatics. He seems to feel that such a thing would be nipped in the bud at his university. I have no such confidence in my own. I end up sounding both paranoid and defensive.

Over my shoulder I watch that the young kids do not fall in the wading pool. I love all my children, but I am fanatically in love with my three-and-a-half-year-old daughter. Just the wrong time for it, as she enters her Oedipal stage. When she falls on her arm and cries, I leap up and glare at my thirteen-year-old son as if it is his fault. I know he has projected some of his animosity towards his own older sister onto the younger half-sister who is, however, an older sister to her own younger brother. I have made a great effort to bridge the distance between this son and me this summer, and with, I think, a good deal of success. Time itself does seem to be healing some of the wounds, many of them originating in the divorce, but he is at a fragile age.

I made an immense mistake the night before, telling him and his much younger half-sister to "quit fighting," when he was, of course, just warding off her playful, but annoying blows. It sounded as if I was putting him back into a childish perspective. He won't let me forget that for awhile.

Usually I wax philosophical to my children somewhere near the end of the second six-pack. Last night I took my son to see *Blow-Up,* against his wishes, and later explained to him that lacking much money all I had to give him was what I had here (pointing to temple) and here (pointing to heart).

I also gave him a lecture, prompted by a joke he told, on tolerance towards gays, and how what they did seemed as natural to them as what heterosexuals did seemed to us. I think everything I said embarrassed him, although I hope not as much as my father's belated treatise on nocturnal emissions.

* * *

Dave has lost twenty-five pounds. He's running regularly and I wistfully spy a barbell in his garage. He looks good and sounds the most at-one-with-himself that I have ever heard him.

I have found his twenty-five pounds and made them mine. My back has prevented me from exercising much the last few years. I've developed a taste for sweet wino wine. I'm self-conscious about the way I look and, in spite of the confidence ny mistress and a little literary success provide, I feel that I am going downhill.

I have become a better parent over the years and, probably, a better person towards other people. Ironically, I felt better about myself when I was young, strong, and a nearly total prick. And I never used words like "mistress" then.

* * *

Before Dave married my sister-in-law, I thought I was in love with her. My present wife is exactly her age. I still like my sister-in-law very much, but I am no longer in love with her. I am still, or again, in love with my wife. This love contains within it the seeds of my destruction.

My wife asks me to carry her purse and a big bag of the kids' things to the car. In front of Dave, a former boxer, I shrug my shoulders beneath the pantomime of a burden of defeated machismo. "Two purses," he says. "One for each of your ears," I reply. I am not bothered at the time though. I'm only a little bothered when I remember that my wife will be getting into the driver's seat of her car. It makes all the sense in the world. I've been drinking and she hasn't, but I don't like the way it looks to Dave.

"We've got to get together more often," I say; "I always feel like I'm talking double-time trying to cover all the ground."

"I feel the same way," he says.

I think we are both telling the truth.

All the way down the four freeways, I am stuffing myself with antacids, but they don't seem to be doing much good. At home I discover I am out of booze. "Have a couple of my beers if it will save you going to the store," my wife says. She likes one Lowenbrau before bed, and I haven't cared much for it since it became Azuzabrau. "Thanks," I say; "I'll see how tired I am." She goes into the bedroom with the kids.

I wait a few minutes and walk out to the phone near the market. I call Tina, ask her about her day, tell her about mine. When I mention that Dave is an analyst, she says, "Oh God, don't you feel uncomfortable talking to him?"

"No," I say.

"Why not? I would!"

"I guess I've just known him too long."

I think I'm implying a bit of superiority in that: that I know he's even nuttier than I am, but I don't hear much conviction in my voice.

I tell Tina that I think I'll be able to see her tomorrow evening. When she hints that perhaps I could come earlier than usual, I reply coldly that I have too much work to catch up on. Part of my attitude is the result of my having read our horoscopes for Sunday. Mine says, "You would do well to separate yourself from a negatively minded intimate." Hers, "A relationship that you have overestimated may be coming to an end."

* * *

I decide not to drive anyplace for booze. I decide I am tired enough to go to bed without drinking any of my wife's Lowenbraus. My stomach is still bad. I take a couple of Gaviscons. They are advertised to work even while you sleep.

But I can't sleep. I lie there soberly thinking the worst about the evening and about myself at this time in my life. I try to divert myself with erotic fantasies. These at first involve my wife. Even with two children also sleeping in the room, I feel strangely alone with her, almost as it was when we were illicit and nightly lovers. I want to touch her but I am afraid to. I try to excuse myself that I am only being considerate, and that it is impossible in front of the children anyway. But I know I am afraid to touch my own wife.

* * *

I decide there is no chance my heartburn will go away while I am lying down. I get up and return to the front room. The last of the liquor stores has just closed. I pick up the book Dave has sent home with me, *Psychoanalysis: The Impossible Profession*, by Janet Malcolm, and I begin to read it.

I notice that Freud includes among the three impossible professions Education.

I think Ferenczi may have been right to have been always kissing his patients.

I suspect that all love is transference, as Freud himself suspected. Does that mean no one should kiss anyone? I know I am a father-figure to Tina, whose own father is a professor. That does not stop me from sleeping with her. I find it surprising, although Freud would not, that she resists this obvious insight. Frankly I can't see the problem about people sleeping with their father-surrogates or daughter-surrogates or mother-surrogates. Maybe I'll see it if I'm ever plagued by a hysterical symptom, knock on wood.

I read, "The concept of transference at once destroys faith in personal relations and explains why they are tragic: we cannot know each other."

In a lecture at Clark University in Worcester, a city where I spent my first year of college, Freud spoke of "What we call a normal man—the bearer, and in part the victim, of the civilization that has been so painfully acquired." Was it Freudian when we called Worcester "the asshole of the universe?"

The humble goal of orthodox analysis remains "transforming hysterical misery into common unhappiness."

The Oedipus Complex "describes the shattering, by fear of castration, of a small boy's dream of making love to his mother, and the formation of the superego as a permanent memorial to his dread."

Women have penis envy, but not the fear of castration. Freud sees them as resultingly less ethical in the ideal model.

* * *

I return to bed, my heartburn sufficiently eased to allow me to doze off, and that is when begins the already partially narrated Nightmare of the Couch.

* * *

You want castration anxiety? I'll give you castration anxiety: I have slept holding my balls since the first night that I was unfaithful to my first wife.

I sort of wake now, holding my balls, as a poem drifts away that I have been composing in my dream. It involves a boy/man who was punished for offending not, as in the original line, his beloved, but, in an emendation, "his Holy Blessed Virgin Mother."

* * *

I remember Dave remarking that most psychoanalysts fail to recognize that they are themselves a counter-culture. We both recall the joke about how many psychoanalysts it takes to change a light bulb. He tells the one his Jewish colleagues have told him, about how it can be proved Christ was a Jew, and which involves his insisting, to his dying day, that his mother was a virgin.

I divert myself back into sleep with erotic thoughts of Tina, and I bring her into my sleeping arms, but then it is my wife who is in my arms, and I am overjoyed. It's been so long, and I realize she has missed the holding, the caressing also, and I kiss her tiny nipples and go down on her and then I am about to enter her when...

...I am half-awake; my arms are crossed; I am facing my wife, and she is lying on her back, turned maybe slightly away from me. I can't tell if her eyes are open, closed in sleep, or closed in death... and I remember the children in the room... and I don't know if I have been talking in my sleep or rolling about, or if I may even have been holding my wife in my arms. I don't know if I've touched her, or spoken to her. My eyes keep closing. I keep forcing them open, trying to see my wife's eyes. I don't know what she has been dreaming all these last few years. I don't know if she's had someone else. I don't know what she wants. I don't know if she suffers. Or whether things are just the way she wants them.

* * *

I go to the kitchen, sweating and shaking, take one of my wife's Lowenbraus from the refrigerator and open it. I take a swallow, find a notebook and pen, and begin to copy down in barely legible scrawl the events of the dream and of the day and their associations.

For instance: "Castration and conscience: mother and wife... Repetition obsession: mother and wife."

As I strike it on the page "Freud" comes out looking like "Feud" but not like "Fraud."

Freud and I and anti-Feminism. Not misogyny. Anti-feminism in its RATIONAL extreme.

In a part of the dream I now remember, Dave was also reading the Janet Malcolm book, and then his wife was also.

Dave had said, "Why have I had to go through ten years of analysis to get to the point she (his wife) has always been at?" Yet she, the youngest daughter of five Irish Catholic children, and a twin to boot, struck me, in her teens, as the most fragile of psyches. She will have her second child in a month, just as I and my wife, at her age, have two.

The beer is starting to fade both my anxiety attack and my memory of the other world. I open a second bottle.

My neck is very stiff. Could my arthritic problems be related to repression in my writing?

Unlikely. Much more likely the result of early athletic injuries, recent sedentary labor, and an ill-advised dip in the ocean.

Must I feel guilty at having a little time to do my own work this next week, having spent the last almost entirely with my son?

The KABC talk show psychologist, Toni Grant, says you don't have to feel guilty about avoiding contact with a domineering mother.

My mother and my wife would get along fine. Have gotten along fine in their little expository and telephonic communication. My first two wives were not at all like my mother. I left them.

The other day Toni Grant recommended to a caller a book on how to get over an addiction to a person.

Over a third beer I look at a prospectus from my tax man about a real estate investment fund. I've never owned an inch of land. I should look into it, but it might mean putting gift money into community property.

I'm returning to the world of external worries. Money is a popular one. I finish the beer and return to stand looking down on my wife. She has almost no bosom, but what she has is the most attractive to me. I deny this to Tina who has large breasts and senses that they don't affect me much. Or is it just that my wife is so private with hers? No, I always loved them. Could it be that she's ashamed of them? Are we so much, as Freud would say, "powerful solitary fantasy systems," that she doesn't know my sexual feelings toward her? Does she think I prefer a mistress?

She opens her eyes.

I say, "I had frightening dreams. Was I talking in my sleep and acting strangely?"

"I don't know," she says. "I was asleep."

I lie down next to her and let the beer drop me beneath dreams and reality.

TO THE SHORES OF SAN CLEMENTE

Every second weekend Jimmy's two kids from his second marriage spend with him. Usually they take a late afternoon bus on Friday up the Pacific Coast Highway to Seal Beach, and on Sunday he drives them down the San Diego Freeway to San Clemente. They used to live in Seal Beach just a few blocks from him. Things were less formal then. It must have been hard for them to leave Seal Beach, where they had lived nearly all their lives, but they have a much nicer, much roomier and safer house in San Clemente, at least for the time being. They've made the adjustment, as they've learned to make all adjustments, without complaint. They are expert at making the best of the situations in which they find themselves.

California is back on standard time, and so it is dark by the time he drops them off with their mother. He chats briefly with his former wife about practicalities concerning the kids, then trudges back down the hill to his Toyota wagon. He is still in pain from his yearly episode of lower-back trouble, but it gets a little better each day. Two weeks ago he couldn't turn over in bed. His back first started giving him trouble twenty years ago, when he was playing high school football and basketball and lifting weights. Over the years, and after a lot more weightlifting, the attacks have become more frequent, more painful, and slower to ease. He hasn't lifted any weights in over a year now, and he misses it. He doesn't like the slackness in his arms. He doesn't like the slackness around his waist either, and he knows it complicates the back problems, but it's the old vicious circle: he knows he should exercise to lose weight, but when he exercises, the weight helps knock his back out. Then he can't exercise at all for a few weeks, during which time he puts on a couple of additional pounds. His physical condition, or the lack of it, is not good for his spirits.

Nor is the situation with his present wife. They've been together many years and have always fought, but now he thinks they may indeed be on the verge of splitting up. She seems to want that. Maybe she's just faking, for leverage in the relationship, the way he managed to keep his freedom for years by maintaining the impression that he was only too willing to cut out at any time. Now that he's made the mistake of letting her know he doesn't really want to leave, she has turned the tables on him. Just this afternoon, fighting over something so ridiculous as whether football or a Sesame Street re-run should occupy the t.v. screen, she says, "You can just get out of here any time you want." When he says, "Is that what you want, though?" she hedges: "I thought we'd been through this... I thought I'd made myself clear... You ought to be able to tell for yourself." He says, "I thought you felt the way that I do, that, sure, either of us can leave if he or she wants, and the other will survive, but that we'd rather we didn't have to separate." When she refuses to speak, he falls back on a recent innovation of his: "Okay, you leave then. Since women's lib, the man doesn't have to be the one to leave anymore. This place will be perfect for a bachelor, and you know I hate apartment hunting."

They have one child of their own, a two-year-old daughter. Brenda is six months pregnant with their second child.

He doesn't want to resume the war this evening. Since she has to get up early Monday morning for work, she'll be in bed by the time he gets home, if he kills a couple of hours before embarking on the hour's ride up the highway. He's been meaning to check out a couple of the San Clemente bars anyway, not that he has many illusions left about there being many great bars, or even interesting ones, in the universe, the famed London pubs included.

The first bar he comes to is at the corner of the main shopping street, near the Greyhound station. He sees a group of young jugheads enter, thinks twice, then shrugs and follows them in.

The clientele is composed mostly of Marines, ex-Marines, Marine reservists, and retired career Marines. There is a fat young cocktail waitress and a handful of other fat women of varying ages sitting next to their men. One man is flanked by two fat women a good deal younger than he is. From the instructions he is giving the bartender, he seems to be the owner of the place. It seems to be the bartender's first night. The place is ordinary and unpretentious, a long bar, three booths, a second room for a pool table and bowling game, rest rooms, phone, and cigarette machines in back, mirror behind the bar. The drinks are not expensive. Jimmy lowers himself with some pain onto one of the barstools and orders a bottle of Bud.

The place would be comfortable enough if it weren't for the wall-to-wall gyrenes. San Clemente must have the shortest-haired population of any town but Oceanside. Nixon must have found a certain security in that, but Jimmy isn't at all sure he likes his kids growing up in a town so unanimously wholesome and patriotic.

The fat women, especially the fat waitress, are turning Jimmy on. He's never had much luck picking up women in bars, but he wonders if he'd stand any chance with the fat waitress. Why do fat women in bars turn him on? Outside of bars, he has no sexual appetite for fat women. He's turned down numerous opportunities to go to bed with fat women of his acquaintance.

The owner gets up to take his two women to dinner. He has been bantering with a young Marine at the end of the bar. As he passes him, he says, "Don't you wish you had a woman on each arm?" and the young Marine says, "If I did I'd be able to do something with them." The owner is too mercenary to risk the luxury of an offended honor. He laughs it off and leaves. When the door closes behind him, someone says, "He was on the Arizona," and someone else says, "Too bad he didn't go down with his ship."

* * *

A hyper kid elbows himself next to Jimmy at the bar and says, "Hey, this is a great bar, isn't it?"

Jimmy shrugs, "I just got here."

"Hey, you got a match?"

Jimmy doesn't.

"Hey bartender, you got a match?"

The bartender turns for matches and the kid clears his throat and hawks into the bar towel. A patron nearby says, "This guy just hawked into your bar-towel, Phil."

The bartender looks to Jimmy for confirmation. Jimmy looks away.

"You're 86'ed," the bartender snaps at the kid, who still has his hand out for the matches.

"Hey, I didn't mean anything..."

"You're through in here."

"I wasn't trying to..."

"Finish your drink and get out."

The kid returns to the table where he's left his drink. Jimmy orders another Bud. A few minutes later the kid returns to the bar. The bartender is serving someone else. The kid clears his throat and spits into a fresh bar towel. He eyes the patron: "You keep your trap shut, fink."

The bartender returns and the patron says, "This guy spit in your towel again."

"You mother——"

The bartender lifts the phone on the wall behind the bar and commences dialing. The kid says, "Hey, that isn't necessary!"

The bartender continues dialing.

"Okay, okay, I'm leaving..."

The kid hurries out the doors, and the bartender asks the patron, "You want me to go ahead and get the cops? He may wait outside for you."

"He'll have a long wait."

"You're the boss."

* * *

Jimmy's on his third beer when he feels a tug at the crack of his ass. His pants have always had a tendency to ride low, especially on barstools, and the old shirt he has on is a bit shrunken. He turns to his left, but his molester, a young Marine from a table of Marines behind him, has gone off to the right towards the men's room. Jimmy turns to the table and says, "I didn't know this was a gay bar."

Fortunately, the young men at the table are all good guys. "He's just a little drunk," one says, and another says, "He's been acting like an asshole all night. Don't let him bother you."

Jimmy grins and turns back to his beer. When the trouble-maker returns from the head, Jimmy follows him over his shoulder. There's some whispering at the table, and then the whole group gets up and heads for the door. Jimmy makes a mental note that this is probably not the place to frequent when his back is really bad.

* * *

After his fourth beer Jimmy wanders down the road to a different bar. He makes a point of choosing a spot at the end of the bar near the entrance, where no one will be behind him.

You see a lot of Jack Sprat-and-his-wife couples in bars. There's such a pair in this one, a scrawny, bespectacled, nervous fellow of about thirty with a girl who must have been very pretty when he married her. Now her biceps are twice the size of Jimmy's, and her ass is thrice. Still a tall, rawboned jarhead is standing next to the wife, flirting with her and just generally trying to stir up a little strife and discord.

"Doesn't your husband ever just grab you and give you a big kiss and make you feel like you're his woman?"

"We've been married nearly ten years."

"Some marriage. I'd never want a marriage like that."

"Have you ever *been* married?"

"Hell, no, but if I ever were, I'd just grab my wife, and drag her off to the bedroom, and make it clear to her that she was my woman. Hey, buddy, you mean you don't ever just grab this beautiful lady of yours and play the cave-man?"

"Do I look sick?"

"What an awful marriage."

"I think we're doing pretty well. How many other people do you know these days that have been together as long as we have?"

"You've been together too long."

"Look, the bartender has only been married a couple of weeks. Hey, Billy, come here. You ever just grab your old lady and give her a big kiss?"

"What would I do that for? Do I look sick or something?"

* * *

It turns out that Rawhide has already been 86'ed by the bartender. All he had to do to get 86'ed was come through the door. Apparently he has a reputation for starting fights. He says he can get served back up the street, but he doesn't seem in any hurry to prove it. When one of the older patrons points out to him that there's no one in this bar both young enough and strong enough to give him a fair fight, any pugilistic inclinations Rawhide may have had are at least temporarily derailed, and Jimmy feels even older and flabbier than when he walked in.

It also turns out that Jack Sprat has that afternoon won a sucker bet with Rawhide. Took him for twenty bucks on the results of a game that had been over for an hour. Now, playing drunker than he is, Rawhide suckers Sprat into a bet that one of the two teams in the NFC championship game will be *in* the Super Bowl. The bet is for twenty dollars. When he realizes what he has agreed (and signed) to, Spratt insists that the bet was that an NFC team would *win* the Super Bowl, but the bet is in writing. Rawhide gloats that Spratt now knows what it feels like to be "taken downtown." Spratt croaks that twenty bucks to him is what twenty cents would be to Rawhide, but his face is pale and his hand is shaking and his wife has fallen silent and everyone is embarrassed for him.

Rawhide tries once more: "Look, Billy, I'm not even close to drunk. At least pour me a coffee or a glass of water."

The bartender goes to the well and returns with a glass of water.

"Oh, Christ," he says, and to Jimmy he tries to say, "He thinks I want to start a fight," but Jimmy is already looking the other way.

* * *

Jimmy thinks, "If it weren't that the blizzard is missing, I'd swear I wandered into the Blue Hotel."

* * *

But Rawhide decides to cease and desist his terrorizing of Jack Sprat, for the time being at least. Maybe an eyeful of Sprat's wife's ass on its way to the ladies' room has dulled his ardor. He goes and sits with a tableful of Marines, probably hoping they can order a surreptitious extra drink. Jimmy figures it won't be long before this bartender too is picking up the phone.

After his next beer, Jimmy goes to empty his bladder before the long ride up the highway. He hopes that he has enough gas that he won't have to stop on the way. Brenda will almost certainly be in bed by the time he gets home. The half-dozen beers, the six pack, such a round and respectable number, have left him temporarily at peace with his world. He'll punch a talk-show or a rock station, just put himself on automatic pilot, lean back and enjoy the rows of bright lights against the black sky. At home he'll continue drinking through the news, and Jim Hill's *Sunday Night Sports Final,* and maybe even a re-run of *The Rockford Files* and *The Name of the Game.* It is imperative for the future of his marriage that he appear as cool as Rockford or Glenn Howard.

Of course, he reflects, neither of them were married. Few heroes since Ulysses have been. Except King Arthur, ha, ha.

He's pleased to have avoided conversation in the bars.

O TANNENBAUM

They have indeed once again managed to get along better, almost like a loving, long-married couple, over the holidays. And Jimmy has once again fallen into the trap of thinking things might possibly continue getting better, that the pieces of their Humpty-Dumpty marriage might be drawn back together, like a film run in reverse, until even the jagged seams would disappear. It is in this spirit that he arrives home the evening before New Year's Eve.

Brenda is doing the dishes and Jocko is watching something furry on the Disney Channel. He has no sooner said hello to his wife when he hears his daughter's voice beginning faintly from the bedroom: "Dad-dy? Dad-dy? Dad-dy?" He can ignore her and hope to keep the truce in effect, or he can open the bedroom door and switch the marital projector to Fast Forward. He asks himself, Why am I still living here anyway?, and remembering the answer, he enters the bedroom.

"Is my sweetheart in trouble?"

"Yes." And she comes from her bed to sit on his lap, tears rolling down both cheeks.

"What's the problem?"

"I didn't know I wasn't supposed to write on our new table."

"You wrote *on* the new table? You mean you wrote directly onto the surface of the table?"

"No, I just wrote and drew pictures on the white paper Mommy covered the table with until she has time to stain it."

"Just on the *paper*? That doesn't sound like the end of the world."

"Mommy says she doesn't have any more of that kind of paper."

"How long do you have to stay in here?"

"I can't come out at all."

"You mean you have to stay in here until morning?"

"And my brother is getting to watch *Josephina the Cat*."

"Have you tried apologizing to your mother?"

"She won't let me come out there to apologize."

"Well, you might as well try."

"Come out with me. I'm afraid to go out there by myself."

"Okay, but I can't promise anything."

So he leads her into the front room and says, "Missy wants to say she's sorry."

"I know she's sorry."

"Can she come out now?"

"No. Being sorry isn't enough."

His daughter returns to the bedroom, sobbing. He closes the door behind them and holds her, saying, "Try not to cry. It will only make you feel worse and it won't help with Mommy."

After a while she gets her voice sufficiently under control to ask, "Can't you do anything to help me?"

And he thinks to himself, I can carry you into the other room myself and deposit you in front of the t.v. and be in the position of having undermined your mother's authority. And you can be sure she'll take it out on you psychologically as soon as I'm not around. Or I could just blast your mother right in the face with my fist, and don't think there would not be a great deal of pleasure and relief in that for me, but then she would be able to have me arrested and divorce me with custody of you guys and get a couple of hundred restraining orders and probably have me paying her damages for the rest of my life, and maybe I'd lose my job as well—the Women's Studies people would love to hear I've taken to abusing women physically as well as in print. Or I could walk out the door with you, and even if I weren't picked up for kidnapping, you'd probably be crying for your mother in an hour.

Sweetheart, he could tell her, a man has almost no weapons at his disposal nowadays, and this disarming was accomplished in the name of progress for young ladies such as yourself.

Instead, he just tells her, "Most of the things I could do would only make things worse."

"At least don't leave me in here by myself."

"All right," he says, "just let me pour myself a glass of wine and I'll be right back."

And in a few seconds he is sitting with her on the bed, one hand holding her and the other a glass of sweet vermouth, and he is thinking, I could also leave your mother, which is exactly what she's been hoping for years that I would do, and in which case I would no longer be able to sit here with you and my glass of wine, comforting both of us, and in fact I might be too broke even to ease my own depression with a drink. And so you see why I put up with...

"This certainly isn't any punishment," his wife is saying as she sweeps by them towards the closet; "you might as well be sitting in front of your movie. Go ahead!"

His daughter hurries out to join her brother on the couch, and Jimmy saunters towards the refilling of his glass and the establishing of his elbows upon the counter.

After the cat film, and on her way to brush her teeth, Missy tries to kiss her mother, and Brenda angrily pulls back her cheek. The child stands there shoulders slumped in defeat, then runs to her father. Jimmy goes down on one knee to take her in his arms with, "I know. I know how you feel."

Brenda comes to the door to glare at them. He waits until she turns away, then tells his daughter, "Go on, now. It won't be you that she'll be mad at in the morning.

*   *   *

He drinks later and has to rise earlier than he would like the next day to pick up his paycheck. The check, dated January 1, cannot be deposited until three that afternoon, so he goes to the office to write a few letters. He doesn't feel like being there, but he doesn't feel like being at home either.

When he returns in late afternoon, the first thing his daughter tells him, with great seriousness, is, "We're not going to the New Year's Eve party, but Mommy says it's not because she's angry at us but just because she doesn't feel like it. But I'm going to get to bake cookies with the bake-set that I got for Christmas, and if we take a nap we're going to get to stay up till midnight for the very first time, and anyway Mommy says that the people at the party are just your friends not ours."

"The party is at Rafe's house. You know Rafe. You've been at his parties and he's been at ours. You saw him just last week at school."

"Mommy!" she cries, "the party is at Rafe's house!" But when no reaction is forthcoming she knows she's said something that her mother doesn't want to hear and she turns to her father with, "Are you going to be here for *our* party?"

"I already committed us to go to Rafe's, and he's already worried that not many people are showing up. I'll stay here as long as possible, and maybe I'll get home before you're in bed, but I'm going to at least show up at Rafe's party as I said I would."

"Ohhhh," his daughter says, clearly disappointed, and when his little boy asks him the same thing a little while later, he has to give the same explanation which, by the younger child, is even less well understood.

* * *

Although he does not get home from the party until nearly four—the sort of family party with kids and dogs and grandparents and friends of decades' standing that Brenda has always claimed to be her ideal sort of party—he arises feeling surprisingly good. Now, however, the wait is on to see if she will also pull out on their ride to visit other old friends—although she's known Raul for fifteen years she'd probably claim that he is really not *her* friend because Jimmy has known him for twenty. Jimmy finds her out front staining the children's table and chairs over which the initial row developed. "What's your schedule?" he asks.

"I don't know. When I finish this I may take the kids for a walk. Then they need baths. I'll need a shower. We'll all need lunch."

He says nothing. Goes inside and plants himself in front of the t.v. He might as well enjoy Doug Flutie in the Cotton Bowl, with occasional flips to the Fiesta Bowl of UCLA and Miami.

* * *

He had hoped to be on the road to Riverside by 1:00, but he considers himself lucky that they're finishing lunch at Taco Bell by a little after 2:00. He can have them to Raul's in an hour. They've never been on time to anyone's yet.

* * *

The day goes pleasantly, Jimmy mostly watching the Rose Bowl in the living room, while Brenda hangs around the kitchen. Raul and his wife alternate between the two rooms, while the four kids parade through the house and back yard. Jimmy knows that his dear old friend, a brilliant physicist, seldom drinks and in fact used these infrequent get-togethers with Jimmy as an excuse for downing a few India Pale Ales and reverting to the insult comedy and silliness they've both enjoyed so many years. Ann, his second wife, tolerates these performances, probably even enjoys them up to a point, and knows it will be sobriety as usual in the morning. Raul is one of the most fiercely loyal of Jimmy's friends, and Jimmy respects him as much as he enjoys him. He supposes he mildly resents the extent to which Ann has tamed his never *that* rowdy cohort, and he supposes he considers his friend's conversion to male feminism as leaving him unwisely vulnerable. On the other hand, it is consistent with his lifelong liberalism, and after all, Jimmy asks himself, how is *he* faring with his own Neanderthal approach to interpersonal relationships.

Nothing comes between the friends except the logistical difficulties of getting the families together like this, especially with the always tenuous relations between Jimmy and Brenda. When Raul tells of having been at a New Year's Eve party at which the feminists subjected everyone to a showing of Johnny Guitar—because the women wear the guns in it— Jimmy says, "Tell me another story like that and I'll lose my appetite," and Raul laughs. Ann does too.

Just before dinner, though—good enchiladas baked by Raul—Jocko comes to the living room to tell his father, "Mommy is saying that you don't share with us."

What's she talking about? Jimmy always makes it clear that she and the kids are welcome to anything of his, whereas she resents his nabbing a kleenex. She's the most possessive of material things of anyone he's ever known. Then he remembers hearing talk from the kitchen of word processors, and he bets that she's been saying that he won't share his new little fifty-buck portable manual typewriter with them. Which is bullshit—she's already used it, and all he asked was that she supervise the kids and not let them pound it to an early death. He doesn't want to sit down to it looking forward to a full day's writing only to discover half the keys are jammed. So now she's taken to bad-mouthing him to his friends.

* * *

In the car in the dark on the freeway, Jimmy considers trying to strike up a conversation. The kids are asleep in the back seat. It's times like this that they seem to do their best talking nowadays. But he's sick of always being the one to make the conciliatory gestures, and he knows she takes them as signs of weakness. He's tired of making up to her for what she's brought upon herself. He looks out the window and neither of them says a word all the way home.

* * *

The next day, as he leaves the house, she is taking down the Christmas ornaments.

* * *

It is another two days before he notices that she has moved the typewriter chair outside and that their living Christmas tree is firmly established upon it. To what depths of pettiness will she not sink in her spite. Strictly speaking it is her chair, but he has been using it as needed at the typewriter for fifteen years. It is about the only thing left in the house that she could have done to further inconvenience him.

* * *

He calls to tell Rafe about the chair. He knows it will help him calm down.

"Shit, Jimmy, we've got chairs to spare around here. Come on over and take a chair anytime you want."

"Nah, I appreciate it but I can get one at Goodwill if I want. Trouble is she's also made sure there's no place left to put one. Of course she's moved stuff of the kids into the likely spots, rather than her own stuff, so if I move anything, she can tell the kids I made it necessary for her to toss out a few of their favorite toys. She's an evil genius. One of these mornings she'll be waking me up to say one of the kids is sick and can I handle it, and if I say, 'Aren't you the same bitch who planted a fucking Christmas tree on my goddamnn typewriter chair," she'll go tell the kids I didn't want to take care of them."

"You'll figure something out."

"Oh, yeah, I'll be okay. I seldom do any typing at home anymore, and if I need to I can put the typewriter on the counter, even if it is a little high. What the fuck, Ernest Hemingway wrote standing up. And there are other little ways

I can return the favor: let the garbage pile up, forget to buy a *T.V. Guide*, pull the drapes all day so that her indoor plants die, not replace the toilet paper when it runs out... God, I hate to descend to her level, though."

"Well, the chair-offer stands if you decide to take me up on it."

*　*　*

Friday she buys Missy a kitten, trying to replace the string of kittens that have died, and, of course, trying to cement her daughter's affection.

But, neurotic that she is, she immediately doses the kitten and the entire house with flea spray, and by the next day this kitten too is suffering from diarrhea. Flea spray is one of Brenda's stubborn points, like insisting that tampax and clumps of hair do not clog the toilet.

The next day the cat goes to the vet who gives it a shot, a fifty-fifty chance of surviving, and presents Brenda with another twenty-five dollar bill.

*　*　*

The system they have worked out is that Jimmy gives Brenda a lump sum at the beginning of each month that is supposed to cover his half of expenses for the household and the kids. A few other items, such as telephone charges and the cable bill get taken care of as they come in. This month, however, instead of tallying what he owes on the phone bill, Brenda circles her calls and leaves the bill on his typewriter. He puts it back on her breadbox. The next morning it is on the typewriter. He tosses it on the breadbox. This is a strange maneuver on her part since she will not be reimbursed for the bill, which she has already paid, until his part of the charges get totaled.

* * *

Since she and the kids are back to school, they are also back to an early bedtime, usually not long after Jimmy arrives home. She is doing her best to keep the kids away from him, even calling them to brush their teeth when he is in the middle of reading them something. So one night when she is otherwise occupied, he turns on a movie on the Disney channel and the kids sit in his arms on the couch while Brenda fumes away in the background waiting for the film to end.

* * *

God, she must hate him. God, she must wish he would leave. But he senses that, with the sick kitten and being back to school and all, she is beginning to realize that it won't be long before she needs his help for something. Even now he's sure she would like to discuss what to do about the kitten with him—he's always taken the load of guilt from her by making the decision when a pet is too far gone to stay with them any longer. One of these evenings he will come through the door to find her talking brightly to him as if nothing in the least had been the matter. Then he'll have to decide how hard to come down upon her over the stinking chair.

* * *

And sure enough, it is only a few days before he comes home to find the kitten dying of uncontrollable diarrhea, and Brenda on the verge of a nervous breakdown trying to clean up after it. "I've had it to the vet," she says; "he gave it a shot and I've been giving it liquid antibiotics. It just keeps getting worse."

"All right," he says, "I'll take it to the shelter while you and the kids are gone during the day tomorrow. And while I'm in that part of town, I might as well pick myself up a typewriter chair at Goodwill, if the other one is going to sit outside permanently with the Christmas tree on top of it."

"Oh, that's not necessary. The chair can come inside anytime you want to help me lift the tree off of it. I just wasn't able to lift anything that heavy by myself."

"But you managed to get it outside."

"I dragged it."

"Okay, I'll take care of it. I thought maybe you were just being spiteful."

"No, it was too heavy for me."

"Next time say something."

* * *

So, he has won the Great Christmas Tree Stand-Off, at the expense of his daughter having to suffer the loss of yet another kitten.

He gets to savor the victory, of which there have been damn few, for about twenty-four hours. The next evening, as he sits sipping his sherry, Brenda and the kids arrive home from the shopping mall and his daughter excitedly explains to him, "Mommy says that she's never bringing another cat into this apartment—that there's something about the place that kills them—but that it's time we moved to a larger place anyway."

FIN DE SEMESTRE

Okay, he will have a new clutch put in the goddamnn car, even though he would much rather trade it in on something brand-new and better. But how much better could he afford? Because he has a daughter who works for Ford back in Ann Arbor, he is eligible for a deal at something like invoice plus one per cent. At first he had been under the illusion that this might allow him a true splurge, perhaps an Explorer, preferably with air-conditioning to make his wife and kids happy and power-everything for those increasingly more frequent times when bursitis and tendinitis and various other forms of inflammation rendered shoulder or elbow or foot virtually useless. Automatic transmission, for instance, so, in a pinch, one could get by with one good leg. Four-wheel drive for blizzards at Big Bear, not to mention periods of civil disorder precipitated by earthquake, flood, or outrageous verdict. These were excellent ways to rationalize what would no doubt end up a very expensive and seldom fully utilized toy.

How expensive he had not realized until he gave a call to a friendly fleet sales manager from whom he learned that even at heavy discount Explorers went for just about twice what he had planned to pay.

How about a nice, roomy, loaded Taurus? Practically as much as the Explorer.

His little red Hyundai Excel two-door, which had listed when he had bought it for the lowest price, save the Yugo, in America, had given him what he had hoped for: six years of relatively inexpensive, relatively trouble-free transportation... but he had just finished sinking money into brakes and tires and a battery, and today it was the clutch, and who knew what it would be tomorrow. He guessed that from here on it would just be one thing after another. And he was sick of squeezing into a car two sizes too tight for him, not to mention moving the seats forward and back every time he had his kids or the dog as passengers.

He would meet his wife at the Arco garage five miles away, back where they used to live but where he still trusted the mechanics. He would listen to the kid who would write up the work order extol the merits of his ageless Subaru four-wheel-drive station wagon. Maybe he would price one of them himself—might be a good compromise. Kid would say his never gave him any trouble, even though he never changed the oil, which seemed odd coming from a mechanic, but maybe not if you considered that he changed other people's oil all week. Maybe dentists never brushed their teeth. Jimmy liked this kid because the kid not only laughed at his wisecracks but even remembered a couple he had made when he was in for a smog check. That didn't sound quite right but perhaps it wouldn't be long before we, as well as our cars, needed annual smog certification. Sooner than that, urine samples to weed out not only the dopers but the smokers and drinkers. Ah well, he shouldn't let himself get started on that chestnut of a theme.

* * *

His wife is ten minutes late, of course, leaving him to bake his swelling feet on the asphalt beneath a ninety-degree sun. She insists she has time to drop him off at home, but he directs her to pick up their daughter first. Her Honda station wagon has great air-conditioning and a first-rate AM/FM/Cassette. The twenty-nine dollar radio he had installed in his Hyundai is busted, and he has never yet owned an air-conditioned car. His daughter, a freshman in high school, has had a day off. She and her girlfriends like to browse the alternative shops and coffee houses that have sprung up along Fourth Street and Broadway. She has dyed her hair blue, but he thinks it looks beautiful, although he has explained to her the social consequences she should expect if she chooses to look different. Few, except for blacks, would know better than he.

She is waiting outside the Tiger's Eye, an occult store. Her girlfriend has been picked up by her mother fifteen minutes early, which does not please him. Like all young people, she has few specifics to offer as to how the previous four hours have been spent: some time among the tarot cards, a fine young man conversed with at Taco Bell, a bookstore at which he hopes she has not located his own titles. When his kids finally begin to read his stuff in earnest, and to let slip to their mother that they are doing so, he may just as well resign himself to divorce.

They are home in time to take showers and cool off a few minutes beneath the Casablanca fan before getting back into the car, borrowed from his wife, for the ride to L.A. He is taking his daughter to the annual awards banquet of a writer's organization. He will not himself be receiving any awards. He has not been on any of the committees selecting the winners. He did have a book eligible in one of the categories. He has never been to a single function of this writers' society, although he does keep up the considerable but tax-deductible dues. Most of their gatherings are priced to raise funds. This one too—fifty bucks a person—but when he showed the invitation to his daughter, who is doing well in English, she recognized a couple of the authors on the letterhead as having penned books she enjoyed, and she surprised him, mildly, by saying that yes, she would like to go; it would be something different. The next day he sent in the tax-deductible check.

Now he asks her, "Should I wear my birkenstocks or this battered pair of walking shoes that I discovered this afternoon I can squeeze into if I lace them very loosely."

"Wear what you want," she says; "that's what you told me."

"I know, but you'll look beautiful in anything. I wish these damn things didn't show so much white sock."

"Are you wearing a sport coat?"

"I couldn't get into it."

"A tie?"

"I'm taking one in the car in case they insist."

"Did the invitation say anything about a dress code?"

"No."

"So it's the white socks and birkenstocks you're worried about."

"Yes. I have a new shirt from the fat man's shop. Size 6-XL. And my best pair of Sears cords. But I've seen the way birkenstocks and white socks serve as magnets to the eye."

"Are writers notoriously well-dressed?"

"No, few real writers are. Maybe Tom Wolfe. Probably not Thomas Wolfe. But a lot of the writers at this thing will be wealthy socialites first and writers second. In some cases their butlers may have written their books for them."

"Tell them to get fucked. Tell them to kiss your ass."

"I'm afraid I've been telling them that, more or less, for about four decades. Pretty much as a matter of principle in my early years. I knew a person of my conspicuous talents would not require tact, much less sycophancy, to prevail in short order. You can see where it's gotten me."

"Is that why you and mom warn me about my *attitude*? Because you want me to kiss ass?"

"No, I don't want you ever to kiss ass. But you might investigate *diplomacy* a little sooner in life than I did."

* * *

The event is being held in a plush athletic club in downtown L.A. He leaves himself an hour and a half to negotiate the rush-hour traffic and spends the first half-hour creeping about five miles up the San Diego freeway. He opts to backtrack northeast on the Long Beach freeway and the move pays off. The traffic is again clotted at the Santa Ana, but he knows his way well enough to cover East L.A. by surface roads. He arrives at the parking garage on time which is naturally, by California standards, half an hour early.

The evening exceeds in stuffiness and boredom not only his own expectations but even those of his daughter. The writers whose works she knows are not in attendance. Very few of the writers that *anybody* knows are there. He has been writing in Southern California for thirty years and there are only three people there of his acquaintanceship. One of them, although they do not allude to it, was a judge of the category in which he was not victorious. One of them, a lively old lady, surprises him, his daughter, and everyone else at their table by exclaiming, "Are you THE POET JAMES ABBEY?" But it turns out they both read at a poetry publication party many years before.

The drinks at the no-host reception bar are four-and-a-half bucks, so he limits himself to two. His daughter is sharp enough to size up the situation instantly and insist that she does not need a coke. He is sure there will be, at the price, at least carafe-wine at the meal. A few people *do* stare at his birkenstocks and white athletic socks, and he is, as usual, clearly the most underdressed person in the place, but once he has a tanqueray in his belly, his demeanor bespeaks, "Fuck you. Kiss my ass." He relaxes and enjoys just being with his daughter, telling her what little there is to tell about this segment of the Southern California literary scene, which is not that of the starving poets. They are, however, fairly hungry by the time an officious maitre d' hustles them into the dining room.

To his dawning horror there are no wine glasses at the table. There is no wine card. There are no sommeliers. There are rolls and butter, an approximation of a Caesar salad (pre-tossed), the death-and-taxes chicken and mushrooms, a medley of sauteed vegetables with something to offend everyone, and an admittedly rather well designed fruit tart. Jimmy never drinks coffee, but, it being the only drug in the place, he swallows two cups of caffeine. These keep him awake through the generally inoffensive awards presentations and acceptance speeches.

There are seventeen tables and they have been assigned places at table seventeen. This is probably less a matter of personal insult than a result of his not having contributed beyond the cost of the tickets. A table nearer the front seems to be having wine poured for them. He hates to make too much of the wine drought in front of his daughter—he would just as soon defer her discovery of the consolations of alcohol a few more years—but it truly is an outrage at, of all things, a fucking *writers'* gathering. What neo-Puritan could have perpetrated such a calamity. No doubt a feminist whose mother was beaten by a drunken father, or who drove some former husband of her own to drunken violence. How clever of the women to gradually deprive their men of all of their escapes from them, or substitutions for them. So much easier to domesticate the sober. A man with a drink in him does not take kindly to being told to fix his own goddamn dinner, or do his own goddamn laundry, or to clean up his goddamn work space. Now if he talks back he can be put in jail.

The mike is working poorly. Table seventeen can barely hear the voices at the podium. What a fucking shame.

* * *

Cruising home on the Harbor freeway above those streets where that weekend alone thirty-five people will, in unconnected incidents, be murdered, his daughter asks him, in reference to his third acquaintance at the banquet, "Why did that small man at our table keep talking about all the people he knew and all the things he had written?"

"Probably you just answered your own question."

"Oh."

"He really *is* very intelligent, and he really *has* written a lot, and he really *does* know a lot of people, and he really *did* used to edit a very fine poetry magazine, and he was very good about including me in its pages at a time when most editors were much less hospitable. He doesn't have to be so insecure, but for some reason he always has been. I once called him a complete fucking asshole at the top of my lungs at a poetry reading because I thought he had insulted a good friend of mine and was going to insult me. The sad thing is he didn't even get angry. Ordinarily that would argue a *lack* of insecurity, but I'm afraid in his case it was the insecurity that caused the clumsy attempts at humor and that the absence of ire stemmed from his acceptance of the truth of what he had been called. But we long ago agreed to consider the whole thing an unfortunate misunderstanding. I'm sorry now that I said it. It wasn't necessary. At the time I obviously felt that it was. Those were combative times, especially for men.

"I'll tell you a more upbeat anecdote though. This time I was at this enormous party he had given at his house to launch one of his literary ventures. He had invited everyone who was anyone, even me, and quite a few people had showed up for the free champagne and hors d'oeuvres. Well, just as it seemed the bubbly had run out, and the host was no doubt happy that people were beginning to drift away, I discovered the secret cache and distributed innumerable bottles all over the place. Everyone was walking around drinking champagne straight from their own bottles. It was too late to re-lock the barn door, so to speak. I'd been introduced at the beginning of the evening to this columnist from a major paper, and he'd told me about the years he had worked in Paris on the *International Herald Tribune*, and now every time I saw him with a new group of people I barged in and regaled them with tales of our wild days in Paris working together on the Trib. He was so drunk himself I think he was starting to believe the stories.

"As you can imagine, knowing me and my appreciation of my own sense of humor, I thought it was the cleverest routine since Abbott and Costello. It's the sort of thing your mother has never seemed to enjoy hearing about."

"Then why do you subject her to it?"

"Because I find that hilarious also."

He plays with the dog in the backyard long enough to calm it down, then settles in front of the news in his tall-backed recliner with a tumbler of cream sherry. It slips down warmly, easily. He kicks off his birkenstocks, yanks off the white athletic socks, elevates his feet on the settee. It is so soothing to be home for the evening. His wife is already asleep. The late news will be on in a few minutes. His little boy has a friend staying overnight with him. They are involved in their world of comic books and drawing pads and Stephen King movies. He hears his daughter in her bedroom, listening to her alternative rock, reading a little, maybe jotting something in her diary, maybe talking softly on the phone with a friend. She must be very tired. The next time he passes her door on the way to the bathroom, the light will be out. He will tap with his fingernails on the door, open it, tell her he loves her, whispering in case she is already asleep. It isn't long ago that she needed him at her bedside every night to kiss her goodnight, and talk with her about anything at all, and maybe give her a little rub on the back of her neck. She told him once it was the best part of her day, and after that he made every effort to be there, even if it meant walking out on a disbelieving woman in a bar. On his drinking nights he would come home from the office to be with her and go back out once she was asleep. Now there were few nights out; he seldom felt like it. He'd done it, done it to death. He remembered how, by the time he met Chinaski, twenty years ago, Chinaski had already learned to hate the bars, although those who didn't know him assumed that he was still a barfly. In those days, Jimmy lived in the bars. It had seemed like a pretty interesting life at the time, and no doubt often had been.

So he was almost always home at his daughter's bedtime now, but she no longer needed him to get to sleep. Just as well—he often fell asleep in his chair ahead of her. And his little boy still liked to give him a kiss on the cheek on his own way to bed.

* * *

It would not be a good weekend. With a three-hundred-fifty dollar clutch installed in the Hyundai, new rattles would announce themselves beneath the hood. At the YMCA pool an overzealous lifeguard, mistaking the circulatory hyper-pigmentation of his feet for dirt, would order him loudly back into the showers. He would talk himself out of attending the graduation party of an attractive young friend, and staying home, would get in a fight with his wife over the disarray of his bookcase, the occupation of the dining room table by her jewelry-making hobby, his subsequent loss of any writing space, and her apparent resignation of any responsibility for the feeding of her young. They would end up slamming things around just to raise each other's blood pressure, and he knew they would not converse in a civil manner for days and she would play games such as rushing to install herself in his chair as soon as she heard him driving up. Ah well, he thought, circulation allowing, I will spend some extended time in the office and maybe get a little fiction written.

On Sunday, at a poetry reading, he would hear that Chinaski had leukemia.

On Monday he would notice that his wife, after his having spent an exhaustingly subtle year trying with some success to repair the damage she had made the summer before to her relationship with her daughter, the relationship she had seemed wrongheadedly bent on destroying throughout her daughter's life, was now trying to erect barriers between his daughter and himself, portraying him as the patriarchal and over-protective Nay-Sayer in matters of what concerts she could go to, what styles of clothes she could wear, where she would be safe on her own. He would have to communicate to his daughter that he was going to refuse to be manipulated into that role any longer, but that he would always be there for her in the background.

My God, you'd think Brenda would have thanked her lucky stars that he was willing to take the heat off her by making a few of those decisions for her. If there was anyone who had proved herself a control freak in the upbringing of their children, it had been Brenda.

On Tuesday his last delinquent directed studies student would finally deliver to his home mail box her only work of the semester, but barely sufficient for him to justify assigning her an Incomplete and finally getting the semester's grades out of his hands and into the department office. It would require his driving over to school. But he would swim a slow, endorphinical half mile in the YMCA pool, under the sloe eye of a prettier, less officious lifeguard. He would enjoy lox and cream cheese, tomato and onion, on a bagel at the little bakery near the university. And he would see about starting a story.

Poems he would be able to write in his chair, and at the dining room table, once he managed to recapture those disputed strategical positions.

CANDY BARS

Jimmy has taken his son to a movie, *Interview with the Vampire*, that he is finding among the most insufferably boring that he has ever committed himself to sitting through, and he has decided to kill a few minutes and give his legs a stretch by going for the free refill of the Jurassic-sized plastic bucket of popcorn they have just shared. It occurs to him to ask if Ziggy would like some candy also. "No," the boy replies; "I don't need any."

"But do you *want* any?"

"Unh-unh. Thanks anyway."

It both pleases and troubles him that he has a son with such will-power or simple lack of a sweet tooth. He wonders if he *ever* said no to a candy bar as a kid. He doubts it. But then, having been born in '41, at the beginning of World War II and rationing, and with his father in the service, his mother on a two-year unpaid maternity leave from teaching, and little expendable income in the family, there were a lot fewer sweets to be had. Even now, not ordering empty calories for himself, he will nonetheless finish up any cokes or milk shakes or desserts that his kids have sense enough not to finish because they are full. If he starts in on a one or two-pound gift box of chocolates, he will have trouble stopping himself before it is half-consumed. So he never buys himself a candy bar anymore, just as he no longer takes a drink. Both are necessary relinquishings, and good riddance to them, though they are not without their rich associations...

* * *

Until a couple of years ago Ziggy and his sister would always ask for Red Vines at the movies. Jimmy knows why:

licorice lasted. That was one of the factors a child instinctively took into consideration. Jimmy wonders if a Chinese kid, under laboratory conditions controlled to exclude extraneous motives, would not also select Red Vines or something similarly lasting at whatever the Chinese word was for the flicks. Jimmy had surely eaten his own share of Red Vines, not to mention Ju-Jubes, Good 'n Plentys, Juicy Fruits, and other chewables meant to stick, if not to the ribs, then at least to the teeth. He still retained the sense memory of having consumed a second box of Ju-Jubes during a matinee of *An American in Paris* at the Loew's Theatre in Rochester, New York, only to emerge into the cold glare of the winter afternoon with a throbbing, nauseous headache. Probably he had been coming down with a touch of flu, or his glasses needed changing, or he'd gone to bed too late the night before, or who knows what, but he'd never eaten another of the colorful, rubbery pellets. He had managed to watch the film on T.V. many times in later life, but never without a recollection of the sickening pain behind his eyes. I am a poor man's Proust, he muses...

* * *

Similarly, he had chewed a whole pack of bubble-gum the Sunday morning that he came down with a unilateral case of the mumps. He was sure, as the pain and swelling mounted in his gland, that he had broken his jaw on the massive wad tucked, like a baseball player's plug, into his left jaw. He and the bigger boy next door had been to Pop's candy store and were trying to decide what sort of trouble to get into in their adjoining back yards when the twinges and hyper-salivation began. Jimmy hated to give up and go inside, but he was soon put to bed in a darkened room in which it would be a good two weeks before he would again chew much of anything. Since he'd grown up to father seven kids, the virus had apparently not, as was sometimes the case, had any effect on his testes.

* * *

As Catholics, it was natural for them to employ Necco wafers as Eucharistic Hosts, consecrating and dispensing them upon each other's tongues in solemn mockery of Holy Communion. *Hoc est enim corpus meum.* For this is my body. Joyce would have approved. Jimmy was himself an altar boy and took his religion as seriously and literally as a medieval theologian. He wondered whether he had ever confessed these blasphemous parodies. Of course the priest would have known that all the kids employed the Necco wafers. Maybe it was before Jimmy's first confession, at seven, the putative Age of Reason. Before that he did not have the capacity to commit a mortal sin. And yet he had, with unutterable shame and relief, confessed impure thoughts at that first shriving. He wonders if the priest believed him. Priests didn't read a lot of Freud in those days. Now they did. More psychology than moral theology. Not many sins left. Some of the priests no longer believe in sin. But Jimmy does. And the Polish Pope. Something they have in common. Jimmy knows that he has sinned against many. But eternal punishments do not seem necessary. You get your share in this life. What goes around comes around. Just none of the visiting of the sins of the fathers on their sons and daughters, God. All the living sons and daughters of. Or you deserve the infinite millstone tied around your own neck. And to be thrust into an abyss of your own design.

No Cafeteria Catholicism for Jimmy. Another thing he and the Politically Incorrect Pope have in common. And why he left the Church and has never returned to it. And never could. Because, in spite of this present pontiff, perhaps the last of the real Vicars of Christ, the Church that Jimmy left is not there to return to. And never will be. *In saecula saeculorum. Amen.*

* * *

The best of course were and still are Snickers. The three others from the same company—Mars Bars, Milky Ways, and Three Musketeers—are also classics. All-Stars, Hall of Famers. They are still a great temptation to him around Halloween, when his wife buys bags of the miniatures to give away to trick-or-treaters. Last year there were a lot left over and he gorged himself for days afterwards. That was all right—he was just out of the hospital for a lung problem and had lost a lot of weight. This year, though, he needs to take weight off— doctor's orders—so he'll have to insist his wife not leave them out staring him in the eye whenever he's watching a ballgame on T.V.

He remembers how often his son came with his mother to visit him in the hospital. And was perhaps the most unsettled of anyone by his being in there. Of course his older kids didn't even know that he was in there. That wasn't his wife's fault— he hadn't wanted them worried or any of their plans interrupted. He hadn't expected to be in so long. Another of his sons had driven over from Phoenix to be there when he got out of the hospital. His sons loved him more than he deserved. Sons forgive a man for being a man. That was a harder thing for daughters to do because they saw things from their mothers' points of view. That was okay—it was perfectly natural. Also there was the feminist indoctrination that had taken the place of education in the schools, he was convinced. Made things worse that could have been made better.

* * *

Oddly, though, he cannot make any immediate associations with Snickers bars. It should have been the champagne of candy bars, the treat of choice for celebrations. The first time he got laid? On the front seat of his mother's car under a tree at the park near Lake Ontario. No, not with his mother. It's amazing his mother didn't uncover some evidence of it. She never missed a scratch or parking ticket. But no, he was sure there had been no Snickers bar to commemorate that milestone. Maybe a Carvel's thick shake.

But after basketball practices—yes, for sure. Waiting for the bus inside the gas station across from the school in the icy, slushy winters. Far from killing one's appetite for dinner, a couple of chocolate bars in those days would barely have tided one over, would have whetted the voracious teenage appetite.

* * *

What about his first date, with Teresa Baldessari, the girl next door who was a year older than himself, a grade ahead of him in school, and a decade more mature? He shocked her by inviting her to a Sunday movie matinee—he still remembers that one-half of the double feature was *The Iron Curtain* with Dana Andrews and Gene Tierney. She went home after the first film. He hadn't tried to kiss her or anything—and only now does it occur to him that maybe that was *why* she left— because he *hadn't*. He wasn't really crushed or anything—he was too young for that, was only mildly embarrassed to walk back up the street alone—he'd stayed for the second film. But women didn't realize what turned men into misogynists. Did they have any idea how much rejection a man experienced from women in his life, starting in the years when he most feared it? How the resentment could build up? Although you ended up taking it out on those who didn't reject you, because the ones who *had* were not around.

Well, that was changing also. The little girls were on the phone to his son all the time. They asked *him* out. And he put them off. He wasn't even playing hard-to-get. Just more interested in other things—his guitar, his CDs, Stephen King, the Comedy Channel. And he had been spared the terminal acne that had plagued Jimmy's adolescence. What a difference tetracycline would have made to Jimmy's psychic development...

But he must have bought himself and Teresa Baldessari each a candy bar: his mother and aunts would have made sure he had an extra fifty cents with which to treat her. A Hershey's bar. Great milk chocolate. A whole city in Pennsylvania named after it. With or without almonds. Not the bittersweet, not at that age. And not the half-pound bar either, not until college. Maybe a Nestle's. Nestle's Crunch. A nice change of pace. But never a Clark Bar or Fifth Avenue or Butterfinger. How did candy bars like those stay in business? For parents? Acquired tastes. Like his grandfather's hard candies. Except that was puritanism—his grandfather was a Methodist. Maybe some people went for inferior products just to be different. Like driving an Eagle or a Mazda. Or were some candy bars cheaper than others? Not at the movies. He drove a Hyundai because it was the second cheapest new car in America. The cheapest was the Yugo. Thank God he hadn't bought a Yugo.

He remembered catching Teresa in the act one time. He saw a younger child heading through their backyard to the Baldessari's garage and when he asked her what she was up to she said, "Teresa's in there—we're playing Queen Bee." So as soon as she closed the garage door behind her he went and peered through a crack. Teresa was sitting in an old plush chair, a makeshift throne, and wore a paper crown on her head. She held a pinwheel like a scepter and beckoned the little girl forward with, "Approach your Queen." Then, "This is how you become one of the handmaidens of the Queen Bee," and she reached beneath the child's short skirt and pulled her underpants down until the little girl stepped out of them. Then she said, "Raise your skirt above your head," and the girl did as she was told. Teresa leaned forward then, and she was fondling the child and Jimmy got very excited and wished that he could be part of the rite but he was also afraid that Teresa would look beyond the girl and be able to see his eye through the crack... so he turned away and hurried quietly back to his own house. He never knew how long Teresa and the girl were in the garage or how much might have happened. But how much could have? How old had he been anyway? Not very. Teresa had probably just reached puberty and he probably hadn't. It was no doubt something both Teresa and the girl forgot. Certainly never mentioned. Just as he hadn't. There wasn't all this fuss about sex and children in those days. Not like today's hysteria. Things went on. Like playing doctor. Too bad more hadn't. Except that, scrupulous Catholic that he was, Jimmy would have felt obligated to confess everything. The guilt would have been worse than the pleasure. Had he confessed what he had seen in the garage? No, he didn't remember doing so. But it wasn't his sin. He may not have thought of it as anybody's sin. Certainly he would not have heard of homosexuality. The last he'd heard of Teresa Baldessari she was married with several kids. The garage had just been a learning experience.

* * *

Tootsie Rolls, with their cartoon advertisements featuring Captain Tootsie, had made claims of providing Instant Energy in times of crisis—and they were certainly more portable than cans of spinach. Jimmy had dreamed in his youth not of becoming Captain Tootsie but Superman Himself. He figured, if you were going to aspire to be a Super Hero, it might as well be the one with the fewest limitations. In the meantime, however, it was wise to keep a Tootsie Roll handy. The placebo effect sent him flying along the wooden bleachers of the playground. It did not, however, render him so foolhardy as to challenge the proto-gangs who lounged around the baseball diamond in the summer. And when an older tough girl twisted his arm behind his back and sent him home in tears, Captain Tootsie's confection took on the taste of ashes.

* * *

That would not have happened if he had by then been friends with Ben Meineke. Ben was a usually-but-not-always gentle giant, already six-five and husky by the later grades of grammar school. He must have been German or Polish, but he had the face of an Eskimo, round, happy, carefree, fun-loving. His mother and Jimmy's were friends, and each no doubt hoped that her son would acquire a bit of the other's traits. Jimmy was the best student in their class; Ben was not the worst, nor was he stupid, but he found his motivation in girls not books. Ironically Jimmy could always best him in sports also, through discipline, desire, and craft. Of course, Jimmy was not small either—he was close to his eventual height of six-one by eighth grade and had begun to lift weights. But no one would have bullied him when he was with Ben anyway, except, on rare occasions, Ben himself, and those were always instances of exuberance, and Ben was always contrite afterwards.

Ben loved Almond Joys and Mounds bars, and frankly, Jimmy could never quite understand why one should settle for the plainer offering, sans almonds. They ate them at the Friday night movies, which were a necking ritual for Ben, whose natural physicality and self-confidence exuded aphrodisia to the wilder girls. None of them cared to sit with Jimmy, but he felt that he was learning something anyway. Later Ben would be one of the first their age to marry, and a child followed shortly. He did not go on to college; in those days fathers didn't. That didn't bother Ben, nor did he put much credence, it was rumored, in monogamy. On a trip back home for his mother's funeral, Jimmy heard from a friend of his eldest son that Ben was making a good living as a salesman, was still a free spirit, still a good guy.

* * *

When did Heath bars arrive? Sometime after the war. No doubt, Jimmy realizes in retrospect, a result of the expansion of British exports, and of the number of G.I.'s stationed in England before D-Day, and of the ones who brought home English wives. And a first step in what would swell into an insatiable American appetite for imports. Today Heath bars, tomorrow the Trade Deficit. And the yachting Prime Minister Edward Heath. And the British big-band leader Ted Heath, with a great sound like Stan Kenton's. And Jimmy's aunt Anna Louise took him to hear Ted Heath at the Shrine Auditorium in high school and they had a grand time. And now there were at least three Heath brothers in American jazz, but they were black. And jazz was still Jimmy's favorite music, well, right up there with the great show tunes at least.

But Heath bars were too small for kids. If you let caramel melt in your mouth, that was another thing altogether, but what kid didn't chew his candy? No, Heath bars were the first taste of sophistication for a certain type of parent, three decades before the Perrier-and-croissant invasion. Because they had spent a semester in Wales, with Jimmy on a teaching exchange, his wife now insisted on English cucumbers. And Bass Ale before bed, though she seldom finished a whole bottle. Jimmy didn't mind—it was a form of nostalgia, and hope for the future, a pinch of spice in her life. Jimmy had never wanted to be the sort of person who lived in the past, in memories, but at a certain age you wish you had even more of them, and had paid closer attention to the ones you have.

*   *   *

Baby Ruths weren't bad, and he was a Yankees' fan. Those were the years of Micky Mantle, Yogi Berra, Hank Bauer, Gene Woodling, Bobby Richardson. Gil McDougald, who ended Herb Score's career with a line-drive back to the mound. Later Tony Kubek, whose own career came to an abrupt end with a bad hop to his Adam's apple. Allie Reynolds, who just died the other day. Vic Raschi. Junk-dealer Lefty Eddie Lopat who always seemed to be starting when Jimmy would insist his aunts make the pilgrimage to the House That Ruth Built in the course of their trips to the Big Apple. Riding into the city on the elevated tracks above the fences in centerfield. Whitey Ford. Roger Maris. Don Larsen. Mel Stottlemyre.

Billy Martin—the quintessential Yankee.

Thurman Munson, the martyr.

Always a trip to Radio City Music Hall, a big-budget feature family film, the Rockettes and Corps de Ballet, vaudeville acts. They'd stay at the Hotel Taft, just off Times Square, and it was only five dollars a night in those days. Walk past the jazz at the Metropole. Because his Aunt Pat worked for a company that owned a television station, they'd have tickets to a live telecast of Danny Thomas or Ted Mack's Original Amateur Hour. Dinner at Stouffer's or Schrafft's or Horn and Hardart's Automat. He thought the RCA Building was the most beautiful. Mass at St. Patrick's Cathedral. And the musicals to which he became instantly addicted: *Gentlemen Prefer Blondes*, with Carol Channing, was his first because it was the only one his aunts could get tickets for that day. He closed his eyes during some of the chorus numbers so that he would not be guilty of the mortal sin of impure thoughts. His Aunt Lucy, who made novenas, said that it was too risque, but his Aunt Pat, who was the only aunt who didn't go to church, and who had friends who were artists, just laughed. In subsequent years he would see Yul Brynner in a revival of *The King* and *The Fantasticks* in the Village, and would take his kids to the renovated Yankee Stadium and to Shea...

Are they still selling Reggie bars, he wonders.

* * *

The Yankees were leading their division this summer, best record in the American League, on course for their first world series in a decade, when the baseball strike ended the season.

* * *

Now the candy bars have names like Flix, Trix, Bix, Big or Tricky Dix.

No Tom Mix, dead along the highway northeast of Tucson.

* * *

He seldom ate a candy bar anymore, but he sometimes read their ingredients.

That was the difference between fathers and sons: kids didn't read ingredients. Even young men didn't.

* * *

He'd never been crazy about Reese's Peanut Butter Cups. There'd been some kind of Marshmallow Cup that was almost decadent but he couldn't remember its name. Some candy bars were like women that you wouldn't kick out of bed. Except that women could feel rejection. They brought it on themselves a lot of times, though, not getting the point that you really didn't want to marry them or to just go out with them exclusively. They got hurt if you told them that, but if you didn't they said you'd led them on, strung them along. You had to look out for yourself, and so did they.

* * *

Jawbreakers. Ballbreakers. Stix. Prix.

* * *

Mr. Goodbar grew up to be a movie.

* * *

There had been no candy for his father, who returned from World War Two a diabetic. Not much of a marriage either.

* * *

He remembers the time his mother gave him ten cents to run in the drug store for a candy bar and he returned to the car with a box of caps for his six-shooter instead, the one he'd gotten for stopping biting his fingernails. And she was furious. What did it matter? Why such a big deal? He should have known, though. It was the same sort of thing that could set his wife off. Both of them bitches really. Of course, you were supposed to take all kinds of things into consideration with women, all the hormonal things. But who could keep track of them? Were you supposed to keep a calendar on the wall? Now that would really piss them off. Because you were also never supposed to allude to their hormones. Biology was not destiny. Horseshit. You weren't supposed to call them the b-word either. It was degrading, abusive. They'd called *him* a few things in his time. Well, his little boy's mother would be excellent preparation for what he would be up against in life.

* * *

At summer camp, Camp Stella Maris, they were allowed one candy bar a day during their rest period after lunch. He usually chose Milk Duds.

And one soft drink in the evening. He usually chose Birch Beer.

The first time he'd gone to camp he'd been deathly homesick the minute his parents had driven back down the lane. He was okay as long as they were busy at sports or in the dining hall or whatever, but during the quiet times the depression would again descend. Campfires especially. Mid-morning free times. He'd tried to make his mother a ring in the craft class but had immediately mangled it. He never had learned to make things with his hands. On Wednesday he finally broke down and asked the counselor to call his parents to come and get him. He was taken to the nurse, a kindly nun, who talked with him. That helped. They did call his parents for him as they promised, but by then he was feeling better enough to say he thought he could stick it out. He didn't really get teased by the other kids, perhaps because he'd already established that he was a better athlete than any of them. And he joined in the forbidden after-lights-out pillow fights with gusto. At the Friday Night Awards banquet he won the Best Camper Award. And the award for best at basketball. Not for softball, although he deserved it. Later his wife would say, "You idiot, don't you know they always give the Best Camper Award to the crybaby who sticks it out?" Maybe she was right. Maybe he didn't deserve that award and did deserve the one for softball. His first experience of politics in decision-making, extraneous circumstances. Good preparation for the academic and literary lives.

On Saturday morning the parents were supposed to arrive between 9:00 and 12:00. Some were early. Most were there at 9:00. Everyone else's by 10:00. After that, he sat alone on a hill waiting for them. Heartbroken. Devastated. Empty. He should have been the one to write "Fool on the Hill." How could they have been so thoughtless, especially knowing how he'd felt.

Later he would realize they were probably making use of their Friday night alone to go out with friends drinking, or to party at home, or just to spend some time in bed. Maybe they'd had hangovers, his father at least. He hadn't let the diabetes stop him from drinking whisky, only beer.

As soon as they pulled up the drive at 12:30 in their very second-hand Dodge, all was forgiven. It was a glorious day being back with them.

But he still hates being left waiting and he did his best never to make his own kids wait more than a few minutes at the most.

* * *

That evening Jimmy sits across from his wife at the Oaxaca, a relatively authentic Mexican restaurant in their neighborhood. They both like it, and Ziggy doesn't, so on a night like this when their son is already full-up with popcorn and desires nothing more than a glass of milk and free time at home, they take advantage of the opportunity to eat here. His wife has always been a light eater, and he has become one. She orders a taco and a margarita, as usual, and he, as usual, the soup of the day, a clear one with fresh mushrooms and cilantro, and the appetizer of the day, a chile con queso, also with mushrooms. Brenda dips a chip in salsa and asks, "How did Ziggy like the film?"

"Better than I did."

"He immersed himself in vampire lore in sixth grade, remember?"

"It still wasn't one of his favorites. He's a good enough little writer already to spot cheap effects and lack of focus."

"Maybe you had to have read her books."

"Yeah, maybe. I'll never know."

"*Hedd Wyn* turned him into a pacifist."

"I know. That's one of the things about the Republicans getting in that scares me. Not that they might put a damper on political correctness, God knows, but that they might dredge up something like National Military Service. You know, 'Make men out of them,' and all that."

"Christ, Jimmy, did you have to give me one more thing to worry about?"

"*I've* been worrying about it. Shit, I would have killed myself in the army, like a couple of my students did during Vietnam. Never even got there. Never made it out of basic training. I almost killed myself at summer camp."

"You're kidding."

"Not by much."

"Would you be willing to up and leave if we saw a draft coming?"

"As a last resort, yes."

"He's such a great kid. Does it bother you he's not an athlete?"

"Not at all; we have so many other things in common. Sports are what I have in common with Will and Mike."

"He's a nicer person than his father, Jimmy. He'll be easier on his women."

"He'll be easier on everyone because he's nicer than his mother too."

She doesn't like that slant quite as well as her own, but admits, "I suppose he is," and lets it drop.

Jimmy savors the spicy broth and looks at his wife who is still trim and attractive, with classic features, but will, in ten years, be old, and the thought that her youth, like his, is over, never to return, saddens him to the point where he is nearly moved to apologize for having stolen her life from her, for not having let her win the long war of their life together unconditionally. But, in fact, she'd chosen her life, just as he had. She had wanted Jimmy, and she had gotten him. She wanted children and she had them. She'd thought he'd leave her with the children as he had his first two wives, and he hadn't. Win some, lose some.

"Ziggy's coming into his own."

"Yes," he nods, "he is."

How, he wonders, will she ever be able to let her children go? And be left with me. The prospect must terrify her.

"Listen," he says, "I need your help with something I'm writing. No, don't react too quickly—I promise you'll never have to read it. It's just that I had this idea about structuring a story around candy bars and a character's associations with the ones of his youth. I want to make sure I'm not forgetting any."

"I suppose you've covered all the obvious ones: Snickers, Hersheys, M & Ms..."

"Almond Joys, Milk Duds, Tootsie Rolls..."

"Life Savers?"

"Life Savers! I forgot Life Savers! How could I have? My mother always carried a couple rolls of Life Savers."

"Let me think..."

What if I kick the bucket, he wonders? Will the rest of her life be better or worse? I'm sure she thinks it would be great, but she's been wrong before...

"Payday bars."

"I don't remember those being around when I was a kid, but I suppose I'll need examples of precisely that: candy bars that came later."

"Maybe you can work in a pun about how few literary paydays you've had."

"Nah—metafiction is dead."

"Just keep me out of it for once."

"As Billy Jack says, 'I try; I really try... '"

SWING SHIFT

The new phone, a thoughtful gift of his college-age son, has a high-tech ring to it. At first Jimmy's sunken consciousness translates it into either one of his wife's garden of clocks or his children's armory of computer toys. These announce themselves all night like an allegory waiting to be written by some illegitimate descendant of E.T.A. Hoffman.

Suddenly, though, a primeval paternal instinct boils into precedence, and he rolls out of bed onto his not unpadded hip, pulls himself Samson-style to his feet in the archway, and stumbles to nab the receiver before the sixth ring. "Hullo?"

"We missed it."

"Vee's school bus?"

"We didn't actually *miss* it... but I *thought* we had missed it and then . ."

"It doesn't matter: She's at the Y?"

"She'll be looking for you at the front door."

"Tell her I'll be there as soon as I can pull my pants on."

"I'm sorry."

"Yeah, well, you did the right thing to call me, but it's becoming a habit and I was up until four correcting papers."

"It's because I can never tell whether the bus has already come and gone or not. And you know how hard it is to motivate the kids to get a move on in the morning."

"I'll be right there."

*   *   *

His first trip is to the kitchen to swallow a couple of Excedrin with as much of a warm can of Pepsi as his stomach will tolerate. Then he hurries back to pull on yesterday's clothes by the side of the bed. In the bathroom he splashes water on his face and rubs some toothpaste across his gumline, almost choking while rinsing. The way his head feels is a luxury he cannot even afford to contemplate, and his eyelids are going to have to stay open without the assistance of toothpicks whether they want to or not.

* * *

His young neighbors across the street, whom he's never met, are dressed for success, driving off in different directions in going-steady Mercedes. They may never have seen him *ante meridiem*. He sympathizes with them: it can't be a pretty sight.

* * *

He clicks on the jazz station. His AM-FM stereo/cassette is a $29.95 job, Kraco of Compton, purchased at a union-busting discount store, and installed by a handyman for twelve bucks. The factory model would have cost five hundred. Still, since this one has no pushbuttons and is hard to tune he keeps it perpetually dialled to the jazz station KGGO, 105.5 FM from Los Angeles, and, if you're tooling to Las Vegas, something at the extreme other end of the AM dial from Hesperia.

* * *

Pulling from the service road into boulevard rush hour traffic, he thinks his Hyundai was a good idea. Cheapest model in America except for the Yugo and the ads were right on - it was a new Excel or one more used car and someone else's headaches. Heartaches! Sure, there was a brake recall, and sure the clutch was out of adjustment at first and still grinds on a cold morning... but the last two years have been glaringly free of major automotive hassles.

Passes Glendale Federal S & L: How far up will the annualized one-year T-bill note be when his adjustable home mortgage is calculated for the coming year?

Passes Bank of America: He should run a balance check on his checking account at a Versateller later today or tomorrow.

Passes the Village Inn: He can't begin to count how many girls he took there in the old days for a first lunch and how many of those led to some form of consummation before sunset. And not because he ever felt he had any idea of how to deal with women.

Passes the Fish Tale: A long time since he and Brenda, childless, shared nearly everything The Oyster Bar could concoct.

Penney's: Where, for his teaching in the 1960's, he was able to purchase his entire wardrobe without straying from the jeans and t-shirts section.

The Los Altos YMCA: Where he had promised himself a swim this very afternoon, and maybe the lifting, very stiffly and cautiously, of a dumbbell or two.

The Los Altos YMCA: Where his daughter, with absolute trust of her Dad, is waiting with her backpack just inside the front door.

* * *

"Hi, you old sweetie-pie, my darling of the ages, I love you so bad and I'm so glad to be here with you."

"I love you too... but do you mean you were glad to hear the phone ring?"

"No, but I'm glad to be with you now, and you're so beautiful all dressed up for school and with your hair combed out so beautiful, and I'm also glad that you know you not only can but should call on me any time you need me, at any time of the day or night."

She kisses him: "I know I can... but watch out for that maniac in the Toyota."

"I see her."

* * *

They pass an accident: a bicyclist forced off the road by a late-to-work motorist.

They turn left into the crosstown corridor of Willow Street and tunnel through the highrise airport developments springing up on both sides of the road.

They purr into Signal Hill, where the oil wells are losing ground to the condominiums and car dealers.

He wonders whether to tell her the long story of the black college athlete hanged in the Signal Hill jail. Decides it can wait until she's a little older. In the area to which she's bussed for school, she may need to trust the police. It's a "magnet school," voluntary integration, an academically accelerated program, lots of homework, too much homework.

"Did you bring your homework?"

"Yes."

"Tired?"

"Always."

"Is it hard to stay awake in class?"

"Only when they lecture."

"They lecture in fifth grade?"

"Mainly just one of the teachers does."

"Do you learn anything from his lectures?"

"No."

"Does anyone?"

"No."

"Do you think he realizes it?"

"No, he's in love with himself."

"Are you still in love?"

"Yes, but all the other girls are in love with the same boy. Is that the way it was when you were in school?"

"Pretty much."

"Were you the boy?"

"No."

"Are we going to be late?"

"No, I think you'll have a couple of minutes to spare."

"Maybe five minutes on the playground?"

"I think so."
"Good."

*   *   *

He parks in the teachers' lot and walks his daughter to the paved recreation area. It is quite large and the committee rules by which the children organized themselves into various zones of it would no doubt be fascinating to a sociologist. His daughter, for instance, has told him she has difficulty getting any of the other girls to accompany her to the basketball area. He knows his daughter is an excellent athlete: he has seen it.

Now she leaves her backpack with the others lining the classroom wall, then comes racing back to leap into his arms for a hug and kiss. They hold each other tight. He supposes it is he who lets go first: "Go find your friends now. Have fun. Love you." She runs off with her long-legged strides looking over her shoulder every ten yards to see if he's still watching her. She is still young enough to believe her father is wonderful. He is old enough to know that *she* is.

*   *   *

He drives home along the other side of the airport, an area called California Heights which borders the old-money Bixby Knolls. Formerly depressed, it is in a current stage of Yuppification as property values soar throughout Long Beach.

It has only been three years since he and Brenda and the kids moved inland from a one-bedroom apartment in Seal Beach to a small house in a residential area a good five miles from the ocean. So he swims at the Y now instead of the ocean. He sees fewer palm trees, but more elms and pines and fruit trees. He jealously guards his half of a garage that he is always threatening to turn into a gym. His kids have their own rooms and a backyard with two bunnies in a hutch and a tortoise beneath an agave plant and their mother's gardening lining patio and walk. Inside they also have two pet rats (a mistake) in a cage, and two goldfish in a bowl, and, in an aquarium, two colorful and intelligent salamanders and a somewhat ugly, slow, and stupid froggie-toad. The salamanders and the froggie-toad require three or four dozen large live crickets from the pet store every ten days to two weeks.

Ironically, there turned out to be few children residing on their block and half of those have moved out, maybe priced out, maybe divorced out. This is a disappointment to the kids, although Jimmy knows they'd have precious little time for play on the street anyway, what with scouts and dance and music and karate and birthday parties and slumber parties. And the cabin.

But overall he has no doubt the move has been a good one for them, and it makes him feel good that he had the wisdom to know it was what had to be done and the strength to follow through with it.

*   *   *

He is never happier than at times like this when he has had the opportunity to perform an act of love for his daughter.

What else is there?

As a writer he is still drawn to unexplored bars and there are a few in the vicinity that he is tempted to pull into.

Ten years ago he might have.

Fifteen years ago the car would have pulled in of its own accord.

Legendary shit-kickin' bars, roughnecks and McDonnell Douglas workers before and after work and on their breaks. Curley's had the wildest, widest reputation of them all. He's heard it's a museum now. The Postmodern Saloon. Jimmy was there once when it was still a real bar, but there wasn't much goin' on that you wouldn't have found him part of in those days of the Gold Rush Tavern, Clancy's, anyplace. That was before 90% of the bars decided they had to either deal coke or attract pussy and chose divergent sides fairly readily and clearly along those lines.

A couple of drinks wouldn't hurt him and he'd probably overhear a poem or two. But he doesn't need to regain a reputation as someone you might find in a bar at any hour. Not with access to his children the possible stakes. And he's seen it nearly happen to himself in the past, when you start out as the observer, the chronicler, and end up an integral part of the subject matter, the phenomenon. Once, a philosopher...

He never cared what people thought of him and still didn't, except for judges. But anyone read "Babylon Revisited" lately?

* * *

At home he brings the newspaper in from the lawn, re-sets the alarm for an extra half-hour's sleep that will still allow him a few minutes at the Y, and suppresses the seduction of a drink or two to ease him back to sleep over the sports section. It's luxurious enough just climbing back under the covers.

* * *

He is chasing a mini-skirted huntress through a woods of mattress-y ferns when the siren announcing the Third World War goes off. This time his eyes and brow are aching, throbbing. A glance through the Clock-o-Rama assures him he's been asleep less than fifteen minutes, long enough, though, for the weather to go gray and humid, no doubt affecting the barometric pressure inside his skull. He lifts the receiver:

"Yes."

"Daddy?"

"Vee! What's the matter?"

"I forgot my flute. I'm really sorry."

"That's okay, sweetheart, I should have thought of it myself. Where is it?"

"Under my bed."

"Okay."

"And the sheet music."

"Anything else you need?"

"I don't think so."

"How soon do you need it?"

"At ten, I think."

"No problem, then, I'll be right over."

"Thank you."

"Just a second—where do I bring it?"

"Oh... I guess my classroom."

"I'll be right there. You did right to call."

* * *

More water on the face, and fingers through the hair, but he can smell himself and he'd hate to see himself in a mirror. He needed a haircut and beard-trim a month ago. His head is throbbing to the point of dizziness. Ten o'clock, huh? He could afford twenty minutes of drinking which would make him feel a lot better without leaving him drunk legally or in any other way. But what if someone rear-ended him? And they routinely tested both drivers? How would it look if he'd been drinking at all before driving to an elementary school? He gags down one more Excedrin with a swallow of coke and heads out the door with his daughter's symphonic career.

* * *

She is not in her classroom.

Mr. Zotner thinks she is doing math with Mr. Brannigan and Mr. Brannigan thinks she is dissecting something with Ms. Powell. Ms. Powell is pretty sure she is at Glee with Mr.

Roscommon, which is where he finally finds her. While the instructor's back is turned to the young tenors, he rushes to his coloratura, transfers his charge, and whispers, "I love you," and, to the wide eyes of our country's future, slips back out, as slippery as a rhino.

* * *

This time at home he does not hesitate. Washes down a Sudafed with a tumbler of cream sherry followed swiftly by another. Squeezes the space between his eyes until some of the hurt goes out of them. When he almost regurgitates the first two drinks, he has a third.

It's all right. He'll be feeling better soon and he's already had a big day. As soon as he can see straight he'll read the paper until he feels like dozing off. The Y will be out of the question now, but he'll be fine before work. If he needs half a Valium, well, he's earned it.

Best to be out of the house—certainly out of bed—before Brenda gets home though.

He won't say anything to Brenda about the flute. He doesn't think Vee will either. His little girl will trust him not to squeal on her.

He's going to have to impress upon Brenda, though, that as willing as he is to help out in any true emergency, she had better start getting their daughter to her school bus on time.

Is she trying to kill his writing time, or is she going for the big kill: him?

He'd better, in his subtle way, communicate to her that just as she long ago rendered herself useless to him as a wife, she'd better be careful not to prove herself expendable as a mother as well.

Yes, subtly, of course.

He pours another sherry and extracts the paper from its plastic bag.

The dollar is steady. Magic Johnson's knee is better. Larry Bird's elbow is worse. Reagan is leaving Washington.

Gorbachev is still in Moscow. There hasn't been a plane crash in a week. No lynchings are expected. A police chief warns of Satanic cults.

His horoscope promises romance in the late hours.

He'll stop by the Reno Room after work.

They say the swing shift will kill you. Jimmy figures that if one shift doesn't then the other shift will.

CIRCUITRY

Jimmy is a little dozy from his hour in the sun in the YMCA pool. The work is piled high on his office desk—it doesn't just seem as if there is even more of it than usual this semester—with the budget crunch and hiring freeze and early retirements, there is simply more of it to be distributed among fewer people, from larger classes to more thesis and directed studies students to more advisement, letters of recommendation, committee work. As usual, things are far from perfect at home—he has brought his twelve-year old with him to the campus on this Saturday afternoon because, just as his wife, after a year of internecine warfare, has decided to mend fences with their teenage daughter, she has concurrently redirected her excessive disciplinary deprivations towards their son. The little boy, used to being her pet, is in a state of shock at having his Nintendo, T.V., Walkman, and comic book privileges revoked after having brought home an admittedly atrocious report card. He is experiencing for the first time his mother's extraordinary twin talents of wrath and withdrawal of affection. Jimmy knows first-hand what the kid is going through. She almost suspended Ziggy's karate and cartoon-drawing classes until Jimmy had the brainstorm of reminding her that they were paid for in advance and non-refundable (not to mention that they constituted a final source of self-esteem). The lengths to which she would go in her irreversible rages were almost comical—one morning Jimmy was afraid she might actually send her son off to school without his pants for forgetting to hang up his laundry. Now Ziggy is working quietly on his drawing pad at Jimmy's officemate's desk. He's a bright kid, an artistic kid, articulate and a reader. They get along. Ziggy shares his father's sense of humor—another thorn in the mother's side—if not his passion for sports. That's fine—Jimmy's older sons inherited the latter. Jimmy's getting a bit old for huffing his way to the cheapest seats of assorted stadiums and arenas anyway. Thank God for cable T.V. and the anaerobic thrills of channel surfing.

Jimmy's groin is clutched by a sudden desperate need to urinate: he has been taking small doses of a diuretic for a *venous stasis* condition that has been complicating the circulation in his feet and ankles. No, it's no fun getting older, but better venous than penis stasis, he muses, although that, like everything bad, is probably also just a matter of time. He grabs a handful of posters for M.F.A. programs, summer writing conferences, and nascent literary magazines which have been channeled to him in his capacity as creative writing coordinator, a two-year rotation drawing blessedly to its conclusion. He wanders down the corridor purging the corkboards of superannuated flyers while impaling their successors with thumbtacks. "Thumbtacks"—what a vivid Anglo-Saxon term, and yet for a moment he has been unable to conjure it. He wonders if he learned too late to replace the aluminum-based Maalox with the calcified Di-Gel.

He drops the past-deadline notices in the large, plastic-lined trash-can recessed in an alcove across from the entrance to the men's room, diagonal to the elevators, and a few feet from the locked doors of the Comparative Literature Department... and he un-zips his fly and absentmindedly directs a flow of urine into the oversized waste-basket. With the first drumming echo, reality crashes upon him. The fearsome rush of adrenaline nearly induces stroke. With sharp discomfort he contracts the urinary sphincter, stuffs his dick back in his pants, and zips up with trembling fingers. Panic-stricken, he surveys the corridor. All the doors are shut except for his. He hears an indication of typing or other activity emanating from the offices, although it has become customary for faculty, especially women, to lock themselves in their office if working on weekends. His son has not followed him into the corridor. The elevators sound motionless. Closed-circuit cameras—that day would come, of course, especially with the increasing thefts of books and equipment, but it is unlikely the university has been able to afford such installations in this era of severe cutbacks.

He rushes into the men's room to finish the job at a urinal, then returns to his office, pausing only to ascertain that, thanks to his having consumed only water since leaving the pool, he can't discern any pungent bouquet steaming from the innocuous receptacle. So far. His little boy—for whom he experiences an overwhelming rush of love—is putting the finishing touches on a sinewy superhero.

He sits at his desk contemplating the clutter as if it were an emblem of his brain circuitry. He has been teaching for nearly thirty years, writing even longer. Three wives, seven children, four grandchildren. Not all out of the woods emotionally yet by any means. Some, to a greater or lesser extent, unable not to blame him, much as they might try not to. Skyrocketing college tuitions somehow to be invested for. His drinking less prolific, but alternately both salvation to and assault upon his nervous system and assorted vital organs. Radically less time, opportunity, or guiltlessness for the seeking of the consolations and tactile comforts of other women. The spectre of AIDS, which (as the campus chapter of the Gay and Lesbian and Bisexual Student Union made sure the rest of the campus did not forget) strikes heterosexuals also. Were the circuits becoming just plain overloaded?

Of course he had a lifelong history of relatively infrequent occasions upon which he had, while sleepwalking, urinated in comically inappropriate places. Once, in London, upon the mantlepiece of a room in a lace-curtain B-and-B. Once in Brenda's closet, upon her shoes. She had not found either of these comic at the time... although, as a matter of fact, they *had* joked about them just a few days before. That must have planted the subliminal impulse.

And then, of course, he had swum enough that afternoon for the blessedly tranquilizing endorphins to have kicked in.

But *Christ*, he hadn't been *sleepwalking* in the corridor.

Thank God the campus policewomen had not, as they sometimes did, decided to swing by and chat with him on their break. That might have made it a sex crime! Wouldn't the Women's Studies gang have been in their glory! It would have been the greatest thing since Hemingway shot himself.

He had even been cold sober.

He had recently had a strangely illuminating experience. He had been standing in line for an ATM machine when he was flooded with sensations which he flashed upon as being identical to when he had stood in line for his turn on the swings at the playground as a little boy. He had hated standing in line in those days, and he still did, but the replication of feelings was more complex than that; it was for a split-second *complete*.

It had explained for him the phenomenon of *déja vu*.

The circuits. The electricity of the consciousness.

"Okay, Ziggy," he says, "let's pack up and go home."

"So soon?"

"I just can't seem to get motivated today. I might as well go home and turn on the Lakers. We can stop for a treat at the vending machines."

"I've had trouble getting motivated to do my homework assignments this year."

"Yeah, well, I think your mother is going to help you to regain your motivation."

"If she doesn't *kill me* first."

"Your mother loves you very much. She just has a temper and once she loses it she has trouble calming down."

"No kidding."

"The worst is over. Just keep your cool. You'll notice things improving in a day or two."

"I guess I have to hope you're right."

"Trust me."

"Dad, did you ever get in trouble in sixth grade?"

"Yes, sixth was the grade in which I got in the most trouble. The sixth grade nun was the only one who ever seemed to truly dislike me. I got in trouble so often that the principle called in my mother to discuss things and, believe me, my mother almost *killed me*."

"What did you do?"

"I cleaned up my act. Enough at least. That's why I'm not dead. Yet."

They stand waiting for the elevator, equidistant from the men's room and the waste bin.

"Whew," Ziggy says, "the men's room stinks right all the way out here."

"Doesn't get cleaned as often as it should. Budget cuts. Let's go."

BECALMED

"I wondered at the time," she says, "how it must have felt when they did that exhibit of your life and work in the library a few years ago."

"Here's how that came about," Jimmy says. "About ten years ago the Special Collections Librarian started a collection of my books and poetry chapbooks. Shortly thereafter the Fire Marshall inspected all the offices in the Humanities building and put a few of us on notice that we had a month to get rid of excess inflammable papers, books and periodicals piled too high, *et cetera*. Actually, he hauled the Dean of Humanities out of his office to survey the wreckage we had made of ours and to inform him that he was personally responsible for the building. The dean notified us in a memo that did not overflow with good will. He had to notify my officemate also, but he scratched an explanation on his that he was fully aware who was the true culprit. I didn't know how I'd ever bring the office into compliance but I offered my twenty years of little magazines, small press books, manuscripts, correspondence, and so forth to the Special Collections Librarian and fortunately he was only too glad to have them.

"Then five years ago my mother died and I brought back scrapbooks, trophies, yearbooks that she had accumulated as I was growing up. The new Special Collections Librarian, who has also been a kind supporter of my work, saw an opportunity to create something unique out of this variety of materials. Thus, the exhibit."

"But wasn't it kind of eerie? I mean, like, didn't it seem like a sort of premature closure to your career?"

"No."

"It didn't give you writer's block or anything?"

"No."

"How exactly *did* you feel?"

"I felt honored."

"So you felt you *deserved* the honor."

"I didn't say that."

"Then you felt you *didn't* deserve it."

"I didn't say that either."

"Oh."

She falls silent then and stands peering into her plastic glass of red wine. For some reason her not drinking *white* wine touches him, as does her slight air of defeat. She is attractive, maybe forty, at the very least pushing it, but you wouldn't know it by the crinkles at the corners of her eyes, surely not from her still trim figure. She must have been a beauty just a few years back—it troubles him that he doesn't remember her. His thirty years of booze, no doubt. Now behind him. This is his first real party since his hospitalization for pulmonary embolisms—blood clots in the lungs—and he feels a little dull, out-of-place, certainly no longer the erstwhile life-of-the-party. He stifles a yawn. Takes a sip of root beer.

"I enjoyed your class," she says.

"Thank you," he says.

"All those contemporary authors."

"Which did we read?"

"Marguerite Duras..."

"*The Lover*?"

"Yes."

"Did you see the film?"

"Not yet. I want to. Did you?"

"I saw it on video one bright Saturday afternoon when the drapes were no defense against the sun. All the love scenes were in the dark, and with the glare and reflections on the screen I couldn't really ever tell who was on top of whom. It's sort of a waste of time watching what is essentially a dirty movie when you can't tell what's going on. Until they start filming in braille, at least, or develop truly interactive video."

"Do you consider sex dirty?"

"Only at its best."

"Oh."

Her gaze sinks again. He wishes she wouldn't give up so easily. Then it occurs to him that hers must have been one of the classes that he gave a free day to for wandering through his exhibit in the library. A couple of them wrote snide comments in the guest book, mainly to the effect that he must be suffering from elephantiasis of the ego. He wondered at the time if they were acquainted with any writers who had been blessed with humility. *He* certainly wasn't. About the best you could hope for was a false or at least ironic modesty. He considered his own delusions of grandeur downright venial compared to those of most of the writers that he knew.

He gazed down at her light bangs and decided that he should make *some* attempt to hold up his end of the conversation: "Are you teaching now?"

"In a sense. I direct a private school."

"Do you have children of your own?"

"One. A son. He's twenty-two."

"He couldn't be."

"Believe it or not I got married when I was fourteen."

"Fourteen! Excuse me, I've got to run home and lock up my daughter."

"That wasn't my parents' reaction. They couldn't wait to sign on the dotted line."

"You don't seem like the wild type."

"Thirteen years as a single parent takes it out of you. I grew up on Catalina Island and fell in love with the idea of living on a boat. It didn't take long to fall *out* of love with that life. There's more to a woman's life than scuba gear. But I couldn't ask my husband to give up *his* life. He's a born sea captain, independent, eccentric, a maverick. He'd die on shore."

"You must have had constant opportunities to remarry."

"I'm old-fashioned: I just feel in my heart that once you marry someone you're always married to him. I could never marry someone else."

Jesus, Jimmy thinks, she sure doesn't look like the sort of woman you'd expect to feel that way. He begins to experience a quickening of interest in her, even as he recognizes the dangers inherent in her absolutism. "Your husband didn't remarry either?"

"No. He's had a string of women, of course; they fell in love with the romance of the boat. Then they got sick of it, just like I did. I can see what Paul likes about it though. He makes enough to keep going just leading whale-watching cruises a few months of the year. The rest of the time he's his own man. He paints. Makes things. He has exactly the life he wants. He's a happy man."

Jimmy thinks, you're still in love with him, but he doesn't say it. Instead he settles for, "It's refreshing that you understand him so well."

"Why bad-talk an ex? It only reflects badly on your own judgement. You're married?"

"Three times."

"Now?"

"Yes."

"And you have children younger than my son?

"I have two teenagers. I'm not sure I'll make it through their teenage years."

"Your health?"

"My sanity."

"Surely your wife is a help."

After what she's said about bad-mouthing one's spouse, he can only shrug: "I suppose so."

"I thought being so close in age to my son would make things easier. But it didn't."

He doesn't follow up on that, and she does not elaborate.

They fall silent again. His mind wanders to his children. It's after ten. His daughter should be home from the coffeehouse. He hopes his son didn't have any trouble with his math homework. He hopes his wife threw the ball for the dog.

The students have put on some ancient but wonderful surfing music, stuff that was popular when he came here to teach thirty years ago. He sways to it, jiggles a little in his shoulders and elbows and hips and knees, his feet remaining stationary. Even five years ago he would have been hurling himself about the dancefloor. Now he takes a step back and faces the woman-younger-than-himself-yet-older-than-the-other-students as if to summon her to dance with him... but before she notices, he feels a tightness in his chest and says, "I think I'd better sit down."

"Oh... well, it was nice seeing you again."

"I'm sure our paths will cross on campus."

"I'm finished. With my full teaching credential. As of tonight."

"Oh... yes... then congratulations... good luck."

"Good luck with your teenagers."

"I'll need it."

He lets himself down into a soft chair and watches her disappear out onto the patio, this good-looking woman who is still in love with the man she married at fourteen. He wonders if either of his former wives is still in love with him. He doubts it. He hopes not for their sakes. He's sure the present one is not.

He feels bad that the woman will think he didn't find her either interesting or attractive. She doesn't need any further setbacks to her confidence. She won't understand that he's not allowed to get drunk anymore. Not while on the anti-coagulant. Which he could be on for the rest of his life.

It's not going to be easy learning to put the make on women cold sober. Is it going to be as awful as high school? Maybe, it occurs to him, in this post-feminist era, even worse. He'd better keep reminding himself that most women haven't changed anywhere near as much as the feminists would have liked them to. Back to basics.

But for now, for the first time in thirty years, it's past his bedtime.

THE HIPPIE SHIRT

Bob MacGregor liked to pick up hitchhikers. It made him feel good. He knew it was no big thing, but it made him feel he had done *something* at least that day for another human being. And it was so easy to do, yet still invariably appreciated. Sometimes he would let himself feel that he was bridging the generation gap, contributing to the bloodless resolution of the class struggle. Moreover, in all the time he had been picking up hitchhikers, he had never been threatened by queer or bandit. He hadn't even gotten the hand upon the knee.

If he had been a smoker, he would have liked people to bum cigarettes from him. What an easy way to do something nice for someone. Alas, he was not a smoker. He was a man of few vices. "Where you heading, sir?" the young man asked him.

"Downtown."

"Yeah? Great. You on your way to work?"

"That's right," Bob replied.

"Hey, my name's Chief. What's yours?"

"My name? Uh... Robert. Robert MacGregor."

"Robert?"

"Bob."

"Well, hi, Bob."

"Hi, Chief."

"Where you work, Bob?"

"Confidential."

"You the CIA or something?"

"No, no." Bob laughed, "Confidential *Insurance*."

"Oh, wow, that's funny. What I thought, I mean. Hey, Bob, you like your work?"

"My work? Yes. Yes, I do."

"What sort of thing you do? You ain't gonna peddle me a hundred thousand dollar life insurance package, are you?"

"No-ho-ho," Bob chuckled. "I'm in the actuarial end of the business." And seeing the look on the young rider's face, he continued. "Figures. Mathematics. Pen and paper stuff."

"Oh yeah... yeah wow. Man, mathematics never was my long suit, as my mother always said. You dig it though?"

"I really do. I really dig it."

"That's your bag, I guess."

"What's yours?"

"Huh?"

"What's your... bag?"

"Mine? Nothing. Doing nothing. Going here and there. Chicks. Smoke a little dope... you know."

"Oh sure."

"You got a family?"

"Yes... uh, *no*. I'm separated."

"Yeah? Paying through the nose?"

Bob nodded, "Naturally."

"You never feel a little trapped... you know, tied down... I mean, the old eight-to-five and everything."

"I guess I don't. I never was much of a traveller or... or adventurer."

"Adventurer! That's me. The last of the great adventurers. Try everything once. Get back up and try it once again. What do you do for kicks, Bob?"

"Kicks? Oh, well... I have a girlfriend..."

"Yeah? Groovy chick?"

"You know, she really is."

"Groovy body, likes to make it?"

"Yes... yes she does."

"Ever make it on reds, Bob?"

"Reds... oh you mean drugs?"

"Seconal."

"No... no I haven't."

"Oughtta try it. Really strings it out."

"I'll, uh, have to try that sometime."

"Hey, you want a handful?"

"Now? You mean you've…"

"Sure, here, put these in your pocket."

"No, please, no I'd rather not… say, uh, Chief, how far you going?"

"Oh, you can let me off at Pine, I guess. You sure you won't accept my little gift?"

"No thanks, Chief."

"I really like to give things. Man, I wish that there was something I could give you."

"That's all right, Chief."

"Don't that get-up bother you?"

"The suit and tie? To tell the truth it does. It seems like every school I've gone to, every job I've worked at, it's been necessary to dress up. It's one thing I could really do without."

"You like my shirt, man?"

"Yes, I do. I've been admiring it. It's… groovy."

"Take it, Bob."

"What…"

"Take it, Bob; I want you to have it."

"But…"

"You know, 'the-shirt-off-my-back.' I've never given anyone the shirt off my back."

"No, really…"

"Whoa, Nellie… this is Pine."

"Chief, put that thing back on…"

"It's all right, there's another in my sack."

"Come back, Chief…"

"Peace, Bob."

"Come back here…"

* * *

Robert MacGregor, actuary, thirty-five years old, sat in the parking lot of Confidential of America fingering the shirt. It was a very plain shirt, but it was a nice shirt. It was a cheap sort of broadcloth, he guessed, and a kind of cream or beige. It had about a half an inch of Indian embroidering along the sleeves. No buttons or zipper—just a V slit at the neck. It was cut large to pull on and off easily. It was the sort of shirt that could hide a little belly without any trouble at all.

* * *

"Oh no," cried Cynthia Fitzgibbon, looking up aghast from her typing, "have you gone hippie, Mr. MacGregor?"

"I haven't gone hippie," Bob replied, flushing.

"Hey, Mr. MacGregor," one of the younger girls squealed, "I think you look groovy!"

"Thank you, Tina," Bob replied, and hurried towards his office.

Even with the door closed, he could still hear muffled giggling... could still hear Cynthia Fitzgibbon gaily reassuring someone, "Yes, he has—Mr. MacGregor has gone hippie on us."

About ten-thirty came a knock upon the door. Bob looked up from a page of statistics to where Mr. Harve Concannon's subtly padded shoulders were nearly filling the doorway:

"Mind if I sit down, Bob?"

"No, Harve; not at all."

"Don't you ever take a coffee break?"

"Oh, sometimes it's easier to work straight through a problem to the end. You know how it is."

"I know how it is; I surely do. Well, how's your love life, Bob?"

"My love... oh, it's fine."

"Still seeing Janey?"

"That's right."

"Lovely girl. A truly lovely girl. The missus and I were saying just the other night how we've been meaning to have you and Janey back to the house but things keep coming up."

"Oh, that's all right."

"What do you hear from Jeannie?"

"Oh, she's all right. I drop in to see her and the kids pretty regularly."

"Jeannie and Janey—that's sort of a coincidence, you know?"

"Yes, I suppose it is."

"Jeannie and Janey."

"Yes."

"Say, Bob, that's quite a shirt."

"Thank you, Harve. I wasn't sure you'd like it."

"Hell, it's a dandy."

"I kind of like it."

"Real... *snazzy*. Or is the proper word 'groovy'?"

"Oh, I guess it doesn't matter."

"Where'd you get it?"

"It's a long story."

"Give me the Reader's Digest condensation."

"It was a gift. This hitchhiker I picked up this morning..."

"This morning?"

"That's right."

"Then I suppose you've got some other clothes out in the car?"

"That's right."

"Well, then, Bob, you know you could do me a real big favor. Would you like to do me a favor, Bob?"

"What would you like me to do, Harve?"

"Well, how about if during the lunch hour you just kind of put your other shirt back on. Oh, I don't care about the coat and tie, you know me, Harve, if it weren't for the old lady I'd come to work each morning in my hunting jacket. But, hell, those goddamn adolescent secretaries, I haven't been able to get an ounce of work out of the lot of them all morning. Bunch of silly gigglers. You know what I mean, Bob?"

"I know what you mean, Harve."

"Great. Then I can count on you, old buddy?"

"Harve, you know that I hate to let you down, but..."

"But? Oh, wait a minute, I understand. I understand just how you feel about it. If you come back this afternoon dressed differently, it will look as if I called you on the carpet. Those silly broads don't understand the way we've always worked together. More like... more like teammates than anything else. Isn't that right, Bob?"

"Yes, well actually..."

"Look, you take the afternoon off. You'll have time to get nine holes in. Tomorrow morning, those empty-headed girls will have forgotten everything. And remember, Bob, as far as I'm concerned you can always dress as *comfortably* as you want."

"Harve, I can't take the afternoon off, I'm so far behind on..."

"Behind?"

"The coronary figures, Harve! You know they're a nightmare."

"Behind, huh?"

"I'm behind the schedule I had set myself."

"Bob?"

"Yes?"

"Can I ask you something rather personal?"

"Of course, Harve."

"You haven't... you haven't gotten yourself mixed up in anything, have you?"

"I don't know what you mean."

"Oh, sure you do Bob, you know this whole... whole hippie business."

"Harve..."

"No, wait a minute, Bob, I'm not so square as lots of people think. I read a lot, you know, and I have read how some of these things have been spreading into the... the respectable classes."

"What things?"

'Dope, for one."

"Harve..."

"Bob, I can't remember when you've ever been behind before."

"But I am not..."

"Is it Janey, Bob? Has Janey gone hippie?"

"Harve, you sound like..."

"Take the afternoon off, Bob. Take the afternoon off, get nine holes in, have a couple of bourbons at the club... and come in here tomorrow looking like the Bob MacGregor that I've always known and... yes, and loved."

"But, Harve, I just..."

"That's all the time I have to talk about it, Bob."

"But, Harve..."

"That's *all*, Bob."

* * *

Bob didn't feel like golf. He didn't want to get started drinking quite so early in the afternoon. Janey would not be home from work yet. Jeannie would most likely have taken the kids to the beach.

He decided to drive out to the Valley to his mother's place.

"What an interesting shirt," was the first thing that his mother said.

The second thing she said was, "Whatever are you doing off of work so early in the day?"

When her son finished his capsule narration of the morning's incidents, she said, "Don't worry, son; I'm sure it will all be forgotten in the morning. You're a valuable man to Confidential, and I'm sure they will forget this little indiscretion."

"Mom," said Bob, "I like the shirt."

"Even as a child you'd sometimes have these days of eccentricity."

"I want more shirts like this," he said. "Do you know where they sell this kind of shirt?"

"You have a brilliant mind," his mother said.

"I think I'll wear this shirt again tomorrow," Bob said.

"You were the first one in the family to go to college."

"After that I'll have to have another shirt."

"Your father killed himself so that we could afford to put you all the way through graduate school."

"Although I guess that I could ask Janey to wash it out for me."

"You've made me very proud of you."

"I wonder if they shrink."

"I know you won't be fool enough to throw it all away."

"It's a little frayed already."

"I know that you don't want to kill your mother."

"I can hardly wait till Janey sees me in it..."

* * *

"*She* gave it to you, didn't she?"

"Who, Janey?"

"Jeannie. Your *wife*."

"My *ex*-wife, Janey."

"You still go to see her."

"Janey, it has been..."

"You go to see her and you bring her presents and you take her to the movies and..."

"But I just try to..."

"...and you give her extra money..."

"But the rising cost of..."

"...and you wear her goddamn hippie shirt."

"She didn't give it to me."

"Sure, that's right, you saw it flying from a flagpole."

"It was given to me by a hitchhiker."

"Oh, a hitchhiker. And what else did she give you?"

"It was a guy. I know this all sounds crazy..."

"I hate the sight of it."

"Janey, I really wish you wouldn't..."

"I associate such things with filth...

"You know I take a shower every morning. Why I wouldn't leave the house without..."

"...and... and narcotics..."

"Janey, when I met you all your friends were..."

"Never mind my friends. I don't have any friends since you insulted them and you won't ever let me..."

"Janey, don't I look all right in it? I think it covers up my paunch."

"You look like someone *trying* to cover up a paunch. You look... you look..."

"What?"

"...you look pregnant!"

"Damn you, Janey, that's enough."

"You've changed."

"I haven't changed."

"You never used to talk to me like that."

"I haven't changed "

"What next, long hair? Beads? Headband?..."

"Janey, I don't want..."

"Dope orgies?"

"Janey, it was always you who..."

"Just one more hassle when my parents were at last beginning to accept you."

"Janey, it is just a shirt."

"It *symbolizes* things."

"Oh God, the English major speaks!"

"Oh you'll be reading soon: Alan Watts, Allen Ginsberg, Alan..."

"Ladd?"

"Get out of here."

"All right."

"Robert?"

"Yes?"

"Where are you going?"

"I am going out. You just got through telling me..."

"You're going to *her*, aren't you?"

"To who?"
"To *whom.*"
"To whom?"
"To Jeannie..."
"Janey . ."
"Jeannie!"
"Janey, really..."
"You're corrupt."
"All right, goddamnit, Janey, I *will* go to Jeannie!"
"Don't come back to me, you..."
"You bet your life, I won't."
"...you FAGGOT!"
"Oh my God."

* * *

Since he'd been gone a number of changes had come over the place. Gradually, he supposed, but he'd not really noticed them before. A couple of half-melon candles hung by leather straps from the ceiling. Incense burned upon an orange crate coffee table. Upon the wall were tacked posters of Che Guevara, Eldridge Cleaver, Albert Einstein, and a mongoloidal Richard Nixon. "Would you," asked the latter poster, "buy a used car from this man?"

He read his daughter three stories from a Richard Scarry book and she went easily to bed. The other child, a toddler, was already sleeping.

"Say," his wife exclaimed, "I really like your shirt."

"Thank you," said Bob.

"Far out," she said.

"Thank you," said Bob.

"Let's go to bed," she said.

"Now, now," mused Bob, "I'm not sure that we ought to get involved again."

"Come on," she said, "that shirt sure turns me on."

"It does?" said Bob.

"You run on in and get in bed. I'll be there in a minute."

"Well..."

"Go on now, hurry up... and leave your shirt on."

"Leave it on?"

"Just take the rest off; leave the shirt on. Hurry up."

"Okay," said Bob.

Bob went in and took his clothes off, all except the shirt. He felt a little silly... but he shrugged his shoulders, pulled the covers back, and hopped up on the sheets, his legs crossed under him.

Five minutes later Jeannie returned with the two young neighbor girls, Phyllis and Dorinda. They were, the three of them, stark naked. "There he is girls," Jeannie said.

"My God, he's beautiful," said Phyllis.

"Just what we've been looking for," said Dorinda.

"Robert," Jeannie solemnly informed him, "you've been chosen to be leader of our cult."

"Of your *what?*"

"Our love cult. Up to now all our auditions have been so depressing.

"You're our man, Bob."

"Super-phallic," Phyllis said.

"A veritable Krishna," said Dorinda.

"Wait a minute," Bob said.

Phyllis had by now come to the bed where she engaged herself in nibbling at his neck and ears. Dorinda gently tweaked his nipples, while his former wife made tentative excursions elsewhere.

"Stop that!" Bob said.

"Ummm," said Phyllis.

"Let me go," said Bob. "Really," he said, "this sort of thing just isn't my... my bag."

"Don't give us that," said Jeannie. "We know every man dreams about this sort of thing."

"I *dream* about it," Bob said, "But I just don't want to *do* it. Honest girls..."

"Prepare the pipe," Dorinda said.

"The what?" said Bob.

"The sacramental pipe," Dorinda said.

"Oh no," said Bob, "I want my pants back."

"You must smoke the sacramental pipe with us," insisted Phyllis, "for you are our guru."

"No, I'm not," cried Bob. "I'm not anybody's guru. I'm just Bob MacGregor and I work for an insurance company. I'm as straight as you can find them, I'm as square as you can find them, AND I WANT TO STAY THAT WAY..."

"Bullshit," Phyllis said, "your shirt shows what you are."

"Your shirt is beautiful because your soul is beautiful," Dorinda lectured him, her tiny tongue a-flickering about his eardrum, "your shirt is the external manifestation of your everlasting soul."

"The sacramental pipe is ready," Jeannie announced.

"I'm not going to become a dope fiend!" wailed the actuary, salty globules streaming down his cheeks, "I will not touch that thing"'

"You will smoke the sacramental pipe with us," said Phyllis quietly, a pinking shears in one hand and his scrotum in the left, "or else."

"Oh God," said Bob MacGregor, as the sacramental pipe approached his lips, "this can't be happening..."

* * *

"Let's see your license, bub," the tall cop said.

"I smell a little something fishy, Rock," the small cop said.

"Get outta the car, bub," the tall cop said.

"He's hopped alright," the small cop said.

"He's loaded to the gills," the tall cop said. "Get a loada them eyes."

"Up against the car, bub," said the small cop, shoving him roughly.

"He's clean," said the tall cop, giving him a stiff rap in the kidneys.

"Bet his glove compartment's stuffed," the small cop said.

"Won't do no good to bust it open," said the tall cop, rapping him across the other kidney.

"Ow!" said Bob.

"Yeah," said the small cop, kicking the legs out from under him, "he'll just get some smart kike to go to court for him."

Bob landed on the asphalt on his face.

"And some dumb kike up on the bench will let him go," the tall cop snarled, beating the proverbial tattoo upon the kidneys of the fallen man.

"Unnh!" said Bob.

"Will you get a loada that shirt," said the small cop, delivering a swift kick to the left side of Bob's rib cage.

"Faggot," said the tall cop, delivering a swift kick to the right side of Bob's rib cage. "Hippie faggot."

"Let's get outta here before I lose my temper," said the small cop.

"Yeah," the tall cop said.

* * *

"Wow," said Cynthia Fitzgibbon, the next morning at the office, "whatever happened to your shirt?"

"And what in the world," said Tina, "happened to *you*?"

"Is Mr. Concannon in?" asked Bob.

"He's in his office," Cynthia Fitzgibbon said, "but tell us..."

* * *

"Bob," said Harve Concannon, flicking off his dictaphone, "I must say this is quite a disappointment to me."

"Harvey" said Bob, "I'm leaving. I came by to get my stuff."

"Where are you going?" Harve inquired.

"I'm going to the Baffin Bay to live among the Ojibwitski Eskimos."

"Come off it, Bob. Be serious."

"I'll spend the summer with the Ojibwitski Eskimos and winter with the Oaxicoatl Indians of the Andes."

"Just supposing for a minute that you're serious... WHY?"

"They wear these shirts. I looked it up in the Encyclopedia. The Ojibwitskis wear them in the summer and the Oaxicoatls wear them in the winter. Winter by *our* calendar, that is."

"I knew it," Harve lamented, shaking his head, "I knew that you were going hippie."

"Among the Ojibwitskis it won't be a hippie shirt. It will be like everybody else's shirt. Among the Oaxicoatls..."

"They will kill you, Bob," said Harve Concannon. "Those savages will beat you bloody."

"Will they?" Bob said.

"WHAT ARE YOU LOOKING FOR?" demanded Harve Concannon. "WHAT OBSESSION DRIVES YOU FORTH UPON THIS ODYSSEY?"

"I'm looking for the straight life," Bob MacGregor told him. "And I love my shirt."

THE MONOPOLY STORY

"three, i say. one two three. baltic. i'll buy it."

"BALTIC!" exclaims inga. "baltic is worthless."

"oh, i don't know," joan says.

"well, you're the banker," hengest chortles.

"and i collect two hundred dollars for passing go."

"well, you're the banker," hengest chortles.

"it is the dawning of the age of aquarius," i add.

"what?" says hengest.

"it is the dawning of the age of aquarius."

"oh, mel," says joan, "how wonderful!"

"what?" i say.

"i didn't realize you were interested in astrology."

"i'm not," i say.

"how wonderful," she says.

"is it?"

"it is the dawning of the age of aquarius," she says.

"what does that mean for me?"

"it means you're going to be in the forefront of the revolution."

"oh," i say, "how wonderful."

"ventnor," says inga, "i'll buy it."

"now just a minute, little lady," says hengest. "it seems to me we might be able to negotiate a mutually beneficial transaction. indiana and illinois for ventnor. then you'll be able to build."

"he'll be able to build also, inga," joan warns her.

"yes," i warn her. "you'd better not let him talk you into it, inga. besides, he has money and you don't."

"i'll throw in the water works."

joan says, "utilities aren't any good. you can't build on utilities."

"utilities are some good, inga," hengest assures her.

"oh dear," says inga, "what to do, what to do."

"going... going..."

"okay," says inga.

inga passes the deed of ventnor to hengest, who reciprocates with deeds for indiana, illinois, and water works.

"you're not angry are you, dear?" says inga to me.

"no, dear," say i, "it would certainly be silly of me to let a little thing like a game upset me. i do feel, however, that you made an error trading with hengest. only time, of course, will tell."

"well, mel," says hengest, "while you're recovering from the shock of that little transaction, i think i'll take a little trip to the bedroom."

"excuse me," says inga, "but i have to go to the bedroom also."

"of course," i say.

"don't rush," says joan. "mel and i will just smoke a joint while you're gone."

when hengest and inga are gone, i say to joan, "your husband is certainly an excellent player of monopoly."

"yes," joan replies, "he is also very young and muscular."

"i imagine he's also good at other games."

"yes," says joan, "he is intelligent and manages to win without giving the impression of being aggressive."

"therefore, he is also very..."

"...well liked."

"i understand your husband owns almost as much property in real life as he always seems to end up with in monopoly."

"oh yes, hengest is quite shrewd in his investments."

"well, well," i say.

"well, well."

"let's talk about me now," i say.

"alright," joan says.

"i'm not very good at monopoly, as no doubt you must

have noticed."

"of course, mel," joan agrees. "hengest and i have often discussed you and our conclusion is that you will never be worth a damn."

"it is, however, the dawning of the age of aquarius."

"what is it you do out at the plant, mel?"

"i'm an existential engineer."

"how wonderful."

"i invented the existential microscope."

"hengest and i have often said you're going to go a long nowhere."

"i count the existential electrons."

"how interesting. and now, mel, why don't we stop talking about you and just enjoy this joint."

when inga and hengest return from the bedroom, i say, "well, well. gone long?"

"relatively," hengest chortles.

"have a good time?"

"oh yes," inga assures me.

"what were you doing?" i smilingly ask.

"we were playing a game," inga explains.

"oh. any game i know?"

"not really," inga further explains.

"hengest certainly is wonderful at games," i shake my head in admiration.

"yes," inga agrees. "you know, joan, your husband certainly is wonderful at games."

"i know," joan nods enthusiastically.

"well," hengest says, rubbing his palms together, "back to the wars."

"ten," says joan. "one two three four five six seven eight nine ten. st. charles place. I'll buy it."

"i already own it," says inga, "you owe me..."

"here," says hengest, handing me a large wad of money. i want hotels on boardwalk and park place."

"certainly," i say. I count the money and present hengest

with a hotel for boardwalk and a hotel for park place. then joan picks up the dice from in front of inga and hands them to me, scratching my palms in the process. i roll the dice.

"four. chance."

i select a card from the top of the chance cards.

"go directly to boardwalk. do not pass go."

"well, mel," hengest chortles, "looks like that just about cooks your goose.

"poor mel," says inga, "poor dumb mel."

"dumb shit," chortles hengest.

"poor goose," says joan. "hengest," says joan," you know i think the poor goose deserves a trip to the bedroom."

"okay," says hengest. "you just run along to the bedroom with the dumb shit while i take a look at the property i'm getting from him."

"come along, mel," says joan.

"okay," i say. "excuse me, inga. excuse me, hengest."

in the bedroom joan says, "well, here we are," and pulls off her blouse.

"yes," i say, smiling genially.

"hurry up and take your clothes off."

"okay," i say. i hurriedly remove my clothes and stand there naked in the middle of the room.

Joan sits on the edge of the bed removing her stockings. when all her clothes are off, she rolls back on the bed and says, "come here now, mel."

"are we going to play the game?" i ask.

"yes," joan says. "fine," i say and join her on the bed.

when we return, hengest says, "hi. how was it?"

"wonderful," i say.

"about as bad as that sort of thing can be," joan says.

"that's about what i expected," hengest says.

"i want to compliment you on joan," i say. "she's a very valuable property."

"i want to express my sympathy to you, inga," joan says.

"no, i'm not at all surprised," hengest says. "you know,

mel, joan and i have often enough discussed you and we reached the conclusion that you'd never be worth a damn."

"that's very perceptive of you, hengest," i grin, shaking my head in admiration. "it's taken me a long time, let me assure you, to reach that same conclusion."

"what is it you do out at the plant anyway, mel?"

"i'm an existential engineer. i invented the existential microscope."

"isn't worth a flying fig, is it?"

"no, hengest, you're absolutely right."

"well, joan and mel, while you were gone i took all of inga's property."

"yes," said inga, who by now has moved over to sit on hengest's lap where she is occupied with unbuttoning his shirt in order to reach inside and tweak his nipple with her chill little hand—"yes, i landed on marvin gardens."

"i think i'll surrender up all my property too," joan suddenly announces. "all i have left anyway is the reading railroad."

"well, hengest," i say, slapping the table for emphasis and shaking my head in appreciation, "it looks as if you've won again."

"yes indeed," says joan, "and i for one think you have earned a little trip to the bedroom."

"sure has," i agree.

"come along, girls," hengest says, lifting inga from his lap, "the three of us will just run along for a little victory celebration and mel can just sit here and tell himself a story."

"fine," i say.

"mel just loves to tell himself stories," inga says.

"do you have a good story to tell yourself, mel?"

"yes, joan," i reply. "i've been saving a dandy for a special occasion and i guess tonight qualifies. now you kids just run along to the bedroom and enjoy yourselves."

while they are gone i light up a joint and tell myself the story of the sweater woman. in this story i am in an old-folks

bar down in the old part of the city and i have sat down to
have a beer next to a woman in a powder-blue heavy-knit
sweater with an eagle embroidered on the back. the woman is
in her fifties but has a big bosom. she turns to me and says,
"hi, young fellow, what's your name?"

"mel," i say.

"i'm mamie," she says.

"hi, mamie," i say, "it's very nice to meet you."

"you see that scrawny little sonuvabitch of a scotchman
down the end of the bar?"

"the one with the crooked arm?"

"that's my husband."

"oh."

"i guess you wouldn't think to look at him that he's the
world's champion arm-wrestler?"

"no, i wouldn't."

"been married to the little runt for thirty years and never
seen him put down. know what his secret is?"

"no, i don't."

"his secret is that he's had to do everything with his one
arm ever since the other one got smashed up on the
waterfront. wouldn't guess it to look at him, but the muscles
in his good arm are like steel cables."

"i see."

"he's defending his championship this afternoon. in fact,
here comes the challenger now."

through the door comes a product of the era of vitamins
and minerals, six-foot-seven and a lean two-hundred-fifty
pounds. his forearms are the radii of wharf piles.

"poor kid," says mamie, "they're all like that nowadays, so
beautiful and full of confidence. but watch what happens."

the kid and the old man take their places facing each other
across the vinyl table. the bartender comes forth as starter and
referee. "go," he says.

the kid slams the old guy's wrist half through the table.

"impossible," says mamie. "his elbow must have slipped."

they set it up again and the bartender says, "go!"

this time the kid slams the old man's arm so hard that he winces and rubs himself.

"stop him," i say to mamie; "stop him before he doesn't have a good arm left."

"he'll never stop," she says, fierce tears coursing down her cheeks. "he's too proud to give in, the crazy old fool."

her husband gets up and reaches to shake the young kid's hand. "youth must be served," he says. "i think i'll quit while I've still got one good arm left."

later, however, at the bar, his drunken shame has turned to hostility.

"who's the bum?" he says, shrugging a shoulder towards me. "who's the young bum you're sucking up to now?"

"arnold," she says, "you shut your filthy mouth or i will take this young bum home with me instead of you."

"you would," says arnold to her. "you really would." to me he says, "what's your name, young bum?"

"my name is mel."

"whattaya do for a living? college kid i bet."

"no sir, i work out at the plant."

"yeah?" he says, interested, his reverse snobbery thawing somewhat.

"whattya do at the plant?"

"i invented the existential microscope."

"yeah? no kidding? whattaya do with it?"

"i count the existential electrons."

"no kidding! you hear the young gentleman, mamie?"

"pshaw, i could've told you mel was well educated."

"well, mamie," i say, "i feel that no one ever really *finishes* his education. i still take an occasional refresher course at the university."

"say, i bet you could answer my question."

"what is that, mamie?"

"well, i've been thinking of taking a course at the university, but i'm not sure if they offer just what i want."

"what's that, mamie?"

"spelling."

"spelling?"

"yes, spelling. you see i make us quite a few extra dollars knitting sweaters, but lots of times people want a little something embroidered on back or over the pocket, some little bit of wisdom, and sometimes..."

"...you make spelling errors. i see. but i'm sorry i don't really know if they teach spelling at the university. you see i spent my seven years there in the existential sciences."

"oh, i'm sorry. i'm just a foolish old woman."

"no you aren't, mamie. on the contrary, you are the salt of the earth. you are the real thing, mamie, the stuff without which sociology, for instance, could not survive."

"isn't he sweet, arnold... you know... i think i'm going to knit mel a sweater!"

"mamie, really, i couldn't accept..."

"arnold, run out to the car and bring in *your* sweater."

"but mamie..."

"hurry up. i want mel to see the sort of sweater i'm going to knit him."

"mamie, i swear you're going to have me in tears."

arnold returns with his sweater. it is powder-blue and heavy-knit has an eagle embroidered on the back...

"well," says hengest when they have returned from the bedroom, "i guess we'll be running along now."

"be sure to drop in again," i say.

"we will," he chortles; "we'll be dropping by in the morning to bring inga back."

"oh," i say, turning to inga, "have hengest and joan invited you to spend the night with them? what a nice chance for you to get out of the house."

"yes," says inga, "and they have even offered to drop me off in the morning in time for me to get you up for work by kicking you in the kidneys."

"hengest and joan," i say with deep feeling, "all i have to say is that i certainly do feel deeply about you."

"bye-bye, mel," says joan, "don't trip over your shadow walking before you."

"bye-bye, mel," says hengest, "don't get goosed by your shadow walking behind you."

"bye-bye, mel," says inga. "if you masturbate in the sink please remember to rinse it out."

i clear the table and leave the dishes stacked neatly on the washboard. i put the monopoly set away in the closet. i remember to turn down the heat and to make sure all the doors are locked. i set the alarm clock.

i go in and wake up our little girl, mickey, so i can say good-night to her, so i can kiss her good-night.

"what's new, old pal," i say to her.

"not much," she says, my two-and-a-half-year-old colloquial daughter.

"are your grends all asleep?" i ask her.

"yes, doddy," she says, and shows me her monkey and her lion and her $.59 doll.

"what're you going to do when you get up?" i ask her.

"i'm going to have gun," she says.

"you're a funny old girl," i say.

"you gunny old doddy," she says.

i tuck her in and go to tell myself a bedtime story.

THE BUMMER

Julian Escargot was a man who had failed to live up to his illustrious name. Only surviving son of a long line of fugitive viscounts, Julian had grown up on a maple-lined street in Westport, Connecticut, taken his B.S. in Business Administration at Cornell, served honorably but without distinction in the boiler room of an aircraft carrier during the Korean scrimmage, and married, upon his return, a trim, domestically-oriented former sigma kap from Ithaca. Together twelve years, they had spaced out three daughters and a son. Mimi had kept her figure. Julian was very proud of her when people remarked on it, as they invariably did.

Monday through Friday, Julian labored without perspiration in the accounting offices of ZXT Corporation in El Segundo, California. The sixteen thou he drew from them allowed him to keep up the payments on two Volkswagens and a house in Torrance. Every Saturday at seven-thirty the same modestly plain girl from down the street came to watch the children while Julian and Mimi rode up to Hollywood for dinner and a film, or down to Newport or Balboa for a party with the gang. At a certain hour each of these parties threatened to degenerate into an orgy... but none of them ever had. Sunday mornings Julian trooped the family off to services at the First Lutheran Church of the South Bay. Sunday afternoons, if the Rams were playing at home, he got the taste of religion out of his mouth sharing a bag of popcorn with his son at the game. If the Rams were away, he watched a couple of games at home, switching channels and glancing at the enormous Sunday Times and smoking a lot of cigarettes.

For a long time, in fact, Mimi had been after him about the cigarettes.

"Honey," she'd say, "do you really enjoy the taste of those things?"

No, he had to admit; no, he really didn't.

"Then why do you bother with them? Did you read the article in the paper this morning?"

Yes, he had read it.

"Cancer, emphysema, heart trouble, chronic bronchitis... even peptic ulcers? And how many years have you been smoking?"

He had started cadging weeds behind the garage when he was in seventh grade.

"Sweetheart, don't you understand? You're the perfect target for any one of those terrible diseases? What would I do if I lost you?"

On this occasion he put her off with a compromise—he would sacrifice his old favorite, the sailor's cigarette, for one of the filter brands. Maybe later he would consider a pipe. Mimi let him off the hook for the time being, but he had to admit to himself that he was a little worried. It was not that he was afraid of dying, for he was an honest, if weak, man and knew that he had nothing to lose. But what if he should fall prey to a progressive, long-term illness. He was very much afraid of pain; he was very much afraid of the humiliation of physical weakness, so less easy to conceal than that of the spirit. It was not so bad to lose one's soul—that was the national condition—but to publicly lose one's body was the ultimate disgrace. He knew he would not have the guts for suicide.

And so he began to think about giving them up... but just to think about it.

It was at a Saturday night party at the boss's place on the Lido that he got his first shock. He had lured the young wife of one of the new men out onto the patio. Nothing would come of it, he knew. For one thing neither of them really had the slightest intention of *letting* anything come of it—they were equally terrified of entering the uncharted forest of an intimacy. For another thing, there was the company principle: NOTHING SHALL EVER COME OF ANYTHING. No, all he was really soliciting was a kiss—the taste of a new lipstick that would transform the evening out of the ordinary. The memory of it might do the same for Sunday morning, maybe even linger into the afternoon.

They kissed and drew apart and looked into each other's eyes... and he felt a bubble working its way up his windpipe. He coughed and clapped a hand over his lips and stumbled towards the garden hedge. Alone for a moment he brought up a great hunk of phlegm... and thought he tasted blood in it.

"Are you all right, Julie?" the girl inquired when he returned.

"Oh sure," he said, squaring his shoulders to repair her image of him. "Guess I've just been smoking a little too much lately."

And they kissed once more; then decided maturely they had better rejoin the party before they were missed.

A week later, while driving home from work, Julian lowered his eyes to light a cigarette and plowed into the fender of a car slowing for an intersection. Fortunately, no one in the car ahead was hurt, but the front of the VW crumpled like a sad accordion. Julian paid for it out of his pocket rather than to risk the loss of his insurance. In a moment of weakness, he confessed the details of the accident to his wife. "But sweetheart," she cried, "how would you feel if you had killed a child!"

A few days later he almost killed four children. Went to bed and left a butt still burning, which fell out of the ashtray and onto the couch. The only damage was to the couch, but, in their panic, he and Mimi had evacuated the children out onto the street (the neighbors in their windows) and called the firemen. This time Mimi said nothing; for a week she said nothing. On Sunday night, after the children had been packed off to bed Julian called her into the living room to iron things out.

"Honey," he cajoled, "you haven't been speaking to me."

"I've been thinking."

"Do I have to give them up?"

"I've decided that you don't have the will power."

That hurt him. It was true, of course, but he hadn't realized she knew him so well. Swallowing his pride, he asked, "Then what?"

"I have a plan. You won't like it, but I'm convinced it's worth a try..."

"Go on."

"Smoke to your heart's content tonight, because as of tomorrow morning you smoke only as many cigarettes as you can borrow."

"For Christ's sake, sweetheart, I hate people who are always bumming cigarettes. You know that."

"That's why I think it might work. You won't have to give up smoking altogether and the few you can bring yourself to bum won't hurt you."

Julian relaxed back into a corner of the couch and took a pack from his shirt pocket. "A bummer!" he sighed. "How I've always hated bummers!"

The next day went just as he knew Mimi must have suspected it would. For the morning he was able to put cigarettes out of his mind altogether. He got as much work done as he used to in a week. He was really proud of himself.

So proud, in fact, that by lunch he decided he deserved a treat. He went with the usual guys to the usual table in the cafeteria and looked around for someone to hit up. Believe it or not, he had never noticed before that Harry Jenkins smoked a pipe and Bill Wheeler cigars. It had never mattered before. Willie Marsden didn't smoke at all. Looking around him in fact, he was surprised to find how few people were actually smoking. Had the notorious cancer report actually had some effect? Of the few people lighting up at nearby tables, all were either just a little too far above or beneath him in the corporate hierarchy.

What the hell, he told himself, I didn't really need one anyway.

By five o'clock he was just about out of his mind. He hadn't gotten a thing done all afternoon. Shamelessly, he had asked Rose the secretary for a Newton and she had given him two of the vile menthols, looking at him as if to say, You know goddamn well you can afford them better than I can. It would clearly be against the rules for him to buy a pack from her. The two smokes, cherished puff by puff, had only whetted his appetite.

Driving home, his hands were shaking on the wheel. An evening without nicotine lay ahead of him. Oh God, he thought, and pulled into the parking lot of the next cocktail lounge he came to.

The tables were crowded but there were only two customers at the bar. One of them was smoking a stogie. The bartender was busy fixing martinis for table service. Julian turned to the fortyish woman next to him and said, "Say, I know this sounds stupid, but why don't you loan me a cigarette and let me buy you a drink?" The face that turned to him was lined with severity:

"I don't smoke."

"Oh, I'm sorry..."

"Cigarettes are the work of the devil."

"Huh?"

"They are spread throughout this country by the Communists."

"Hey, really..."

"They deprive our men of their virility, our women of their..."

"Now listen..."

"You want a cigarette? You really want a cigarette?"

"Yes," said Julian, "Yes, I really do."

"Then follow me to this number," she said, and scribbled an address on a napkin. While he looked at it, she got up from the stool and headed for the door. Julian looked up long enough to decide that she had, as to say in *Virginia Woolf*, kept her body. The address was all the way up in Echo Park. Nah, he thought, and ordered another drink.

Two drinks later he left the bar and turned his VW back towards the freeway.

It was an old one story house at the top of a very steep hill. A somewhat gothic willow obscured the porch. The woman met him at the door and ordered coldly, "Follow me!" Inside the bedroom, she said, "Take off your clothes; I'll be right back." And locked him in the room.

The next time the door opened there was silhouetted against the light a masked figure of black leather tights and a bare pointed bosom. In one hand she held a gun; in the other a whip. "Turn over," she said.

"What the . . "

The woman raised the gun and Julian flipped over.

"The devil has possession of your body," said the woman, and Julian heard the knotted tip of the whip being drawn across the floor...

Strange to tell, when she let up long enough to ask him if he felt the devil going out of him, he told her, "Not yet; his claws are tearing at my bosom; heal me, please heal me..."

When he returned home, Mimi was sitting up in bed. She took one look at him and cried, "Oh, honey..."

"I got drunk trying not to smoke," he said. "I was attacked by juvenile delinquents. I don't ever want you to speak of it."

"Sweetheart, let me get you a cigarette, . ."

"No," he said, "I'm determined to show you I can stick to it. Now go to sleep . "

The next day he avoided the bar where he had met the woman and drove to another in Hermosa Beach. He was relieved to see that there was not a woman in the place. To Julian's delight, the fellow next to him did not even wait to be asked before proferring his pack of *Gauloises*. Fellow turned out to be very bright and witty—an artist. Julian's best friend at Cornell had been an artist. The guys at work were such bores that he couldn't remember the last time he had enjoyed a decent conversation. After a few drams of Courvoisier, Julian's new friend suggested they amble across the street to his studio, where Julian could tell him what he thought of his recent collages. Julian was very complimented. Why not, he mused; why the hell not...

Friday evening he stopped along the PCH to give a ride to a hitchhiker, a hippie chick with hair like noodles, an epidemic of freckles, but not, as they say, unattractive in her own way.

"You smoke?" he asked.

The girl observed him sternly. "You the heat?"

"The what?"

The girl relaxed. "Hey, mon," she said, "why don't you loosen your tie a little?"

Okay," he said, "but what about that cigarette?"

"Tell you what, mon," she said; "you give me a ride to Seal and I'll turn you on to some real fine shit."

Besides the fact that he didn't know what the hell she was talking about, Julian was appalled by her language. This younger generation—if he ever caught a daughter of his talking that way he'd wash her mouth out with a bar of Ivory. But it had been that kind of week. And he was dying for a cigarette, no matter how shitty it was. "Seal Beach?" he said; "I guess I can take you that far..."

The party was a kick, couples making it four at a time on the double bed and everyone so happy.

It sure beat the old Saturday night parties as far as Julian was concerned. And the girl he had given the ride to turned out to be a very sweet person. He found himself wanting to be in love again. That was just before she offered to split a cap with him...

Two days later Julian arrived home.

"Where have you been?" cried Mimi. "I've been calling everywhere. I even called the police and..."

"The heat?" he laughed, a new edge as of emerald to his voice. "The heat are no doubt chasing their own tails as usual."

"Julian Escargot, WHERE HAVE YOU BEEN!"

"Just bumming around," he said.

"Oh Julian," she said, "let's go back to where we were. I'll never bother you about your cigarettes again."

"Cigarettes," he said; "hell, I've given them up."

THE GOLD RUSH

She had never owned gold, except for a few pieces of jewelry, very few. She and her husband, both academics, had in their early days together doled out their meager funds on the necessities of keeping spirit and flesh together while the obstacles of their respective graduate schools were, in what at the time seemed like slow motion, hurdled. Later, travel became uppermost in their priorities, a series of partially tax deductible educational visits to Ireland, the United Kingdom, and the Continent. Since having their two children, it had been necessary to postpone— not, they hoped, indefinitely— further travel plans.

Their children became the center of their existences, but children today were an enormous expense, and it was never too soon to start putting a little something aside for their own college years. Above all, they wanted their children to have all the educational and cultural opportunities that they had had. They were the first in their families to finish college, let alone graduate school.

Yet, everyone all of a sudden seemed to be buying gold. Everyone in California at least, the Golden State of the Gold Rush that had brought the ancestors of the Golden People who now basked in the Golden Sunshine—the California of Sutter's Mill, Knott's Berry Farm, of Calico and Bodie. Everyone they knew was laden with gold chains from which impended every conceivable shape of golden pendant.

Among their mildly affluent neighbors the conversation ran to the comparative advantages of the Krugerrands, Maple Leafs and fifty-peso pieces, while the doctors, lawyers, and real estate brokers hinted vaguely of more speculative approaches, of futures.

There was something glittering, yet solid about the talk itself that sent a thrill through even so anti-materialistic and politically-to-the-left a presence as that of Mary Beth Kinnerly. She had to remind herself that the values of her husband and herself lay elsewhere, and that even if they'd been of a different cast of mind, they simply had no extra money. They could not afford anything so tangible. It was fantasy, masochism, not-at-all healthy to pleasure oneself with even the mildest of such longings.

Still, on her husband's birthday, she presented him with a twenty-inch cobra chain in a small velvet box.

"It's... it's very nice," he said. He was stunned. Their gifts to each other, at their most extravagant, ran to professionals' semi-utilitarian-luxury conveniences such as the two volume Oxford English Dictionary

"It'll look good on you, Karl," she said, "and it's something of... of an investment."

When her birthday rolled around, he presented her with a twenty-inch Victorian chain. Anything less would have made him feel cheap... and perhaps cheapened him in her eyes. For Christmas, they exchanged gold pendants—of a unicorn and a mermaid. From then on they routinely presented each other with items of gold on occasions of gift-giving. They seldom wore them in public, though. Besides the dangers of loss or theft, they feared their possessions could not compete with the more expensive jewelry of their friends. No matter—they felt no need of a display. There was a pleasure just in having what they had, in knowing that what they had was, after all, a good investment.

Then the windfall arrived in the form of a thousand-dollar check for retroactive pay that had been held up in the courts by the forces behind the tax-limitation movement. The money had been delayed so long that Mary Beth and her colleagues had despaired of ever seeing it. Most of them had forgotten about it. Mary Beth certainly had. What a surprise this would be for Karl!

She began to list in her mind several things they had needed, but had not felt able to afford: a new sofa, more bookshelves, new musical instruments for the kids... but none of these things seemed necessary anymore. They were all things the family had managed to do without for quite a while... and could presumably continue to do without for a while longer. What's more, it was unlikely that Karl would be aware of the back pay. It had not been an issue at the private institution where he taught. Mary Beth skimmed the *Times*, but she found no story about it. She and Karl shared the expenses of the family equally, but what little was left over they kept individually for their own clothes shopping and other personal expenses.

She got out the phone book, and looked up "coin shops" in the Yellow Pages. There was one on the other side of town. She copied the number on a note pad, put the phone book away, and sat there in a state of nervous excitement.

She stood up and paced the room, then turned quickly on her heel, strode to the phone, and dialed the number.

"G and L Coins."

"Yes... yes, I'd like to buy a gold coin, and I haven't bought one before, and I wondered how I'd go about it."

"Krugerrand?"

"No, I couldn't... no, not a Krugerrand."

"Canadian? Fifty-peso Mexican?"

"What would that cost me, a fifty-peso Mexican gold coin?"

"Changes every day. Today we're buying at seven-twenty-two and selling at seven-fifty-two."

"How do I pay?"

"Cash."

"Are there any taxes or other charges?"

"Just bring in cash, and we won't worry about any of those other things."

"How late are you open?"

"Six o'clock."

"Thank you."

Mary Beth... Mrs. Kinnerly... Professor Kinnerly... was not a problem drinker, but when she hung up the phone she went to the liquor cabinet, and poured a little whiskey and water in a glass. She finished it quickly, then poured herself another. When she'd finished that, she straightened up the house, and went out to the car.

She couldn't remember ever having been in such a state before, not on her wedding day, or the day of her doctoral orals, or waiting outside of class the first day she'd ever taught. She had to remind herself not to run any red lights on the way to the bank.

The teller hesitated when she told him that no, she did not want a cashier's check or money order, she wanted cash, please. He went to get some hundred dollar bills, and the transaction was quickly over.

Her nervousness grew on the way to the coin shop. She was seriously worried she might lose control of her bladder, and have to return home. She locked the doors because she had heard of purses snatched from women drivers in this area. She searched the faces of pedestrians and other drivers for threatening signs. She drove right past the coin shop, and had to return to it. The eyes of construction workers followed her from the car to the shop. She forgot she was an attractive woman, and men often followed her with their eyes. She almost ran inside.

Although there were only a couple of other customers in the place, she had to wait a minute before a thin young man waited on her. After she told him what she wanted, he went into a back room from which he did not immediately emerge. When he did, he had a coin in his hand, and a little paper envelope. He set them both on the counter, and waited for her to count off the seven hundred-dollar bills, two twenties, a ten, and two ones. He placed the coin in the envelope and handed it to her. Could that be all there was to it? She thanked him, turned, and left the shop.

She tried not to seem to be in any hurry, but she breathed a sigh of relief when she was safely locked in her car.

When she was in a better neighborhood, she pulled over to the curb, turned off the engine, and took the coin out of her purse. She fingered it, tossed it a few inches in the air, flipped it as for heads or tails. It was heavy, heavier than an ounce. It was an alloy, no doubt, probably gold alloyed with copper. She put it back in her purse, and drove to her savings and loan. Five minutes later, the coin was safely sequestered in her safe deposit box.

She tried to appear nonchalant that evening, but it was impossible to conceal entirely her excitement. When her husband remarked on it, she said she was just looking forward to delivering a freshly prepared lecture to one of her classes the next day. In reality, she was hoping to calm herself sufficiently to concentrate on the reading she had still to complete for that same class. Her hyperactivity communicated itself to her mate. After the kids were in bed, he urged her into bed with him. Although her mind was on other things, she didn't want to further rouse his suspicions, and, as it turned out, the sex had a tranquilizing effect on her. Afterwards, alone in her study, she managed to maintain enough of an attention span to get through her reading in about twice the time it would ordinarily have taken her.

Of course, she still had the extra couple-hundred dollars that remained from the thousand-dollar windfall. She left her office hours early the next day in order to return to the coin shop before closing. This time she purchased a two-peso piece for thirty-seven dollars. The next day she bought another. The day after that, two more. The smaller denomination coins, she reasoned, would come in handy should the American currency collapse altogether. Even if the government managed to right the ship of state, there would be an emergency period in which the possession of precious metals might actually spell the difference between life and death. Of course, one should have a handgun to prevent one's gold from simply being taken away. Karl would never allow a gun in the house. Gun control was one of his most ardent causes. It was illegal to carry a concealed weapon. Maybe she would take one of those all-day courses after which you were allowed to carry mace. She could tell Karl she was afraid of being raped on campus. She would have to look into that.

After the surplus from the back pay was exhausted, Mary Beth began to put aside a little of her own biweekly paycheck, locked in her office filing cabinet. When she had what she thought should be sufficient for a coin, she called the shop to check that day's prices, and whenever the price was right, made her now familiar trip to the coin shop and safe deposit box. She was always a little distracted these days, but she wore absent-mindedness well, like a sensuous perfume. Ironically, even as Karl enjoyed her more often and intensely in bed, he became suspicious that she must be seeing someone else. When he confronted her with his accusation, however, her denial was so genuine, so full of astonishment, that his mind was set at ease on that score at least.

In fact, she had been approached by two attractive men at the university, one a colleague, the other a precocious student. She had turned them both down, kindly, but definitively. There was no room in her consciousness for an affair.

Soon, however, her obsession began to manifest itself in a different way. The dinner menus had gone from steak to ground beef to hamburger helper. The table wine was of a supermarket variety that came in four-liter jugs. The kid's toes were poking through their tennis shoes. Mary Beth had taken to cutting their hair herself, and it was not her forte. When Karl suggested they rent a cabin for the family at Yosemite over the Easter break, she said she had too much work piled up. For Father's Day, she did not buy him gold. She said he must be sick of the same old presents, as he unwrapped a swirling tie from Penney's.

Finally, near the end of the semester, Karl looked up from a tumbler of Gallo sherry to where Mary Beth was desultorily grading a stack of student essays: "Whatever happened to that retroactive pay you people were supposed to receive?"

"Retroactive? Pay? I don't know. It may still be in the courts. We probably lost the case. I don't think any of us ever seriously expected we'd win."

"Oh," he said, and picked up a journal.

Did he know? Mary Beth sighed, and returned to her papers. It didn't matter if he knew.

For Mother's Day he waited until the kids were in bed before letting her open her gift: a gold anklet, a gold slave bracelet. He told her to put it on right then and there, and he actually carried her over the threshold of the bedroom. By the time he was finished with her that night, she had almost forgotten her top priority.

When he asked her to put it on again the next night, she said, "Oh, it was much too valuable to keep around the house. I took it to my safe deposit box this afternoon."

A couple of nights later, she remarked while doing the dishes, "You know I loved my anklet... but... if you're buying me something like that again sometime... gold coins are a much better buy, a better investment."

He knew her secret then. He had had his suspicions for quite awhile, but knowing was one thing, and knowing what to do about it was another. He thought of going to the university counseling service for advice, but Academe was a tight little world, and confidentiality was not always absolute. The Daniel Ellsberg break-in was only one extreme example of what could happen in lesser ways and degrees. He did not want to rush into a course of action that might prove a grave professional embarrassment to his wife.

One Friday afternoon Mary Beth arrived home late. She had been to the hairdresser's. Her formerly auburn hair was now blonde, a dazzling, lustrous yellow-gold.

Her husband didn't hesitate a moment longer. "You've got to cash them in."

"Cash what in?"

"The coins."

"What coins?"

"The gold coins. You know what coins."

"I don't know what you're talking about."

"Yes, you do."

"I can't."

"Yes, you can."

"I won't."

"Then leave. Get out of here in the morning. You're sick. You're too sick to be around the children any longer."

She slept in the guest room that night, but she didn't sleep. In the middle of the night she went into the children's bedroom, and stood there quietly above them. Then she went to her husband, who hadn't slept either, and said, "All right. I'll sell them tomorrow."

Her savings and loan was open until noon on Saturday. She was in plenty of time to transfer the horde of coins from her safe deposit box to her purse. She drove dully to the street of the coin shop. It was locked up and deserted. All the signs had been taken down. There was no forwarding information.

Her heart bounced off the concrete. She went down on one knee, and began to weep. After a while she got in the car, and drove back home, all the life gone out of her.

Her husband simply held her. "We don't know for sure they're phony,' he said.

"Of course they are. I don't know why it never occurred to me they might be counterfeit. I was just so wrapped up in... in... I don't know what."

He held her a long time, then brought her two Valium and a glass of water, and put her to bed.

When he heard her breathing heavily, he took the coins out of her purse. He drove to a different coin shop, and poured the coins on the counter in front of a man who was wearing a green visor and thick glasses.

"How much are these worth?" Karl asked.

The man did some fingering and scrutinizing and fiddling with a calculator. "Sixty-five eighty-two."

"Sixty-five dollars and eighty-two cents?"

The man looked at him as if he had heard that joke one time too often: "Sixty-five hundred and eighty-two dollars. No cents."

Karl stood there looking at the coins. Then he scooped them back up. "I think I'll wait awhile, and take a chance on a better price."

The old man shrugged. "If you don't need the cash, you're smart to hold onto them. The price will be going back up. It'll be going way up."

Karl's savings and loan was open until three on Saturdays. He had time to deposit the coins in his safe deposit box and cash a check.

Mary Beth sat up when he came into the room. He handed her a hundred dollar bill. "This was all I could get for them," he said. "I drove all over town. I'm sorry, but it's over now, and I don't want you to blame yourself. You're a wonderful wife, and I love you. It was just a lesson to be learned, a lesson to be learned the best way, the hard way, by both of us. Now let's try to put it all behind us."

NOT TO WORRY

It was shortly after filing his final grades for the semester that Professor Martin Baldwell received the message on his Voice Mail: "You have an Unsatisfied Degree Requirement. You must return to campus immediately to fulfill said requirement in order for doctorate to be re-issued effective 7-1-94. Re-certification of M.A. contingent upon re-issuance of Ph.D. Re-validation of B.A. contingent upon re-certification of M.A. Residency mandatory for satisfaction of unfulfilled doctoral requirement. For further information contact Associate Dean Malcolm M. Malcolm at (555) 555-5555, Extension 555 between the hours of 5:55 and 5:55."

Martin Baldwell found this communication, as misdirected as it must be, extremely troubling. This was the stuff of academician's nightmares, and it was true that he, like, he assumed, all but the most arrogant of his colleagues, had suffered from the fear, no, the *dread*—that he did not really deserve his degree, that it would somehow be taken back from him—for many years after the ultimate sheepskin, the "union card," *The Degree*, had in fact been conferred upon him. But it was almost to the day the thirtieth anniversary of his Defense of Thesis. He had been teaching with distinction at an accredited (if not acclaimed) university for all those years. He had been at Top-Step-Full for more years than he could count. He had generally kept his nose clean. If he had ever transgressed the Education Code, such lapses had gone either unsuspected or unproven. Of course it was all the result, no doubt, of some easily remedied computer glitch but really, with all of one's professional responsibilities and the ever-increasing paperwork, not to mention the endless struggle to remain not merely current in one's field but technology-literate, who really *needed* such distractions, such, as his students would phrase it, *hassles*. To borrow another of their multi-purpose formulations, *it sucked.*

Fortunately he was accessing his messages from home and would therefore not be stymied by the eight-mile telephonic circumference to which the faculty had been restricted by budgetary exigencies. It was a more-than-minor comfort to realize that the annoyance was within seconds of being extirpated from his consciousness. Then he could begin the mental and emotional adjustment to "getting some of his own writing done." He dialed (555) 555-5555 and, in response to a recorded command, Extension 555:

"Office of the Associate Dean."

"Yes, ah, my name is Martin Baldwell, that's *Doctor* Martin Baldwell, returning a call to my answering machine from Associate Dean Malcolm Malcolm. A very serious error seems to have occurred somewhere along the line at your end. According to the message I received, some unfulfilled requirement for my doctorate has cropped up. But, you see, I have had my degree for thirty years, so obviously..."

"Many things which appear to be obvious are later found to be not-so-obvious, Mister Baldwell."

"*Doctor* Baldwell."

"Could we compromise on *Martin*, Martin?"

"No we couldn't, Dean Malcolm. How would you like it if I addressed you as Malcolm and we've never even met?"

"I wouldn't like it at all."

"Well, there you have it."

"I wouldn't like it at all because I'm not Dean Malcolm. Now if I *were* Dean Malcolm..."

"You're *not* Dean Malcolm? Then who the hell are you?"

"I'm the Particles Technician."

"Particles? As in Sub-molecular Physics?"

"No, as in I dust the offices. I was just dusting Dean Malcolm's desk when his phone rang. I decided to be Mister Good Guy and answer it, but obviously my little attempt at

Service Above and Beyond the Call of Duty has gone grossly unappreciated."

"Oh for Christ's sake, I thought Dean Malcolm was available between 5:55 a.m. and 5:55 p.m."

"No, but yours is an all-too-frequent misunderstanding. Dean Malcolm is available between 5:55 *p.m.* and 5:55 *a.m.*"

"He works nights?! What kind of a dean works nights?"

"The Associate Dean for Nocturnal Technicality Searches— that's the kind of dean who works nights. But he'll be at his desk in just a few hours now. Till then, Martin, have a nice day."

"Wait…"

Martin heard a click. The Particles Technician had hung up. When Martin re-dialed, he got a busy signal. The Particles Technician was either using the phone himself or had taken the receiver off its hook.

*   *   *

Martin Baldwell did not enjoy the hours until 5:55 p.m. He tried reading, but could not concentrate. He snacked unnecessarily and felt guilty. So he drank a few glasses of water, because it was supposed to be healthy to do so, and he ended up bloated. He flipped on the t.v. to the financial cable network where he learned that even his literal fortunes were in decline. Most of the commercials were for mutual funds, but one was for a bottled water and specified the diverse toxicity of the tap water which was sitting in his stomach. It was with relief that he re-dialed Associate Dean Malcolm:

"Yes, ah, this is Doctor Martin Baldwell at Pacifica State replying to your message regarding some glitch in the recording of my degree…"

"No glitch, *Mister* Baldwell."

"What?"

"The records are accurate: you are one-tenth of a semester unit short of the sixty graduate units required for completion of your doctoral studies."

"That's ridiculous—how could I be a tenth of a unit short of anything? How could I have earned nine-tenths of a unit of anything? That's the most absurd thing that I've ever heard."

"Our sentiments precisely, Mr. Baldwell: ridiculous and absurd and a damn embarrassment to our university, the first of its kind. Because of you we are on the verge of losing our accreditation, and it's a miracle that we ever received it in the first place. You'd better get your sorry ass back here in a double-time hurry."

"But I don't even know what unit I'm one-tenth short of?"

"Look, Baldwell, this is too important and complex a case to be handled via electronic communication. We are dealing with a *residency* requirement here."

"How soon does this have to be cleaned up?"

"Yesterday. Yesterday at noon was the unmitigatable deadline. But I'm granting you an indefinite deadline."

"You mean I can take all the time I need, that there's no definite deadline?"

"No, I mean it's not definite when I will decide to reimpose the already past-due statute of limitations. In fact, your other units may start falling off tenth by tenth or chunk by chunk. After all, we do have a seven-year rule here, and your courses were all completed at least thirty years ago. Hell, we could decide to invalidate the entire fifty-nine and nine-tenths units at any moment. And if we lose our accreditation because of your disgraceful lack of attention to details, then this whole miserable excuse for an academic institution is kaput—you, me, the Council of Seven Thousand Deans—just like that, poof, click, do you hear me snapping my fingers, shazam, obliteration, nothingness, the void..."

"I'll be on the earliest possible flight. Give me directions to your office."

"My office? By the time you get here my office will be in receivership. I'm taking early retirement, the golden handshake, before your scandal breaks."

"Then whom shall I seek out?"

"How should I know? You got yourself into this mess, now get yourself out of it. We are in a state of flux. You can never step into the same flood control channel twice. On the other hand, you've seen one flood channel, you've seen them all. If I were you, I'd ask around when I get to the campus. If there's still a campus when you get to it. And of course I'm *not* you. In a very real sense, I'm not even *me*. And yet it might also be posited that we are all one. Have you ever walked a mile in *my* moccasins? No, I bet you're a Birkenstock Man. Do you remember the Marlboro Man? Ah, *la nostalgie de la boue!* Of course one man's gutter is another man's flood control channel. Was it Baudelaire who said, 'We are lying in the flood control channel, but our eyes are on the communications satellites.' Well, good luck, sucker..."

"Dean Malcolm, Dean Malcolm, just one more thing..."

But the line had already gone dead. All the lines to his alma mater proved defunct, deceased.

* * *

Martin Baldwell had great difficulty in making his flight reservations. For one thing all the flight attendants were on strike. Also all the pilots. So all the travel agents had gone on vacation. In a panic all the holders of frequent flyer miles had decided to cash them in. This had catapulted all the airlines into Chapter Eleven. Chapter Eleven had been written by Jacques Lacan. But since Chapter Ten had been written by Jacques Derrida and Chapter Twelve by the Tony-Award-Winning Team of Michael Foucault and Dion Boucicault, the majority stockholders decided to continue trying to decipher Chapter Eleven.

Martin Baldwell set out walking.

* * *

Halfway across the Mojave, Martin encountered Cabeza de Vaca. The role of Cabeza de Vaca was being played by Charles

Bronson. By now Cabeza de Vaca had only one follower. The Follower was being played by Charles Bowden, but he was following at such a distance that he was actually in Guatemala. The white horse of Señor Viva Zapata was still in the hills. Martin Baldwell asked Cabeza de Vaca how things were going.

Cabeza de Vaca said, "Moo."

* * *

When Martin reached the thousand acres upon which the proud campus had once stood, he found a combination mall-theme park-casino-auto center-cinema multiplex-light industry development. It was called *Our Town*. He found the Information Office and stood in line for ten hours. When there were only two people left in front of him, the Information Window slammed shut. A hand hung a sign inside the window. It said, "Come Back Sometime."

He asked the somewhat bovine woman in front of him when she thought the window would re-open. "You never know," she said. "After all, that's what makes a window a window."

Martin did not entirely understand that, although it had a ring of cryptic revelation. So he asked the woman where he could find the nearest school.

"We haven't had schools for centuries," she replied. "Naturally, however, every household has access to the Interactive Information Highway."

"So there's actually a high level of literacy?"

"Oh no, nobody can actually write. In fact nobody has learned much of anything in years. The highway has never been used much for learning. Mostly we play games on it. And shop." She began to salivate.

"But you can shop here."

"Well, yes, a person does have to get out of the house once in a while. Don't you agree? Or we'd all go nuts."

"What, if you don't mind me asking, were you going to ask at the Information Window?"

"Oh, I wasn't going to *ask* anything."

"You weren't?"

"Oh no. You don't go to the Information Window to ask questions. You go to be told answers."

"What sort of answers?"

"Well, the last time I actually made it to the Window I was told, *Every Good Boy Deserves Fellatio.* And it's true, isn't it? Have *you* been a good boy?"

"A good boy? But Goodness is rather a relative concept, isn't it?"

"Oh no—*incest* is. But there goes your blowjob, blowhard."

"Wait a second—I *have*, as a matter of fact, been an almost disgustingly good boy. Except for one stain on my record—I apparently have one-tenth of a unit to complete in order to legitimize once and for all my Ph.D. Would you have *any idea* whom I should see to rectify this oversight?"

"Why I just happen to be the person appointed to Rectumfy All Academic Degree Irregularities."

"You are?"

"Yes indeed—I am the Secretary of Education."

"You are? Then what can I do?"

"Let's see—you could start dictating."

"Dictating?"

"Unh-hunh. At secretarial school I was first in my class in dictation. I can take dictation at the rate of thirty words an eon."

"I'm afraid I don't have an eon."

"Of course you do. That's why there's no rush. But listen—what's your discipline?"

"English."

"Oh—then probably you'd prefer a good spanking. That's the discipline of preference in Whitehall."

"I'd rather just pass an examination."

"You would? Excellent. No one's passed an examination

here in eternities. Just drop you pants, turn your head to the side, and cough."

"Not *that* kind of examination. I want to demonstrate my knowledge of English Literature."

"You do? Fine. Who wrote *Beowulf?*"

"No one knows the answer to that."

"No? Well, you can't expect us to hand out no Ph.D.s to no one either."

"Isn't there any way I can prove I deserve my degree?"

"Frankly, no; there isn't."

"You mean I will have to live out my life with these lingering doubts?"

"You should have learned long ago that the most important lesson that you learn in any graduate school is that you are undeserving."

"So, in fact, I don't deserve my doctorate."

"The fact is that you don't deserve shit."

"Can I at least continue to teach?"

"Sure, you're no more undeserving than the next s/he. But you'd better get back before you're canned for going AWOL."

* * *

Martin Baldwell recrossed the desert to Pacifica State only to discover that his position had been filled by Cabeza de Vaca.

RETURN OF THE HIPPIE SHIRT

He had no sooner emerged on the outskirts of Long Beach from the car that had brought him the last four hundred miles south when, thumb extended, he watched the black-and-white cruise up to him. The tall cop turned the ignition off and the flashing lights on before exiting the driver's side. The small cop made a studied effort to remove himself from the passenger's seat no less slack-jawed, loose-jointed, and lazy-brained. They approached him and the tall cop said, "Bring down that thumb."

"All right," he said.

"What's your name?"

"Robert MacGregor. Sometimes called Bob."

"Your driver's license?"

"I don't drive anymore."

"Driver's license revoked."

"No, it was never revoked or suspended or anything else. I just quit driving so I let it lapse."

"Well then, your state I.D."

"I'm not from this state. Not for twenty years, that is."

"What state are you from, Bob?"

"The last state I was in before this one was Oregon."

"You've been residing in Oregon?"

"No, that was just the last one I was in before this one. I was only in Oregon for a few hours. This time."

"What state were you in before Oregon, Bob?"

"Washington."

"You were a permanent resident of the State of Washington."

"No, I was just passing through."

"Bob," the tall cop said, "I am a patient man, but I have my limits."

"Let me at him," the small cop said, but the tall cop calmed him with a benedictively raised hand.

"Now, Bob, let's make this simple: I would just like to know in what state you have most recently claimed residence."

"California."

"Fine, now we're getting somewhere. How recently was that?"

"That was twenty years ago."

"Bobby-boy," the tall cop sighed, "don't test me, okay?"

"I'm not trying to."

"Now let me guess: You've been living in Canada. You were a draft evader—and please note that I did not describe you as a dirty rotten commie draft-dodger—during the Vietnam War era and you are only now returning to the states."

"No, I was living north of Canada. I was spending my summers with the Ojibwitski Eskimos on the most northern reaches of the Baffin Bay—I suppose you would call it *unincorporated territory*—and I was wintering, if you could call it that, among the Oaxicoatl Indians of the Andes."

"And why were you living among the savages?"

"I was living with these people because they wear these shirts."

"You went there to wear that... piece-of-shit rag?"

"No, I was wearing this shirt—or one like it—when I went there."

"You're pushing me, Bob."

"I'm not trying to."

"What would you call that kind of shirt, Bob?"

"Well, among the Ojibwitskes and the Oaxicoatls it was just called a shirt."

"What was it called here, Bob?"

"It was called a hippie shirt."

The small cop said, "How I wish I'd been a cop in those days!"

"You're telling me," the tall cop said, "that you lived among primitives for twenty years because of a shirt?"

"It started that way," Bob said, "but sometimes the most advanced ideas are the oldest."

"We could beat you bloody," the small cop said.

"I'm afraid he's right," the tall cop nodded.

"Oh, you already have," Bob cheerily informed them. "It was twenty years ago and, well, it wasn't you two guys exactly, but it was, you know, your prototypes, and actually it had quite a bit to do with my leaving."

"Why did we... I mean, they... beat you?"

"Because of my shirt."

"That was all?"

"Yes."

"They were *real cops* in those days," the small cop shook his head in admiration.

"What makes you think we won't do it now, Bob? You think because I have a degree in criminal justice that I'm some kind of wimp?"

"No. I think if I were black or brown or homosexual, you still would."

"Maybe we're equal opportunity brutalizers. Maybe we kick ass without discrimination."

"Probably you'd like to be, but... in this case... the whole world is watching."

The tall cop and the small cop became dead pale. They stared into each other's faces, then they glanced in all directions.

"Bob," the tall cop said, "are you wired for sound?"

"I never said that, officer."

"Where are the video cameras hidden?"

"Did I say anything about video?"

"Listen, asshole, we're going to body-search you and then we're going over this terrain with a fine-tooth comb for surveillance devices. And when we don't find any, you'd better start saying your prayers."

"Gentlemen, do you think you are serving and protecting the pre-industrial communities of the Ojibwitskis and the Oaxicoatls? Don't you realize that we can be observed in perfect detail by satellites orbiting the earth?"

"And why would they bother?"

"That's for me to know and you to find out."

"Larry," the small cop said, "there's something weird about all this. Remember that sting operation *60 Minutes* pulled off? I'm for getting out of here."

"Hitch-hiking is illegal in Long Beach. We can at least cite him for that."

"As a matter of fact," said Bob, "we are not in Long Beach. We are a few feet over the border into what once again is designated an *unincorporated territory*."

"So who's to know?"

"The whole world is watching."

"Goddamn you."

"Oh... and listening."

"Listen, you smug motherfucker, the courts are changing. The last liberal justices are barely breathing. The voters are scared shitless that the country's being overrun not only by drugs but by funny-looking people who can't speak English until they take their college entrance exams. We'll have our way with you yet."

"Believe me, I'm all too aware you may be proven right."

*   *   *

From his room at the Motel 6 he dialed Janey.

"Bob? That can't be you!"

"Yes, it is."

"After all these years... I was sure you must be either dead or... you know..."

"In jail?"

"Well."

"But I have never been a lawbreaker."

"I know, but... you insisted on wearing that shirt that... oh, how I wish I could forget it... it *changed* you so... it *ruined* everything."

"A *shirt* did that?"

"*She* gave it to you! *She* turned you into a hippie! Because *she* couldn't have you, she tainted you for me!"

"I guess I was very easily tainted."

"I suppose you got in touch with her as soon as you hit town."

"No, I haven't seen her or spoken to her. Actually it was you I got in touch with as soon as I hit town."

"Oh. Oh..."

"Tell me about yourself... I mean, you know, your present circumstances."

"Well, I'm married."

"Good. Congratulations."

"Aren't you even going to ask if it's a happy marriage? Isn't that what you always ask?"

"The answer to the first question is no. To the second: you would know better than I."

"Then, no, I wouldn't say I'm happy or unhappy. He's quite a bit older than me, but I'm no spring chicken either. There were a couple of affairs that went nowhere, but none lately and first there was herpes to worry about and now AIDS. I never had any children and, as the result of what is referred to as major surgery, I won't be having any. I helped Frank with two from his first marriage, but I'm not close to them. And *please* do not mention adoption."

"I wasn't going to."

"I quit teaching, which I'd come to hate anyway, because Frank makes more than enough for us both. I always thought I'd like my own little crafts business, but I found out there's a difference between embroidering animals on nighties for birthday gifts and competing in the marketplace. Aren't you going to ask me what I do now?"

"No."

"What I do now is drink. And watch soap operas. And replant the garden which is a lost cause because nothing can grow for long in this goddamnn California soil, which is in fact nothing but sand, without a personal hook-up to the bloody California aqueduct. These activities are of sufficient civic significance to constitute my excuse for never cooking, an art at which Frank has consequently had to rise, if not to the pinnacle of Master then at least to the plateau of stoic journeyman."

"Maybe you need a new life."

"Is that an offer?"

"No."

"That's all right—I was just teasing. I wouldn't even want you to see me now. Not that I've turned into some kind of hag but... oh... I hope you'd admit I was not too far from being beautiful when we were... young."

"You were beautiful... a rare beauty. And I'm sure you've taken care of your appearance. If anything, you may have always been a bit *too* concerned with your appearance."

"Buddy-boy, all I've ever *had* is my appearance. Or did you fall for my personality. And physical warmth. Come on, Bob, I'm the Wicked Bitch of the East, you know that. And I won't be starting over in any new life either. Frank and I will play the cards out as we've dealt them. And I have better days than today. Thank God I don't have any worse."

"I've got to hang up now, Jane."

"Don't rush on my account. This has been good for me. Like lancing a boil. But what about you? You're the one who's been off having the interesting experiences. Are you... why are you laughing?"

"Oh, I was just reminded of a punch-line I heard the other night. Some woman comedian whose name I don't remember: 'Now let's talk about you! What do you think of me?'"

* * *

A couple of days later he called Jeannie.

"My God, it's Robert, isn't it?"

"Yes, Jeannie. How are you?"

"Oh shit, I can't complain. I mean I could, but what good would it do?"

"The kids?"

"Mindy graduated from Brown a year ago and is in the Peace Corps in Nigeria. Zorba's in his second year at the University of Hawaii. Hey, thanks for keeping up the child support. How'd you manage that?"

"I discovered gold in the Arctic and silver in the Andes ."

"Then you weren't sending nearly enough, bastard."

"Actually I just taught what I know. English. Math. And helped them out a little in their dealings with the outside world."

"Like Deborah Kerr in *The King and 1.*"

"Kind of. Except I was lucky enough not to have had to waltz with Yul Brynner."

"I bet you did your share of tangoing. We all know about Eskimo hospitality and I bet you helped revive an ancient Inca rite or two!"

"Like Chaucer's Clerk: 'Gladly did he lerne and gladly teche.' How about you?"

"Oh, you know, they come and go. The good times and the bad. The laughter and the tears. The Agony and the Ecstasy."

"Wild World of Sports."

"Wild World of Sports."

"You'll always be okay, Jeannie. How's the photography?"

"I'm painting more these days. Even sell a few. But guess what I do to keep flesh and spirit together?"

"You sell real estate."

"How did you guess?"

"Just a statistic I read."

"I'm not that bad at it. And north San Diego County's all construction."

"And Mexico?"

"I can't save Mexico. So beautiful and so tragic. I hope the Mexicans can."

"Can Mindy save Africa?"

"No. But you can't raise a kid with altruistic values and then tell her IBM is where it's at. She'll be okay if she takes her anti-malaria and anti-tsetse pills. And she's the only one of us who wouldn't forget to."

"Maybe Zorba will bring civilization to the Lahaina Yacht Club."

"He's really matured, Bob. You'd be shocked. And he's still gentle, loving, lovable... and a hunk."

'Do you think they'd want to see me some day?"

"Absolutely. As soon as practical."

"I suppose they hold my leaving against me."

"Surprisingly, Zorb doesn't seem to. I think it's something about being a man that he recognizes in himself as well. A daughter, on the other hand, is bound to feel a little bit abandoned, no matter how much she's told it was not a rejection of her and not caused by anything she did wrong."

"I've come to understand that."

"I'm not trying to lay a guilt trip on you."

"You don't need to and you never did."

"How long will you be in town, Bob?"

"I'm not sure yet."

* * *

He turned on the t.v. to wind down before bed. In Stockton a young man in fatigues with a Russian assault rifle had gunned down a classroom of children of Southeast Asian refugees. Five days before the Super Bowl there were riots in the ghettoes of Miami. The Supreme Court had announced decisions tightening censorship laws, allowing police greater latitude in search and seizure, and returning to the states some authority over the funding of abortions. Rocks and bullets were flying between Jews and Palestinians. Libya was denying the construction of a chemical warfare plant. A commentator was noting that the outgoing president, once the idol of fiscal conservatives, had tripled the national debt. A popular film was portraying the F.B.I. as heroes of the Civil Rights Movement. Interviewed white children had no idea why they were out of school for Martin Luther King Day. The bombing of a commercial passenger jet that killed all on board and two dozen on the ground was still unsolved. The first pick in the NBA draft would be out a year with knee surgery. The incoming president, a seemingly decent and well-educated man, was under subpoena to testify regarding the latest Washington scandal. Presidents Kennedy, Johnson, Nixon, Ford and Carter were spoken of in the same breath. Foreign investments in America were at an all-time high. Black admissions to universities had declined, presumably as a result of the conversion of grant programs to loans.

Bob MacGregor sipped a sherry, wishing it were the hot blood of a freshly slain polar bear.

* * *

When he finally tracked the most recent residence of Harve Concannon (old Harve seemed to have come down in the world), a woman Bob did not recognize answered the door. It took them a couple of minutes to get things straight. Harve had died six months ago of the third in a series of heart attacks. This woman had been his second wife and her name was Maggie, nee Flynn. She invited Bob in for coffee. She had been fifteen years younger than Harve and was eight years younger than Bob. Harve had lost one of his children by his first marriage in Vietnam and the other to drugs. It hadn't been long then before his wife had died in a careless traffic accident. Maggie said she knew Harve could be a real asshole around the office, but that he wasn't a bad guy away from work at all, especially after a couple of drinks, and that she'd never minded the cocktail hour herself. She had two early-teen daughters by Harve and they really kept her young. Harve hadn't left her much except his retirement funds, an inadequate life insurance policy, and ridiculously low house payments by today's standards, but there had been enough to let her quit her computer job at Confidential Insurance and return to the university with a student assistantship in, of all things, acting. Did Bob think she was crazy?

No, Bob did not think she was crazy.

Now, she would have to be freshening up for school, but wouldn't he come back and have dinner with her and the girls that evening.

Yes, he would love to. If he could bring the wine and dessert.

"Hey, Bob," she said, "I really like your shirt. But who did that astonishing needlepoint?"

"An Ojibwitske woman did the front," he told her, "and an Oaxicoatl woman the back. The one needle was of shark tooth; the other of condor beak."

"Oh well," Maggie nee Flynn laughed nervously but with tentative acceptance, "you must have a lot of stories to tell."

"I tried to leave myself open to experiences that would not destroy or permanently damage me."

"Maybe you could write a play for me to star in."

"Maybe I could."

"Maybe a film."

"Maybe."

She kissed him then and he held her small breasts. then ran his hands over a shape kept firm by exercise although naturally trim since childhood.

*   *   *

Late that evening, in bed, he asked her, "When do you sleep?"

"I don't."

"Well, I do. I have to get going now."

"But you'll be back."

"Yes, I'll be back."

"But you'll be staying... in this area... in the country."

Bob nodded yes. "I've done the leaving. This seems a time for staying. Otherwise, what good will the leaving have been for?"

Photo by Vanessa Locklin

Gerald Locklin has published over eighty volumes of poetry, fiction, and literary essays including <u>Charles Bukowski: A Sure Bet</u>, (Water Row Press) and <u>Go West, Young Toad</u>, (Water Row Press). Charles Bukowski called him "One of the great undiscovered talents of our time." <u>The Oxford Companion to Twentieth Century Literature in the English Language</u> calls him "a central figure in the vitality of Los Angeles writing." His works have been widely translated and he has given countless readings here and in England. He teaches at California State University, Long Beach.